FAYE'S SACRIFICE

MADELINE MARTIN

April 1341
Castleton, Scotland

F aye Fletcher had an uncanny knack for getting more from her coin than others. She scanned an assortment of fabrics, eyeing a blue wool that would suit her as well as her younger sister, Clara.

"How much?" She settled her fingers on the bolt and raised her eyes to the shopkeeper.

He was younger than she'd expected, and his cheeks colored when their eyes met. "It...it's, uh, three farthings a yard."

She gently caressed the fabric. It was of good quality, the color rich as a summer sky. "Three farthings?" she asked, putting an edge of concern in her voice.

The shopkeeper's brow furrowed, mirroring her expression. "Aye."

Faye bit her bottom lip in pensive concentration, and his gaze lowered to her mouth. "I need a dozen yards, but—"

An old man in the alley caught her attention, the same one who had been watching her earlier. He was tall and proud, with a head of red hair threaded with white, and wearing a fine black doublet atop leather trews.

His stare bored into her, unabashed and unflinching.

"Mistress?" the shopkeeper asked.

A shudder squeezed up her spine. "I..." She looked to the fabric once more and shook her head. "I've changed my mind."

She left the man's stall without bothering to hear his reply. If he returned to the market another time, she was confident she could smooth over her abrupt departure. Mayhap even use it to elicit sympathy for a further reduction in the cost of the fabric.

Disappointment pricked her. It *had* been fine wool.

She flicked her attention to the alleyway and found the man no longer there. The tension did not ease from her shoulders, however. Instead, wariness tapped at the back of her mind.

She quickened her pace to where she would be meeting with her brother, Drake, on the outskirts of the village. He'd gone to see about getting a cow for them while Faye attended the market.

She glanced over her shoulder and found the old man behind her, mere paces away.

"I'd like a word with ye." His voice was gravelly despite his Scottish burr and imbued with the same confidence as his squared shoulders.

She walked more quickly and discreetly slid the dagger from her belt. While she preferred the cut of her own sharp tongue, in a pinch, the blade did quite nicely.

"Mistress Faye Fletcher."

Her name on the stranger's lips made her step falter. She spun around. "I'm not someone ye want to trifle with."

He lifted his brows with apparent amusement and swept his gaze over her. "Ye've grown into a bonny lass."

"And ye're a leering old goat."

He tsked. "Is that any way to speak to yer grandda?"

The apprehension in Faye's gut drew into a hard knot. She met his green eyes, a shade disconcertingly similar to her mum's. Prickles ran over her flesh.

She'd heard enough about him to be wary. He was Chieftain of the Ross clan, a man with power and greed running in his cold veins. He was so cruel and self-serving that Mum had risked her family starving rather than take her children to live near Balnagown Castle in the Highlands, even though doing so sacrificed Drake's claim to the chieftainship.

Faye glared at him. "My grandda is a dishonorable cur who rules with fear and manipulation. If ye are indeed who ye claim to be, I want nothing to do with ye."

The mirth fled his expression, and his face went red under his rust-colored beard. "Impudent chit." He narrowed his eyes at her. "It doesna matter what ye want. I've come to fetch ye to deliver ye to yer betrothed."

She tightened her grip on her dagger. Betrothed?

She scoffed derisively to cover her unease. "Ye're mad, and I dinna have time for this."

Turning away, she strode swiftly toward the large tree where she'd planned to meet Drake, hoping to God he was already waiting. Her grandda's strong, wiry grasp caught her arm and spun her back toward him.

She rolled her arm over his and gripped his thick wrist, twisting it sharply. He grunted in pain, but she didn't stop there.

This was exactly why she carried a blade. Quick as a blink, she put the point of her dagger to his withered throat. "Leave me be and dinna bother coming to find my family, or I willna stop my blade next time, aye?"

He grimaced, his teeth yellow beneath his thin lips. "Let go of me, ye foolish lass."

She shoved him from her, then backed away.

"Ye willna go unpunished for that." He glowered at her, then slipped between two homes, disappearing.

Faye slowly exhaled, and a tremble softened her limbs. Was he the man he said he was? Her grandda? And what was his claim of her being betrothed?

She kept the dagger clutched in her grasp as she made her way to the large tree. Drake was already waiting for her with a velvety brown cow whose soft eyes were large and framed with long lashes.

Drake frowned as she approached. "What is it, Faye?"

There was a single moment that passed where she considered telling him what had happened. But only one before she resolved to keep news of their grandfather's presence in the village to herself.

Drake was the eldest of the four of them and had been visiting the last sennight. The following morning, he was due to return to the English side of the border to resume his duties as Captain of the Guard at Werrick Castle.

His job was one of great importance and brought him an abundance of pride. It was not the knighthood he'd hoped to obtain as their father had, but it was an honorable position in a noble household. One that afforded them all a much better life than what they'd had before. No longer were they forced to wear threadbare clothes that left them chilled in the winter.

Nor did they go without food so long that their bellies snarled with hunger.

She was grateful for what he did for them but did not care for him being gone so long or being so far away—especially at the place where his heart had been broken by one of the earl's daughters. Her handsome brother should have already had a wife and children, and she suspected his lack of procuring one had a good deal to do with Lady Anice.

If Drake knew their grandfather was nearby, and that Faye had been approached, he would undoubtedly delay his return to Werrick Castle. She wouldn't have Drake risk his job on her account. Not when they were finally doing so well, in a stone manor outside the village with some livestock and enough food and clothing to be comfortable.

"'Tis only that I'm sad ye'll be leaving us on the morrow." Faye gave her brother a perfect smile. A lifetime of practice had rendered the expression convincing.

Drake's worry lightened into an endearing expression, and he ruffled her hair. "I'll be back before ye start to miss me."

She smoothed her fingers over her tresses to ensure his affection hadn't left her mussed. "But I already miss ye, and ye've not even left yet."

He chuckled. "Ach, my honey-tongued sister. One day ye're going to get yerself in trouble with such pretty words."

"I'm sure I'll find a way out of it." She grinned.

Together, they wandered down the trail leading to their home Drake had constructed for them two years prior. It had taken considerable time to save enough, but the home provided them with protection for themselves, as well as their livestock.

Faye's meeting with the chieftain churned in her thoughts, though she'd tried to set it aside. He was nothing she couldn't handle. After all, how much of a threat could one old man be?

Sutherland, Scotland

EWAN SUTHERLAND, CHIEFTAIN OF THE SUTHERLAND CLAN, was getting married. Again.

Or at least, he would be promised to the chieftain of the Gordon clan's daughter once he affixed his signature to the lengthy agreement set before him. The quill remained perched in his fingertips; the point not quite settled upon the page. A drop of ink slid from the sharpened tip and beaded on the parchment before absorbing into a blotch of black.

"Ye dinna want to marry the lass?" Monroe asked from his seat opposite Ewan's desk.

Ewan lifted his head to regard his advisor as he considered the question.

Mistress Blair Gordon was fine enough. Ewan had met her several times at feasts held by the Gordon clan. She'd been a talkative young woman whose face dipped demurely to the ground any time her father was nearby.

There had been a girlish excitement about her, not at all like the formal stiffness of Lara. The thought of his first wife brought an uncomfortable tightness to his chest.

Why then was he so opposed to signing the damn betrothal contract?

Ewan set the quill aside.

"Ach, that's what I thought." Monroe's dark brows twitched. "There may be another option."

"I canna remain unwed," Ewan grumbled bitterly.

He didn't want a wife. But he needed an heir. And alas, one could not come without the other. Or at least, not a *legitimate* heir. And he wouldn't complicate a lad's life with having him be born a bastard.

"I dinna mean ye should remain unwed." Monroe smoothed a hand over the heavy wooden chair arm and scanned the capacious solar as though seeking to ensure their privacy, despite their being alone. "Though yer uncle remains curiously quiet over the matter."

"Curious," Ewan repeated bitterly. "I dinna expect him to support a union where an heir might prevent him from inheriting the title of chieftain should I die. We all know he's been eyeing it since my da passed."

Ewan rubbed at a knot of tension at the back of his neck. Having his uncle in his close council allowed Ewan to maintain a watchful eye on him, but it didn't mean the task was easy or pleasant.

Ewan's cousin, Moiré, kept him abreast of her father's activities to ensure they were not nefarious. She had come to be something like a sister to him. Without any sisters of his own and his elder brother having passed years ago, Ewan found himself often seeking her counsel and relying on her to perform the duties of the castle's mistress since Lara's death.

"Ye received a missive from the Chieftain of the Ross clan." Monroe withdrew a folded bit of parchment from the pocket of his doublet. "It arrived by messenger moments ago. The lad informed me it had something to do with yer betrothal."

"My betrothal?" Ewan took the letter, cracked the thick seal depicting a hand holding a laurel wreath and unfolded it to read the contents within.

Once done, he lowered the parchment to the top of his desk in wonder. "Faye Fletcher."

"I'd nearly forgotten about her," Monroe confessed.

"As had I." Ewan pushed up from his hard wooden seat and approached the fireplace where the flames licked over dry tinder. "But our betrothal contract was never signed by her mother. 'Tis no' binding."

He hadn't seen Faye since they were children—when she'd left after a visit from England and had never returned. It was why she'd slipped from his thoughts for so long.

Faye Fletcher had been a quiet, sweet girl who had always seemed so delicate with her slim frame and pale blonde hair and blue eyes. She'd be a biddable lass; that's what his da had said of her. Granddaughter to the Ross Chieftain, she and Ewan would bring peace to their clans. Their union was made to dissolve the hatred of the last two centuries and unite the clans as one.

Ewan recalled his hope at such an idea. But he was no longer a lad swayed by fanciful notions. He was a man who led other men. His decisions dictated who lived and who died.

"What does her dowry offer?" Monroe asked.

Ewan folded his arms over his chest. "Coin, much more so

than what the betrothal with the Gordons, as well as lands to the west of us and...peace." He sniffed at the ridiculousness of the latter.

Unfortunately, the offer was a tempting one. The lands to the west were rich and ideal for raising sheep. With the cost of wool rising, it would be an opportunity to amass wealth. As of late, the constant battles between clans had been expensive.

A marriage to Mistress Faye Fletcher would resolve both issues, as well as hopefully provide him with an heir.

Monroe turned in his chair to face Ewan and his dark, smooth hair gleamed in the firelight. "How much land does the Ross lass bring?"

"A considerable amount." Ewan returned to his desk and regarded the letter once more. "More than they'll get from Berwick. I dinna know why they've wanted that land for so long." Berwick was over a fortnight's journey away and overrun with reivers and thieves. The Sutherland clan hadn't bothered to maintain any sense of order there. Such a feat was nearly impossible.

"Ross insists that I consider the betrothal and meet with him next month to discuss its renewal." Sutherland glanced at the agreement beside the letter, the one that would seal him to Mistress Blair Gordon.

The girl Faye had been rose in his thoughts. What kind of a woman would she be now? Had her skinny body blossomed out to be more robust? Had her white-blonde hair stayed fair or turned the color of wheat?

"What will ye do?" Monroe asked.

Ewan's chest constricted at the thought of marrying again. Lara had been a good wife to him. She had not bickered or complained, nor had she desperately clung to him as some men's wives did. She had performed her duties at the castle promptly and in good order. Aye, she had not given him a bairn in their three years together, but she had tried.

It had been almost two years since her death, and Ewan was

not getting any younger. He required a wife and a son and had two contracts lying at his fingertips. He heaved a sigh that sent the parchments shifting over the desk.

"Aye," he said, at last, his mind finally made up. "I'll meet with Ross to discuss the possibility of marriage to Mistress Faye Fletcher."

Faye bent the bean shell in half over the bowl until the snap sounded sharp in the stillness of the room. The manor was always extraordinarily silent after Drake's departure.

She sighed and reached for another handful of pods.

"'Tis too quiet," Kinsey complained. The youngest of them had red curls that she didn't bother trying to control. She propped her cheek on her fist, so her mouth stretched up the left side of her face.

"Yer face will freeze if ye keep it like that." Faye popped another pod open and let the beans plink into the bowl.

Kinsey rolled her eyes in reply. "Why is he aiding the English anyway? They've done nothing but cause us strife."

"'Tis English money that's paid for this house." Their mother joined them at the large wooden table and shooed her hands at Kinsey.

Kinsey moved with her elbow dragging across the table's surface to keep her face propped in her hand.

Mum took several pods and scooped out the beans in a deft,

practiced move. She'd had blonde hair like Faye when she'd been younger, though most of it had gone white early on, not long after Faye's da had been killed.

"The English have been kind to us." Clara took the bowl full of shelled beans and swapped it for an empty one. She was only one year Faye's junior, her color favoring their father's dark hair as Drake's did.

"Kind to us?" Faye ripped open a fresh pod so the beans spilled out violently, rolling in errant directions before settling at the bottom. "Do ye recall how they shunned us after Da's death? How we dinna have food to eat or—"

"Enough." Mum's gentle rebuke stilled Faye's words but did nothing to cool her ire.

"I only meant Lord Werrick has been good to Drake," Clara said gently. "I thank God every day he is in such care."

Faye's cheeks were hot with outrage, but she bit back her angry words. She was not as forgiving or patient as Clara, who was practically a saint. Nay, Faye was still raw with unhealed wounds left by how quickly friends had turned on them after Da had been killed in combat. He'd been an English knight, honored by his people, a man who died bravely in an effort to keep them all safe. Those very people shunned Mum for being Scottish, and Faye and her siblings for being of mixed blood.

Mum's hand rested on Faye's forearm, cool and dry. Her eyes found Faye's. Green as grass in the summer. Just as the man who claimed to be her grandfather had.

"Mayhap ye'd like to go for a walk to cool yer blood?" Mum suggested.

Faye gestured to the bowl. "The beans—"

"I can do them for ye," Clara offered with a genuine smile. "Ye know I didn't mean to offend."

Faye gave a grudging nod and scooted off the bench.

"Can I join ye?" Kinsey asked.

"Nay," Faye and her mother said at the same time, albeit Faye replied with more force.

Kinsey dropped her head back with exaggerated lamentation.

Faye pulled her cloak from the hook on the wall and banged out of the front door. The cool afternoon air hit the heat of her face. She breathed it in, letting the fresh crispness of it revive her, and began to walk.

The path was the same she'd strode down before for the same reasons. She knew she should wish she could release the pent-up hurt from all those years ago, but it lingered like a picked wound. And, in truth, she wanted to hold onto it. The wall she'd erected around her bruised heart would keep it safe.

A warning suddenly tapped in the back of her mind. She jerked right, but it was too late. Something akin to a stone wall slammed into her, knocking her to the ground.

The world spun around her as her thoughts reeled.

Before she could think to retaliate, the iron grip of arms tightened around her torso.

Her body acted on instinct and Faye drove her elbow into her attacker. Never had she been more grateful for the lessons Drake had taught them after seeing how skilled Lord Werrick's daughters were at fighting.

Whoever held her grunted and the tension around her loosened. Faye pulled her arm free and slammed her elbow back once more, this time meeting with the unyielding surface of a bony face. Pain shot up her arm, the mark of a solid hit.

She leapt to her feet and pulled the dagger from her belt. Three men stood around her, surprise evident on their faces as they looked from her to the skinny man writhing over his injuries on the ground. Their shock lasted only a moment, and in the time Faye spun around to flee, they were already grabbing for her.

She stabbed the first one in the shoulder, but as he released her, another man caught a fistful of her hair and yanked her backward. She went with the momentum of his tug and shoved into him, using her elbows once more, this time on the middle of his neck, so he choked and gasped for breath.

The final man was larger than his friends. Despite her efforts to evade him, he managed to lock her in a grip so firm, she couldn't even wriggle one elbow free. She twisted in his hold, lunging her torso to the right and bit his arm.

His sleeve was filthy, sour with mustiness, but she didn't let go. She'd rather die than give in to these men. It was widely known what happened to abducted women.

She sank her teeth more savagely into his skin, tasting the metallic copper of his blood. He growled, a low, animalistic sound that reverberated through her and rattled loose deep fear. Panic nipped at the fraying edges of her control. She had to keep a level head, or she would surely die.

But no matter how she locked her jaw on him, he did not release her. Indeed, the harder she clamped, the more he squeezed until she could scarcely draw breath.

A flash of pain exploded at the side of her head, and everything went dark.

❦

FAYE AWOKE IN A LARGE WOODEN CRATE THAT BOUNCED ABOUT like a wagon crossing rugged terrain. A weight had settled over her wrists, cutting into the skin. She squinted in the darkness where slivers of light sliced into her prison. Metal shackles bound her wrists together.

Her frantic breath huffed around her, echoing against the wooden box.

She'd been captured.

Taken from her family. Drawn away from her home. Every roll of the clattering wheels took her that much farther from Castleton. But to where?

And why?

Her panting breath dug into her fear and exacerbated it. Would her mother know she'd been abducted? Would her family think she'd left in anger?

She clenched her teeth, and determination grew inside her with visceral force and she threw her body weight against the side of the crate. The whole thing rocked on its side.

Outside, someone cursed, and the movement drew to a stop.

"She's a fecking hellcat," a man said.

Faye clasped her iron-bound hands together. They had no idea how much of a "fecking hellcat" she could be.

A clatter came from the left side of her crate as the latch was lifted. She edged toward it, held her breath and waited. When a crack of light appeared, she lunged through the opening and slammed her manacled hands at her captor's head. The man dropped to the forest floor like a sack of grain.

Strong arms wrapped around her, locking her in place as they'd done before. "I'm wearing leather this time," the man said in a low, menacing voice. "Even ye canna bite through that."

"Faye." Her name was barked with the authority of a father figure scolding their bairn.

She glared up at the man who dared call her thus and met the familiar green eyes of the Ross Chieftain. Her own grandfather.

"Ye've abducted me," she accused. "Ye've stolen me from my home and my family."

"I am yer family," her grandfather said in a gravelly tone.

"Ye'll never be my family." She kicked out her legs, but the man behind her only tightened his hold.

"Where are ye taking me?" she demanded.

"To yer betrothed." Ross crossed his arms over his chest and frowned at her. "Because ye're too damn stubborn to listen to reason."

"How is there any reason for this?" She shook her shoulders to free her captor's hands off her.

Her grandfather nodded at the man. "Ye can release her."

"If she bites me again, I'll beat her," the man warned.

"Do ye hear that?" Her grandfather raised his brows at her. "I willna stop him."

The warrior released her with a shove. She staggered to remain upright and looked around for the first time. They were... nowhere. A scattered forest surrounded them, without a house or person who might help in sight.

She had no idea how long she'd been in that damn box, or how long she'd been knocked out senseless. Her head ached with each thrum of her heart; the beat reverberated in her skull.

"Ye're to marry Ewan Sutherland, Chieftain of the Sutherland clan," her grandfather explained carefully. "Ye've been promised to one another since ye were bairns. Do ye no' remember visiting me in Scotland? He almost never left yer side when ye'd come. He always protected ye, being champion to ye like a fine knight, thinking ye too fragile to defend yerself." He chuckled. "He'll have quite the surprise when he meets ye. Eh, Dougal?"

The man behind Faye grunted and spat on the ground.

Her body remained tense, ready to run. Even still, she could not stop her mind from plunging into memories she'd long since forgotten. A savage land of vivid green grass and brilliant blue skies with patches of amethyst heather sprinkled like shadows through the mountains.

And a boy, older than her, light brown hair falling into his hazel eyes as he looked earnestly at her and held out his hand. "Ye dinna need to be afraid. I'll always protect ye."

As soon as the recollection was there, it was gone, like a slight ripple on a still pond.

"We've got a long ride ahead of us." The Ross Chieftain heaved a great sigh, and lines of fatigue showed on his aged face. "Be a biddable lass, and we can keep ye unbound. Or I'll be forced to keep ye chained and boxed for the next three weeks."

Three weeks?

Faye balled her hands into fists. She would be compliant long enough to earn their trust, but as soon as they least expected it of her, she would fight back. She would gain her freedom and not stop running until she was home.

⚜

EWAN HAD NOT BEEN ON ROSS LANDS IN MANY YEARS. EVEN HIS horse seemed wary as they made their way toward Balnagown Castle. Certainly, his cousin Moiré had warned him against even considering Faye as his wife.

"If ye decide no' to wed her," Monroe said from his side, "I'll ride out posthaste to inform Gordon ye'll accept the marriage to Mistress Blair."

Ewan nodded. Though he was not interested in either prospect, he knew a decision must be made. And the Chieftain of the Gordons was growing tired of waiting.

The journey to Balnagown had taken Ewan and Monroe into the afternoon. Now, the castle rose before them, spires stretching up toward the brightly lit sky. The woman Ross claimed Ewan had been betrothed to since childhood was within those cold, stone walls. Unless Faye's mother had signed the agreement, which Ewan was not aware of, the contract was not binding.

"I dinna like this," Ewan said under his breath.

Monroe cast him a guarded look. "Her dowry is substantial," he replied hesitantly. "It would do considerable good for our people."

Ewan didn't reply. He didn't have to. They both knew what this union would bring. Not only fortune but things more price-less than land: peace. As long as the Ross clan kept up their end of the terms. Which was doubtful.

A short, round man met them near the stables and bade them follow. They were led into the Great Hall, where a lingering fetid odor bespoke of rushes that hadn't been changed in some time. Shadows of smoke scarred the whitewashed walls above the wall sconces, and thick wooden beams lined the ceiling above like the rib cage of a great beast.

Ross sat at a dais in a fine doublet, looking down at them from his steepled fingers. He stood as Ewan and Monroe approached.

"Sutherland." His voice was still as heavy and ragged as Ewan remembered from their few interactions.

They clasped forearms like allies. For soon, they might well be.

"Thank ye for coming." Ross grinned at him, revealing yellowed teeth beneath his russet and white beard. "It heartens me that ye're finally keeping yer word on yer betrothal after all these years."

"The contract wasna ever signed by the lass's mum," Ewan said.

Ross's chest puffed out. "'Twas signed by me."

"Which was no' binding," Monroe pointed out.

Ross slowly shifted his gaze to Monroe with quiet irritation before returning it to Ewan. "I want to honor my part of the agreement. I'd like to think ye're man enough to do the same."

Ewan ignored the blatant goad. "I thought Mistress Faye had left Scotland for good."

"She's back." Ross's smile became more of a grimace. "And she's ready to make good on the betrothal, same as ye."

"It wasna—"

"I signed it," Ross growled.

"Ye're no' her guardian." Ewan glanced around the great hall, expecting the lass to make an appearance.

His curiosity had been teased awake by the prospect of seeing her again. Though it had been a good sixteen years since they'd known one another, he could still recall being awed by her beauty.

Ross surreptitiously scanned the doors along the side of the

Great Hall as though he'd expected them to open at any second. They did not. A moment of heavy silence passed.

The older chieftain cleared this throat. "Ye should know, she may be different than the lass ye knew. She's been living on the borderlands between England and Scotland. 'Tis a hard land, as ye know. She is no' as—"

A door opened and a woman in a homespun gown entered the room. She was of a sturdy build, like a farmer's wife, with tufts of blonde peeking from beneath her mob cap. Her face was hard with a determined set that was not entirely pleasant. He met Monroe's eyes, but his advisor kept his expression blank.

"Fetch me Dougal," Ross snapped at the woman. "And get us some ale, aye?"

She started in surprise. "Aye, sir." She bobbed a short curtsey and practically ran to do as he bade.

Ewan's shoulders relaxed somewhat. The woman was a servant. Not Faye.

"It shouldna be much longer." Ross indicated the seats at the dais, and they all settled at the long table in the otherwise empty room.

The woman rushed back, a flagon in one hand and three goblets in the other. With practiced efficiency, she laid them out on the table and quickly poured the ale. As she was completing her task, a tall, bald man entered the Great Hall. Presumably Dougal.

He kept his back straight and proud as he strode toward them, but it did not mask the stiffness of his limp. As he approached, Ewan realized that was not the extent of his injuries. His left eye had gone dark with a violent bruise.

"Where is my granddaughter?" Ross demanded. "And what the feck happened to ye?"

Dougal slid a look toward Ewan and Monroe before replying, "If we could speak privately, sir."

Ross issued a curse and pushed up to his feet. He led Dougal to a rear corner where the two proceeded to whisper.

"What do ye make of all this?" Ewan asked his advisor.

Monroe tapped a long finger on the table's marred surface. "'Tis...extraordinary." The diplomatic answer was given with care and followed by a sip of ale.

Ewan grunted in reply, no more amused by the passing of wasted time than he was Ross's inability to produce Faye.

The chieftain returned to them; his mouth pressed in a firm line beneath his overgrown beard. "It would appear yer intended bride is missing."

Even Monroe lifted a brow at this.

"Missing?" Ewan repeated.

"Aye, she escaped from her room early this morning." Ross's already ruddy face went a new shade of vivid red.

Escaped?

"Ye make it sound as though ye were holding her captive," Ewan replied.

Ross drank from his goblet before bothering to reply. "The lass is willful."

"I'll no' wed a lass being forced to marry me." Ewan got to his feet, and Monroe stood at his side. "Leave the lass in peace. I've other prospects."

"Nay," Ross growled. "Berwick is mine. Ye promised it to me."

"No' like this." Ewan stepped away from the dais.

"Aye, like this." Ross slammed his fist on the table's surface. The sound slapped off the stone walls and made a servant freeze in fear.

Ross leaned over the table menacingly. "Ye'll no' get out of yer contract with us, Ewan Sutherland. If ye refuse to wed her, I'll ensure ye pay dearly for yer negligence."

"Are ye threatening me?" Ewan demanded. "For a contract that doesna hold bearing?"

Ross glared at him. "If ye dinna follow through with our agreement, I'll see ye're properly punished."

"There is no agreement." Ewan glared back at his enemy, a man who he'd intended to secure peace, not start a war. This had all gone wrong.

They couldn't afford to anger the Rosses further. Not when the Ross clan attacks were already so brutal. Not with their own stores already reduced after all the years of fighting they'd endured.

Something niggled at the back of Ewan's mind about Faye Fletcher. He came back to the dais. "Ye said she was from the borderlands, aye?"

"Aye." Ross grimaced around the word.

"How long has she been here?"

Ross lifted his ale and took a swig. Foam dotted his beard around his mouth when he lowered his goblet. "Nigh on three days."

Dread crept through Ewan. "Ye mean to say the lass is now somewhere outside the castle, alone and in a land she doesna know?"

Ross nodded once, appearing more enraged than concerned for his granddaughter.

The girl he'd known as a boy rose to the forefront in his mind once more. She'd been a slight thing—delicate with small, fragile hands he could easily tuck entirely against his large palms. He'd vowed to protect her then and had always kept that promise in the times she visited with her grandfather. Even from the wolf that had set on them once. The scar at his forearm burned with the reminder, and he could not help but recall how she had shivered afterward with fear.

And now she was alone in the wilderness of Kildary, a land both foreign and dangerous.

"How long has she been missing?" Ewan asked.

"As of early this morn." Ross set down his goblet. "My men

have been looking for her and assumed they'd have her back already. Which is why they dinna tell me until now." He glared at Dougal, who kept his soldier's gaze set in the distance, his face impassive.

Ewan let a curse slip from his mouth, something he rarely did.

"Does that mean ye'll help find her?" Ross's thick brows rose.

Ewan drained his ale before giving the answer he somehow knew he'd deeply regret. "Aye," he replied. "I'll help ye find her."

❧ 3 ❧

Faye was freezing. Her breath puffed white as the snow covering the dead, straw-like grass at her feet. All around her, trees rose like spear shafts, too skinny to block out the bitter wind and too dense to let in a bit of warmth from the sun.

She'd stopped shaking some time back. A bad sign. With fingers she could no longer feel, she smoothed her unbound hair, trying to look as presentable as was possible. She wore a new dress, which her grandfather had procured so that she might look "bonny" for Ewan Sutherland. A man she hoped never to be forced into meeting.

Mayhap she looked fine enough to impress someone—anyone —who might offer her aid.

Her hopes, however, were fleeting. Especially when she hadn't happened upon a soul for hours. Not since she'd hidden in a half-rotted log to evade her grandfather's men. They'd given up some time ago, but they would be back.

She continued to walk on, certain she would come across a village at some point. The grass was thick and patchy underfoot. Her feet had long since gone numb, making it difficult to walk. A particularly rough bit of earth caught at her toe and sent her sprawling against a large rock.

She pushed off the damn thing, leaving behind a smear of red. Anger and frustration whipped through her.

How could such a place be so desolate? She would never have been able to walk this long on the border without encountering at least a handful of other people. This was not how her plan was supposed to go.

Tears prickled hotly in her eyes.

She'd spent the three weeks of travel being well behaved with the men, anything to be let out of that horrid crate. They only trusted her enough to remove her shackles a few days prior. Even then, she hadn't had the opportunity to attack Dougal and steal the key until that very morning.

A sob choked from her throat, which was now raw from breathing in the frigid air. She would die out here before she returned to her grandfather.

A heaviness settled in her limbs, so she was nearly weighted down with exhaustion. It was not the first time. She blinked slowly in an attempt to stave off the sensation, to prevent it from overwhelming her. The tiredness came in waves, each one a stronger pull of temptation than the last to lie on the hard ground and close her eyes. To sleep. To be warm.

Warm.

She couldn't imagine ever being anything other than cold ever again at this point.

She wanted to curl into a ball beneath a tree where the snow hadn't settled, against a wide trunk that might block the wind. Only for a moment. To just rest for a quick second.

Her footsteps slowed, and her eyes slid closed, ready to slumber even as she walked on. Something rolled under her foot, and she pitched forward again. This time, there was nothing to catch herself on, and she landed hard on the icy ground. Snow chilled at the bare skin of her chest, where her cloak had fallen open. The chill snapped her back to awareness.

She pushed herself up and swept at her heavy wool kirtle to clear away bits of dead grass and frozen crusts of snow. The thick fabric and the squirrel-lined cloak were no doubt the only reasons she'd not frozen to death.

Yet.

Movement in the distance caught her attention. A rider.

She stilled, uncertain whether to call out or to hide.

If it were one of her grandfather's men, they would haul her back to the drafty castle and lock her in her room until she could be forced into marriage. Exhaustion tugged at her again, threatening to drag her beneath the quiet, dark surface of sleep.

Sleep.

Warmth.

She staggered and snapped her eyes open. The rider was closer now. Enough to discern his face and realize he was not one of her grandfather's men.

He turned toward her, clearly having seen her.

Energy shot through her, propelling her to her original goal: appeal to someone who might offer her aid. Her fingers slid over her belt, where her dagger usually hung and met with nothing but the smooth leather belt. She silently cursed her grandfather for leaving her unarmed.

The rider approached, and Faye ran her fingers down her hair, hoping the chill had left her cheeks and lips red. She had to look alluring.

"Please," Faye pled softly. "I need yer help."

He stopped his horse and leapt from its back. He was a large man, quite handsome with brown hair and hazel eyes. His shoulders were broad beneath the bulk of his fur-lined cloak.

"What's happened?" he asked. "Are ye alone?"

His voice had a deep timbre, and he spoke with the authority of a man whose requests were obeyed without question. Not only was his clothing made of fine quality, but his horse was also exceptional with its black, glossy coat. He was evidently a man of means. One who would surely fall upon the codes of chivalry and aid a woman.

"I've been taken from my home." Faye had meant to summon tears for effect, yet when they rose to her eyes without effort, she realized they were genuine. "I don't know where I am and need help returning." She gazed up at him, imploringly. She knew just how to do it, widening her eyes, softening her mouth, pushing her breasts out ever so slightly. Complete supplication and innocence.

A muscle worked in his jaw, but his attention didn't slide to her bosom. "Ye're on the border of the Sutherland lands."

Her back straightened. "Sutherland lands?" She forced herself to remain in place rather than stepping back. "Who are ye?"

"Ewan Sutherland." He held her gaze with his intense hazel eyes. "Chieftain of the Sutherland clan. And ye're Faye Fletcher, aye?"

Her quickened breath was evident in the frozen huff of air blooming before her mouth. She shook her head, and this time, she did step back.

He held his hands out to his sides, palms facing her, showing he did not hold a weapon or shackles. "Faye." This time when he spoke, his voice was tender with kindness. "I'll no' force ye to wed me. If ye want to go home, I'll see to it ye're returned back to where ye came."

She watched him, indecision warring in her mind and mingling with fear so tangible that it left an ugly, metallic taste in her mouth.

"I'll no' take a wife that doesna want me." He remained standing where he was, cajoling her with his words, but not trying to reach for her.

A gust of wind blew, cutting through wool and fur alike until it seemed to shake her bones inside her skin. She shuddered.

Sutherland held a single hand out to her, his fingers

outstretched in offering. "I promised always to protect ye. I dinna know if ye recall it—ye are younger than me. But I mean to hold true to that vow."

She looked at his extended hand. It didn't seem threatening. *He* didn't seem threatening. She wanted to trust him. Dear God, she wanted it with all of her soul.

"I'll keep ye safe," he said earnestly. "I'll protect ye."

The wind shoved at her from behind again, far more aggressively than the last. It pushed her in his direction, so she was forced to put one frozen foot in front of the other in an effort to remain upright.

He caught her by the shoulders, his grip strong, yet somehow gentle. "Let me care for ye, Faye."

She nodded, unable to voice the words that brought her too much unease. For how could she possibly trust the man she was supposed to wed? Was he not part of the betrothal negotiations?

But what choice did she have, other than being left to freeze to death?

He helped her onto his massive horse and swept up behind her. His arms framed her body on either side, and he pulled his cloak around her. The heat immediately enveloped her, spiced with something masculine that mingled with the scent of leather.

His hold on her was that of a protector, not a captor. As he'd promised.

Time would tell how well his vows held.

The warmth of his body at her back wilted her resolve to remain stiffly away from him. Before she could stop herself, she sagged against his chest as the exhaustion of the day dragged her down with a force she could no longer fight.

But even as she fell asleep, the last few thoughts that tumbled through her mind were ones of worry and doubt. For what would become of her once she arrived at wherever they were going?

RAGE TWISTED THROUGH EWAN, STARK AND RAW. FAYE HAD lain back against him the first minute of their ride back to the castle. By the second minute, her head had lulled to the side in slumber.

Exhaustion bruised the delicate skin beneath her eyes, and she weighed next to nothing where he held her to him. She could stand to eat a few hearty meals, aye, but that was not what angered him the most.

When he'd aided her onto his horse, her sleeves had pulled back to reveal the chaffed skin of her wrists. As though she'd been shackled.

The moment that Ewan realized Faye had been held captive and was being forced to marry him, he had resolved not to go through with the wedding. Now, seeing exactly how she'd been treated, he resolved never to return her to her grandfather.

The lass *would* be returned safely to her family at the border.

Monroe appeared in the distance on his horse and trotted over to Ewan's side. "Ye've found her."

"Aye, but she'll no' be going back to Ross." Ewan glanced down at Faye as she slept. Something in his chest stirred. She looked so precious and innocent, where she lay against him. Her golden hair and fair skin gave her an ethereal look, like a goddess of old. He knew her eyes to be blue as a summer loch, wide and rimmed with thick, sable lashes.

His memories of her as a girl did not do justice to the woman she had become.

His malcontent toward Ross swelled anew.

"The beast had her chained," Ewan ground out.

Faye stirred on his chest, her brow flinching. He instantly regretted the harshness of his tone. The last thing he wished was to frighten the lass.

God knew she'd been through enough.

"Once she's with us, ye could keep her safe," Monroe said

cautiously. Even as he spoke, however, his expression was one of uncertainty.

"I'll no' marry a lass who has been chained up in an effort to force her into marriage." Ewan glanced down at Faye once more. He kept doing that, he realized, as though it was impossible to stop gazing upon her beauty.

"It would be war," Monroe warned.

Ewan sighed. "Aye, I know." He turned to his advisor. "It's no' right."

Monroe nodded, acknowledging the truth of Ewan's words. It wasn't right.

Riders appeared in the distance.

"Shite," Monroe muttered under his breath. "Go on to the castle. I'll try to head them off."

The riders' pace increased, racing toward Ewan and Monroe.

It was too late. The men had already seen that Ewan had found Faye. Still, he held tighter to Faye and brought his horse to a canter. The Ross clan would be soon upon them, but it would be enough time to get her into Dunrobin Castle and secure her in a place where she could remain protected.

She sat up abruptly, alert, her head whipping from side to side. "What is it?" She clung to one of his arms and glanced over her shoulder, her eyes wide with fear. "Have they found me?"

"Aye," he said. "I'll get ye inside where ye'll be safe."

She sucked in a breath and nodded; her face beautiful even with the set of determination. God, she was bonny. Plush lips, red from the cold, the bottom plumper than the top. How he'd like to suck it into his mouth and trail his tongue over it.

His cock stirred, and he halted the direction of his thoughts.

She was not to be his. Not under the circumstances laid before them. And the last thing she needed was a cockstand jabbing her in the rear from the man who'd promised to protect her.

Jesu, what was his problem? He snapped the reins and called out for his horse to race the last bit of the way to the castle.

Once there, he dismounted from the horse and helped Faye from the destrier's broad back. Ewan put a hand to her slender shoulders and guided her. "This way."

She looked about as he rushed her through the castle, shouting orders to the servants as he did so to prepare for an assault from the Ross clan.

"Sutherland," Ross bellowed from outside.

Ewan ignored the call.

"Let me in to speak with ye, or I'll kill yer man here."

This time, Ewan did stop.

Monroe. Damn it. Ewan should never have allowed him to remain behind.

Faye put a hand to Ewan's chest, and those wide blue eyes lifted to his. "Don't let him die for me. Speak to them. Please." Her speech came across with more English to it than Scots, more so than when they'd been bairns.

"Aye, but no' with ye here." He flagged down a servant. "Let Ross in."

The servant nodded and ran off to comply with his order.

"This involves me as well." Faye walked with Ewan.

He squared his shoulders. "I told ye I'd keep ye safe."

She lifted her chin, her eyes glinting with resolve. "I refuse to be shoved in some room while ye handle my future."

He hadn't thought she could be lovelier than when she slept against his chest. He was wrong. As demure as she'd been asleep, she was now bright with passion, like dry tinder that had been struck with a flame. Wild and bonny.

"Sutherland," Ross's voice was closer now. Just inside the Great Hall.

Footsteps pattered down the hall, and Moiré appeared, gasping for breath in her haste. "What has happened with the Ross clan?" she asked, her brown eyes wide.

"I must speak with Ross," he said to his cousin. "Stay with Mistress Faye, aye?"

Moiré looked at Faye, and the confusion in her gaze deepened, but she nodded.

"This is my cousin, Moiré," Ewan said. "Ye can listen all ye like but stay here. Away from them."

When Faye opened her mouth to protest, he took her slender shoulders in his hands. "Stay here."

She remained quiet, and a shiver ran through her, reminding him of how cold she'd been. He drew off his cloak and draped it over her shoulders.

She tugged it more tightly around her and gave a nod. He wasn't sure if it was in compliance or thanks, but she offered no further protest.

Assured she would remain hidden while he handled the situation, he left her in the corridor and pushed through the door leading to the Great Hall. He secured it closed behind him and made his way to the dais where Ross and several of his men waited.

"Where is my granddaughter?" Ross demanded with a scowl as he pushed Monroe to Ewan's side.

Ewan narrowed his eyes at the older man. "I'll no' marry a lass being forced to wed me. Especially no' one who has been held captive and abducted from her home."

"Berwick is mine." Ross's shout rang off the walls around him, and his face turned a dark shade of red. "If ye refuse to wed her, I'll attack yer people until every last one of them is dead."

The threat sent a chill scraping down Ewan's spine. Regardless, he folded his arms over his chest and scoffed. "We've endured yer fighting for years. We'll do so again now."

"Give her to me," Ross demanded.

"So ye can sell her into another marriage?" Ewan widened his stance. "Nay."

Ross took several menacing steps forward, his hand on the hilt of his blade as though he meant to draw it free and slay Ewan where he stood. Still, Ewan held his ground and met the icy glare of the older chieftain.

Ewan had anticipated more threats, mayhap even an attempt at gutting him. He had not expected a shrewd expression to cross Ross's face or the question that followed. "What if there was another option?"

❧ 4 ❧

Faye leaned against the crack in the door. Her ear ached from pressing it so firmly to the wood, but her grandfather's words had become difficult to discern.

Ewan's cousin stood at her side, in deep concentration as she also tried to listen. She was a pretty young woman with light brown hair and dark eyes, mayhap older than Faye, though only slightly.

No doubt, she was worried about what she heard. Faye would be if she were of the Sutherland clan.

Ross had threatened war. He intended to kill them all, and still, the Sutherland chieftain had stood his ground. Protecting Faye. Just as he'd promised.

Her chest squeezed. Could she have so many deaths on her conscience simply because she refused to wed a man who was willing to risk his people to return her to her home?

She gritted her teeth, determined to remain as stoic as Sutherland.

"What other option?" Sutherland asked, his voice wary.

"A more biddable lass," Ross said. "Another of my granddaughters."

Faye's blood chilled. Even the heavy cloak Sutherland had draped over her shoulders could not quell the coldness frosting in her veins.

"I'll no' marry anyone ye force my way." Sutherland's reply was resolute. Heroic.

"This one is a good lass," Ross continued. "She'll do as she's told and is as bonny as her sister, but with hair dark as peat."

Clara.

Nay.

"I told ye," Sutherland said. "I'll no—"

"Nay." Faye pushed out into the Great Hall before she could stop herself. Before fear drowned out the last of her bravado. "I'll marry him."

Sutherland frowned at her, but her grandfather grinned. "I knew that would lure ye out." He chuckled. "But make no mistake, I'll take that sister of yers for a marriage if ye manage to worm yer way out of this."

"Promise me that ye'll leave my family be." A storm of rage and sorrow swept through her and nearly made her voice quaver. "No more marriages, no more abductions. Ye leave them be."

Her grandfather stared at her as if she were a child attempting to rebuke him. "Ye're no' in a position—"

"I'm not done." Faye wanted nothing more than to lower her gaze from the steely cut of his glare but refused to give him the satisfaction. She would win this battle.

After all, he'd shared his weakness. Berwick. And she was the key to obtaining his greatest desire.

"This marriage will stop all fighting between the Ross and Sutherland clans." She looked between the two men. "There will be peace."

Her grandfather sputtered his disbelief and looked to Sutherland as if seeking confirmation to what Faye had demanded. She nodded at the man she would marry, letting him know her mind was set.

"Give the lass what she wants," he said solemnly. "And I'll wed her."

Ross studied them both as the options weighed and counter-balanced against one another in his mind. "The wedding will take place now," he said finally. "Followed by a bedding ceremony."

"A wedding with no bedding ceremony," Faye countered before Sutherland could speak.

Her grandfather turned his green eyes on her. They weren't soft with tenderness like her mother's, but hard and unyielding, like chips of emeralds. "A bedding ceremony as well to verify the marriage canna be annulled. That, or I walk from these doors and send my men in two directions. One here to kill every Sutherland they can find, and another down to Castleton to bring me the rest of yer sisters."

"Enough," Sutherland snarled. "Ye're mad."

"Aye." Ross turned a wide-eyed gaze to Sutherland. "And I'll no' be duped by a false marriage."

"Fine," Faye said abruptly. It didn't matter if people saw her in her chemise.

But despite her attempt at bravery, a hum of nervousness vibrated within her.

Ross gave a low growl of irritation but finally held out his hand. Sutherland clasped forearms with him.

"To the chapel." Ross indicated for Sutherland to lead them.

Moiré said from Faye's side, "Surely ye can allow her a moment to prepare. It is her wedding day, after all."

Faye regarded Ewan's cousin, unable to say when she had approached. Especially in light of all that had transpired in the meeting.

"'Tis already late afternoon." Ross indicated the large doorway of the Great Hall. "To the chapel, so there will be time to sup and celebrate our alliance."

Moiré tossed a sympathetic frown in Faye's direction. While it had been kind of Moiré to help, Faye was grateful her grandfather had insisted on their immediate wedding. For with time to consider her choices, she might find herself lacking the strength to go through with it all.

Her mind was a fog of exhaustion from her attempt to escape. Her limbs were weak with weariness, and her stomach growled with savage hunger. She scarcely had the fortitude to remain upright, let alone wed a man she didn't know.

A husband she didn't want.

She'd never wanted marriage. Not after having seen what her mother had gone through after loving a man, then losing him. When Faye's da died, it had nearly killed her mum as well. Mum had never recovered, not fully. There was always sadness around her eyes, and an inability to truly laugh, to enjoy life. It was as though part of her had died along with Da.

Faye had long ago sworn to never be like her. No one would ever have such power over her so as to hurt her so deeply. Throughout Faye's life, she'd had enough pain.

Sutherland approached her. "Ye dinna have to do this," he said in a low voice.

She didn't allow herself to soften lest she caved. "Aye, I do."

"I'll be a good husband to ye, Faye," he vowed. "Nothing will happen to ye while with me. I'll keep my promise to protect ye. Always."

The image of the boy he'd been flashed in her mind again. His earnest gaze was so similar, despite how his boyish face and body had sharpened into that of a man.

She nodded, uncertain of what to say. He was too handsome, too considerate. The kind of man who would seek the heart she was so unwilling to give.

Even still, she could not stop her fingers from smoothing over her hair, which must be frightful after the hours she wandered through the brutal highlands. A glance down at her kirtle confirmed it was streaked with mud and had a tear at the neckline with several threads jutting out like sparse hairs. Aye, she looked a mess.

Sutherland didn't appear at all bothered by her rumpled state and offered her his arm. She slid her hand into the warm crook of his elbow, and they walked through the castle toward their fate together. The castle was dark, its shutters locked tight, blocking out cold and light alike. Candles lit the corridors and cast heavy shadows within the thick walls as well as an odor of smoke. Their footsteps were silent on the thick layer of rushes, silencing their ominous march.

To be married.

The thought stole her breath.

Married.

Panic fluttered in her chest. Everything in her screamed to grab the dagger tucked into Ewan's boot and escape. If she stole a horse, she could cover more ground. Mayhap find a village. Get help.

And then what?

Then, her grandfather would go back to Castleton and appeal to Clara. All he needed to say was that her sacrifice to move to the Highlands and wed a chieftain would save lives, and Clara would come without a moment's hesitation.

Damn Clara for her goodness.

They entered a small stone chapel. Colorful glass lined either wall, providing more light than any candle within the castle. A man stood at the front, wearing dark robes. His head lifted in surprise at their approach, and his gaze flitted between their party before settling on Sutherland. "May I help ye, sir?"

Faye did not miss the way Sutherland's body tensed before replying to the clergyman. "We're here to be wed."

UNDER THE WATCHFUL GAZE OF EWAN'S ENEMY, HE MARRIED A

woman who was little more than a stranger. The ceremony was a short affair, rushed through by the local priest who'd had no time to prepare the vows properly.

While Faye had readily agreed to the vows, Ewan had faltered. She had been stolen from her family, chained for weeks of travel and hunted down like sport—all for this moment so that he might marry her. He hated the circumstances. No woman should be treated thus.

She met his eyes and nodded. Only then did he force the words from his mouth and allow their souls to be bound to one another.

The priest pronounced them man and wife and bade Ewan kiss his new bride. She regarded Ewan with a searching stare, as though trying to learn who he was in that brief span of time. Her blonde hair settled like gold cloth around her shoulders and fell over the small tear in her dress. He'd noticed her sweeping her fingers over her tresses to cover the spot, in an apparent self-conscious attempt to appear presentable despite the situation.

It warmed him to the core that she should care. It made a powerful yearning spring forth within him, one that longed to draw her against his body and let his lips play over hers. With a flash of regret, he recalled his ceremony to Lara. It had been well-planned, but he had not been hit with the same urges for his demure wife.

A fresh slice of pain twisted in Ewan's heart at the thought of his late wife.

He lifted Faye's slender hand to his mouth, rather than kissing her lips. He would not presume her affections, especially in light of how readily she'd already been taken advantage of.

Ross did not protest the kiss, and for that, Ewan was grateful. Maybe the old bastard had a heart after all.

Ewan offered Faye his arm once more, and they returned somberly to the Great Hall, where Moiré had done her best to create something of a celebration.

The costly table runners used for good company had been set on the trestle tables, and several silver candlesticks and salt cellars glinted in the firelight. The simple dinner of stewed vegetables and roasted quail the cook had prepared was laid out like a fine feast.

Moiré caught Ewan's eye as he entered the Great Hall, conveying with her gaze the words he could hear in his head. *I told ye so.* And she had—before his departure to Balnagown, she had warned him not to consider Ross's proposition.

If he'd wed Mistress Blair, he'd be with a woman who had wanted to be with him, under far better circumstances.

But he'd been too curious about Faye, his interest piqued by the pretty girl he'd known. What was worse, he'd been correct in his assumption that she had only become more attractive.

He walked her to the dais, where she sat at his right side. His clan members settled at the surrounding trestles in oppressive silence; their shuffling feet gave off a sound like the downpour of rain. They looked to him with solemn faces, expecting a grand speech, but what was he to say on such an occasion?

Instead, he lifted his goblet of hastily poured wine and said simply, "To peace."

They all drank as a pathetic band of minstrels quickly set up and filled the silence with a tune far too cheerful for the occasion.

Beside Ewan, his bride maintained a smile that quivered at the corners and contrasted the dullness in her eyes. No doubt, her thoughts were reeling from the turn of events as much as his. It had all been done too fast to process fully.

"Would ye care to dance?" he asked.

Her gaze moved first to the empty square of space for dancing before turning her attention to him. "I suppose it is expected," she replied at last.

"I dinna think anything is expected in this madness," he replied.

Her eyes brightened somewhat with a more earnest smile. "I think it should be a pleasant distraction."

It was all the answer he needed. He got to his feet and extended his hand to her, which she readily took.

They approached the dance floor and stood opposite one another, where she curtseyed, and he bowed. Amid the trill of a pipe and the gentle pluck of stringed instruments, they came together and spun about to the sweet rhythm of the music.

"Do ye recall much of me from when we were children?" she asked as they stepped toward one another.

"Aye." He caught her slender waist and lifted her briefly before setting her on the floor. Her breasts gave a slight bounce that he could not help but notice. "I only saw ye on the few occasions ye visited Scotland to see Ross. What of ye? Do ye remember anything of me?"

She studied his face with an openness he liked, as though trying in earnest to summon his younger self into her mind. "My only recollection is of a boy with brown hair and hazel eyes who promised he would always protect me." Her cheeks had gone pink, but he could not tell if it was from a blush or the exertion of their dance. He found himself hoping for the former.

"I supposed I havena changed so verra much." He smiled at the jest toward himself.

Her gaze dipped downward and shifted away as an unmistakable blush crept over her cheeks. "I wouldna say that," she whispered.

His cock twitched in response. He was not an unattractive man, he knew. Women had offered to become his leman after Lara's death, though he'd never accepted. There had been too much weighing down his thoughts with the ache of her death and the insistent press of his uncle's desire for leadership of the clan.

Knowing his appearance pleased Faye, however, brought him more pride than he'd bothered to consider in a long time. For he certainly found her alluring.

The music drew to a close, and they drifted apart to bow and curtsey one final time. As he led her back to the dais, he caught sight of Moiré sitting at a table by herself. She lifted her brows and waved him over.

"Forgive me," he said to his new wife. "I must speak with my cousin a moment."

Faye nodded and lifted her waiting goblet to her lips as Ewan departed to join Moiré.

"She's beautiful." His cousin tilted her cup in celebration toward him. "Felicitations."

He nodded his head in thanks as she drank deeply from the goblet. "I'd hoped for yer assistance in making her feel welcome."

"Of course," Moiré replied readily, as he knew she would.

"She's been taken from her family and forced into this, as I'm sure ye've gathered."

Moiré nodded, her eyes softening with sympathy. "Aye. The poor lass. I'll do anything I can to help."

"Including showing her duties as mistress of the castle, aye?" he pressed.

After Lara's death, Moiré had taken on the responsibility of running the castle. Faye would, of course, be assuming the task now that she was his wife.

"Ye need no' worry, Ewan." Moiré gently patted his arm, her demeanor as good-natured as ever. "I'll show her what she needs to know."

The tension drained from his shoulders. He'd hoped she wouldn't be offended at Faye assuming the role Moiré had spent almost two years handling with smooth efficiency. He should have known better. Moiré was always considerate and accommodating.

"If I might make a suggestion?" she offered.

Ewan nodded, grateful for any recommendation regarding his new wife and their marriage by unusual circumstance.

"Ye may wish to have a care with how ye handle Lady Sutherland," she said. "To ensure she knows ye care for her." She glanced toward Faye, her eyes sparkling. "As I feel ye will soon care for her greatly."

"Let her know I care for her?" Ewan repeated with uncertainty. "What do ye mean?"

Moiré shook her head. "I shouldna have said anything."

"I wish ye would."

Moiré's pleasant expression dropped, and she nibbled on her lower lip. "I dinna think Lara felt as though ye cared," she replied slowly.

Ewan's face went cool as the blood drained from it. "Why would ye say that?"

Moiré's brow crumpled. "I shouldna—"

"Why would ye say that?" He demanded, more harshly than he'd intended. "Did she..." A band of tension squeezed at his chest. "Did she tell ye that?"

Moiré held her breath and nodded. "I'm sorry."

An ache clawed within him, ripping old wounds open. He nodded and patted her shoulder, unable to summon anything to say.

"I'm sorry," Moiré repeated in a horrified whisper.

"I needed to know." He swallowed at the stubborn lump in his throat. "Was that why..." He couldn't even bring himself to say the words. Instead, they hung in the air, unspoken.

Was that why Lara had taken her own life?

Moiré closed her eyes, and a tear trailed down her cheek. She blinked her eyes open and regarded Ewan with a pained expression. "Be good to yer new wife, aye?"

Ewan clenched his hand into a fist and vowed that he would care for Faye and leave no doubt in her mind that he fully intended to love her.

$\cancel{\mathfrak{F}}$ 5 $\cancel{\mathfrak{F}}$

F aye didn't want anyone to notice her discomfort, and yet
how could they not when she was set on display? The dais
sat higher than the trestles lining either side of the Great
Hall.

It was finer than anything she'd ever dined on. Blue runners
ran along the polished wood and silver glinted among bits of
heater that had been plucked to adorn the table.

She had never been around such costly things, nor had she
been put in a position where all eyes were set upon her. Sutherland was gone only minutes, though it truly felt like hours. He
spoke first to his cousin, then to Monroe, before he returned to
her. Through it all, she sat alone with only a goblet of wine and
plate of food for company. And all those eyes, gazing up at her,
wide with curiosity.

No doubt waiting for the bedding ceremony.

She wished they would start it, get the ordeal over with. Let
those cold, curious eyes feast on her in her most vulnerable
moment. A knot of emotion settled as an ache at the back of her
throat, but she discreetly swallowed it away.

"Forgive me," Sutherland said as he returned.

Faye relaxed somewhat as he settled by her side. Not that she knew him well enough to find comfort in his presence, but he was someone—anyone—who would take some of the gawping attention.

Her grandfather rose with his goblet of wine in hand, which he tapped with his open fingers, so his ring pinged sharply against the metal. The room went silent as people turned to him with expectations.

He lifted his drink high in the air in a silent toast toward the dais. "Felicitations to the happy new couple." He smirked. "Let us put these two to bed."

Faye's stomach clenched, and her head swam with a light-headed sensation that threatened to make her slide from her seat. She didn't want to be here. She didn't want to be in this situation. She didn't want to be married.

But she was. And there was nothing for it, but to stand with her plastered smile and her quivering insides.

This was no battle she could win or conversation she could flirt her way out of. Sutherland got to his feet first and offered her his hand. She accepted and stood on shaky legs.

His people had consumed a good amount of spirits, and though some remained quiet at the stunning turn of events, others threw up raucous and ribald cheers. The chants and jeers filled the large room and buzzed in Faye's ears.

The crowd followed them, pressing at their backs, forcing them up narrow stairs she had never climbed to a capacious chamber she had never entered. A bed stood at its center, a massive thing with thick posts at each corner and heavy curtains hanging from all sides. Her heartbeat slammed so hard in her chest that she was certain the revelers could hear it over their own happy cries.

Two screens had been erected at opposite sides of the room, no doubt where they would prepare. Faye hesitated, uncertain of what to do. These were customs of the wealthy, and she'd not been wealthy a day in her life. Aye, they lived in a manor in Castleton, but it was for protection rather than power. A means of keeping them safe from reivers.

She was breathing too hard; her heart pounding too ferociously. White spots bloomed in her vision, and she regretted having had more wine than food. But her stomach had been nervous and her mouth dry.

A cool hand closed over hers, and Moiré was there with a gentle smile. "Come with me. I'll see to ye."

Faye allowed the other woman to lead her behind a screen, a flimsy barrier between her and the people who had so willingly invaded her privacy.

"This is wrong." Moiré frowned and patted Faye's forearm. "Ye're doing fine. Mayhap better than I would, were I in yer situation."

Faye simply nodded, too numb to say anything else. How had this happened? Just one month prior, she'd been at Castleton with her family, shelling beans and getting upset with Clara for bringing up the English. Clara, of all people, who didn't deserve anyone's scorn. Theirs had been a quiet, mundane life that had been violently upended to this shocking moment of undressing before strangers in lands she didn't know.

That stubborn ache returned to the back of her throat.

"I brought ye one of my nightrails," Moiré said. "'Tis all I could find with such sudden notice."

The other woman was a good two inches shorter than Faye. Still, an ill-fitting garment was a far cry better than being naked.

"Mayhap, my chemise..." Faye glanced down at her mud-stained skirts, and the words died on her tongue. Her chemise would be in no order to be put on display.

She put her back to Moiré and allowed the other woman to help undress her and slide the sark on. It was a thin garment that showed the hardness of Faye's nipples against the white fabric and only came halfway down her calves. She immediately crossed her arms over her chest, but it did little to make her feel any less exposed.

Moiré set to work on Faye's hair next, quickly brushing the blonde tresses and carefully arranging them down Faye's shoulders to cover the peaks of her nipples. Once done, Ewan's cousin peeked around the screen and nodded to Faye.

It was time.

Faye hesitated a long moment, drawing a breath and whatever strength she could scrape up from the dregs of her courage.

She stepped around the flimsy screen, and cheers rose up. It was one thing to entice a man into conversation with the swell of her bosom over the neckline of her gown, and quite another to be put on display in such a manner. Her face blossomed with heat, and she averted her eyes from the crowd to avoid their stares sliding over her. Not that it mattered. She could feel them. Like ants creeping over her skin, crawling over every inch of her, until she wanted to hide in a corner and scream.

Across the room, Sutherland wore only his trews, his chest bare. Though Faye's nerves vibrated with an onslaught of anxiety and fear and humiliation, she was not blind. Her husband was a finely built man. Thanks be to God that he was not old and fat.

She kept her footsteps slow as she made her way toward the bed under the weight of so many viewers, her head held high.

The priest who had wed them began to pray, his words a drone beneath bawdy jests and laughter. Faye lifted the heavy coverlet and slid into bed as Sutherland did too. She covered herself high enough to shield her breasts from view but still could not relax. The priest finished his prayer and made the sign of the cross over their bed.

Not much longer.

Or so she hoped.

Servants moved on either side of the bed, drawing the curtains around them until the light outside was snuffed out.

Footsteps exited the room, and silence took its place, filled only with the steady, gentle breath of the stranger beside her.

She blinked back the sudden threat of tears at her relief and swallowed. "Are they gone?" Her voice was small in the over-bearing darkness. She winced.

Would he roll over onto her and press his husbandly rights upon her?

She gripped the blanket tighter, wishing she were home in her shared room with her sisters instead of here. With this man. In this horrible situation.

A crack of light appeared, and the ropes creaked as Sutherland left the bed. A heavy thunk of wood sliding on wood interrupted the quiet—a door being barred.

Faye started at the sound in spite of herself.

The curtains drew back on all sides, letting in the light once more. Sutherland stood beside the bed, now wearing a fresh leine over his trews, covering his naked torso. He offered her an apolo-getic smile that bordered on sheepish. "I'm glad that's done with."

"As am I," she said softly.

He held up a heavy robe in his hands in an invitation for her. "I noticed ye dinna eat much at supper and had Monroe bring some food. I thought mayhap we might share it and become reac-quainted."

Faye hesitated at his kindness. She didn't desire to become reacquainted. He seemed to be a good man. But good men were oftentimes a disappointment.

More than a disappointment, they had been a source of great pain, an opportunity for incredible hurt. Still, as much as she loathed the idea, the thought of being blanketed in a heavier garment was too tempting an offer to refuse.

She slid from the bed and allowed him to wrap her in the heavy robe. The layer of clothing might be a small thing, but to her at that moment, it was a reminder of her own awareness. Of whom she was and what she was capable of. It put her back in control of her senses.

She would do what she must as a wife, but she would not allow herself to trust this man. And most certainly, she would bar her heart from even considering the notion of caring for him, let alone loving him.

৩৯৩

EWAN COULDN'T TAMP DOWN THE PROTECTIVE URGE THAT ROSE inside him. Faye had looked so vulnerable at the bedding ceremony, her eyes wide in her pale face, even as her back had remained straight and proud.

He led her to the table by the hearth and retrieved the platter of food Monroe had smuggled behind Ewan's screen. It was only a bit of meat and cheese with two loaves of bread, but it was better than the few bites of vegetables he'd seen her eat earlier.

He led her to the small table and set the food in front of her, then poured a goblet of wine for each of them. His actions were loud in the quiet of the room, compensating for all the things he had no idea how to say. When at last, the table was properly set, the silence became oppressive. Music and the hum of indiscernible chatter from the Great Hall floated in, muffled by the thick door.

Ewan cleared his throat and scrambled for something to say. "'Tis a lot of years to cover." He took a loaf of bread, broke it in half and gave her one of the pieces.

"We don't have to." She plucked off a small chunk and slid it into her mouth, the movement slow and carrying an unexpected sensuality.

"I'm sure ye've changed from the lass I knew." He bit into his bread.

"How do ye think I have?" She lifted the goblet to her mouth and took a delicate sip of wine that left her lower lip glossy.

"I dinna recall ye sounding so English," he offered.

She gave a little laugh at that, though it appeared without mirth. "The English think I sound Scottish."

"Ye live near the border, aye? On the English or the Scottish side?"

She lifted a sardonic brow. "Scottish."

"I take it ye no longer do as ye're told," he said.

He'd meant it as a jest, but her mouth lifted at the corner in a half-smile as she eyed him coyly. "Nay."

She said it like a challenge she wanted him to try. His cock stirred with interest.

"Do ye prefer biddable women?" she asked in a throaty voice that put heat into his blood.

He swallowed. "I prefer a woman who knows her own mind," he stammered, feeling foolish for the genuine response to the flirtatious question.

He tried again to put Lara from his mind, but it was nearly impossible to keep from comparing them when the two were so different. Lara would never have played with words in such a way with him, each of her replies open and honest.

"Why did ye agree to marry me, Sutherland?" Faye asked. "Ye hadn't seen me in years."

He smiled at her use of his surname, which was also now hers. "Call me Ewan."

"Ewan." Her lips moved around his name, making it far more alluring than it had ever been before.

"We've been at war with the Ross clan for well over a century," Ewan said, forcing his thoughts from her mouth and what he'd like to do with it. "From the story I've been told, a Sutherland chieftain and his brother stole the hearts of women promised to sons of a Ross chieftain. The battle of wits soon became a battle of blades, and lives were lost."

"'Tis a high cost for love." Faye tilted her head back in thought and put the long column of her slender throat on display. Her skin was as flawless as cream and left him with a sudden desire to kiss the length of it all the way down to the generous swell of her breasts.

Ewan drank a sip of wine to wet his suddenly dry throat. "I imagine if the love was true, it was a worthy sacrifice."

"Over a century of war?" Faye pressed her lips together, as though to still her words.

"I dinna like war, nor do I like how ye were treated." His gaze lowered to her hands, where the sleeve of the large robe had fallen back to reveal the chaffed skin along her slender wrists. "I hope this marriage changes all that."

She regarded her damaged flesh.

"I'll never hurt ye," he vowed. "I would no' ever have allowed ye to be brought to me like this if given a choice. Yer grandda reminded me of the betrothal and considered it legitimate though yer mum had no' signed it. He invited me to Balnagown to meet ye, to go over the original agreement."

She tilted her head. "And ye came."

"Before I knew ye'd been dragged here." He couldn't keep the anger out of his voice.

"Why did ye go?" The way she asked the question was with a gentle sweetness that set him at ease.

He allowed himself a moment to openly admire how the firelight played off her flawless complexion and gleaming blonde hair. "I was curious."

"Curious?"

"When I was a lad, ye were the bonniest lass I'd ever seen." His shoulder lifted in a shrug. "I wanted to see what ye looked like now."

"And?" She raised a brow.

His face heated to say aloud what he actually thought. It was not something he often did. However, it was something he should have done, especially with Lara. He wouldn't make a similar mistake again. "Yer beauty as a lass doesna compare to yer loveliness as a woman."

He leaned forward over the small table and settled his hand over hers. Her skin was smooth and warm. As soft as he'd anticipated.

"Tell me about yer siblings," he said. "Ye have an older brother. Drake, aye?"

She nodded.

"And at least one sister."

"Aye, two," she replied. "Have ye any siblings?"

"Only Moiré, who is more sister to me than cousin," he replied. "I had an older brother who died before my da. 'Twas only several months before. The healer suspects the blow of Ragnall's death is what killed my da."

"I'm sorry to hear it." There was a quiet sadness to her tone when she spoke, as though she were mourning the men as Ewan did still, after almost a decade since he'd lost them.

"Do ye remember them?" he asked.

She shook her head, her face grave. It was then he realized it wasn't that she knew them, but that she knew loss.

"I was sorry to hear of yer da's passing as well." Ewan wrapped his hand around hers in a gentle show of support.

Her fingers moved over the back of his hand, featherlight, a caress that traveled through him like a jolt of lightning. Her touch continued to play over his skin, shifting the sleeve of his leine up as the delicate scrape of her nails whispered up his forearm. It was hardly an intimate gesture, but it set his blood on fire.

She hesitated over the scar just past his wrist. "What was this from?"

"If I tell ye what every scar is from, 'twill be a long night."

Her forefinger traced the outline of the scar, following the teeth marks from the wolf all those years ago.

"I anticipate a long night." Her gaze met his and seared straight to his groin.

His prick swelled at her suggestion.

"What is this one from?" she asked again.

"Do ye remember it?"

She shook her head.

"We got lost trying to find a fae glen." He shifted in his seat, an attempt to be more comfortable despite his hardening cock. "A pack of wolves came upon us, one bolder than the rest. He got my forearm, but I had my dirk on me, and the beast dinna live out the night."

Her lips parted. "Was this my fault?"

Before he could try to set her mind to ease, she slid from her chair, so she was on her knees before him and bent over his forearm with her eyes locked on his. She lowered her plump, red mouth to the scar, bestowing upon it the most tender of kisses.

"Forgive me." Her sweet breath fanned over his skin and made a shudder of desire tease down his back.

His cock was fully aroused now, teased into the full staff of lust by the innocent suggestion of her kiss. Her stare settled on his trews, and her lips fell open, her expression impossibly innocent.

He cleared his throat. "I..."

She didn't move from where she kneeled by his legs. "Did ye like my kiss?"

He'd liked her kiss too much. It made him want more, but not chaste ones like what she had delivered to his scar. Nay, he longed to unfasten the ties of his trews and let his prick spring free. To feel the brush of her breath over his hot skin, the flick of her tongue—

He swallowed and helped her to her feet. "Ye're a maiden."

"I'm yer wife." She tucked her full lower lip into her mouth and slowly let it pop free. "I'm yers to take."

God help him. His heartbeat came faster at the thought of stripping the robe from her body, revealing those hard, pink nipples he'd been able to make out through the thin fabric of her nightrail.

She bent over him and slid her hands up the back of his neck. "Kiss me," she whispered.

With a groan, he lifted his head to do as she'd asked. Their lips touched and ignited like blades that clashed and sparked against one another in the heat of combat. Her lips were pillowy soft and warm. He moved his mouth over hers, tasting the ambrosia of her kiss as his tongue brushed the seam of her mouth.

A little moan sounded in the back of her throat and she opened for him, tentatively caressing the tip of her tongue to his.

He gripped the thick wool robe she wore as if it might aid him in holding onto his control. She was so damn lovely, so supple in his hands, beneath his mouth.

His woman. His wife. His to bed. Soon. So very soon.

❧ 6 ❧

Faye had kissed several men before. Most were chaste kisses, a brief touching of lips, or upon a scruffy cheek for a better price on eggs or other goods that helped keep her family alive and fed.

Once it had been with a man she'd found attractive, a baker's son who had a honeyed tongue and elicited genuine blushes. It was with him that she'd discovered she enjoyed kissing. Mayhap too much. The rush of desire had frightened her, and she'd never returned.

It was one thing to play a coquette, and quite another to be one.

Now though...

She slanted her mouth over Ewan's, their tongues mating with eagerness as a sensual fire coursed through her veins like winding silk. She let it consume her and luxuriated in its allure.

This time, she would not have to force herself to stop. This time, that thundering insistence between her thighs could be slaked by more than her hand.

He grabbed her to him with a growl of desire that made her toes curl. *This.* She wanted this rather than the previous conversation. He was handsome and considerate. Knowing how good he was might pull down the defenses she was not ready to release.

Nay, this was far better. No emotional feeling, only physical lust.

She deepened her kiss with a determination to push the man he was from her thoughts and focus only on how her body responded. In her eagerness, she tilted forward and hovered for a precarious moment before tipping into a fall.

He caught her, his hands at her hips. He guided her downward into his lap. She parted her legs over his chair to avoid kneeing him in the stomach, and the short nightrail rode up over her knees.

The hardness of his arousal pressed into the sensitive place between her thighs, spread open by the way she sat on him. It was brazen and wanton and glorious.

She caught his face between her palms and kissed him hungrily, not bothering to hide the force of her passion, of her need. His hands were still on her hips and now he pulled her forward, so their pelvises bumped against one another. The hardness of him ground against the softness of her.

She gasped in pleasure and moved of her own volition, squirming in his lap to get closer to him, her hands braced on his torso to steady herself. He groaned, and the vibration hummed against her palm. He explored her body, gliding over her robe at first, then under it as he cupped her breast with only the thin linen separating them.

His thumb swept over her nipple, sending a ripple of pleasure over her sensitive skin. He kissed her neck, his breath warm and spicy.

"Do ye like that?" his voice rumbled in her ear.

She swallowed and nodded.

"I want to learn everything about ye." He caught her earlobe between his teeth in a gentle nip. "What ye like." He trailed his mouth over her collarbone as his finger curled around the ribbon at her neckline. "What ye want."

He pulled the ribbon, and the nightrail fell open. "What pleases ye." He brushed aside the thin cloth and cradled one naked breast in his palm.

"That." Faye pressed her chest forward, toward his touch.

He lowered his head and drew her nipple into the heat of his mouth.

She closed her eyes against the intensity of such pleasure. "That," she said again, her voice husky with lust.

His hips lifted as he suckled her breast, so his arousal ground against her. Her eyes flew open with delight.

"Ye please me," she whispered. "Like this, touching me, kissing me."

His large hand hovered over her knee, and his blunt fingers swept over her skin as gentle as a breeze. "I want to touch all of ye."

His fingers slowly crept up her inner thigh, higher and higher. Her breath caught as her muscles trembled with the effort of straining toward him.

Her hem rose up her thighs as he ascended her legs, revealing more and more of her to him until he reached the apex. His gaze lowered to the thatch of blonde hair covering her most intimate place.

Mayhap another would feel ashamed to be so on display, but Faye had never been like other women. She knew the power women held over men came from their bodies, and there was no part of a woman with greater allure than what no one ever saw.

And though she hated to admit it to even herself, she was helpless to its power as well, to the thrum of lust so great, it nearly consumed her. Gaze fixed on his task, Ewan swept his thumb over her center, a light graze that made her hips instinctively flex forward.

His attention flicked back to her face, where he watched her with an appreciative concentration in his heavy-lidded eyes. His fingers moved again, tracing the slit of her sex.

Faye gasped and widened her legs, eager for more.

"Ye're verra wet," he groaned. "Ready for me."

"Aye." Faye grabbed his shoulders to hold herself upright.

He paused at the top of her sex and circled his thumb over an area that made stars dance behind her closed lids. She cried out and arched into him, needing more.

"Ye like that as well, aye?" His voice was gruff, his breathing ragged, the arousal between his legs so wonderfully hard.

He probed a finger inside of her as his thumb played over the swollen bud of her core. "And this?"

A whimper of helpless desire slipped from her lips. "Aye," she panted.

"I want ye so damn bad, Faye." He moved his hand against her, and inside of her, until everything in her began to tense.

She opened her eyes slowly as she lowered her head to gaze at him with the full force of her sensuality. "Then have me."

He slid his touch from her, leaving her hot and aching to be sated.

She flexed her body against his. "Tell me what to do."

The corner of his mouth quirked up in a half-smile. "I thought ye said ye werena biddable."

She lifted a brow. "I'll decide if I want to obey or not."

"Feisty lass." He grinned. "Stand up and take off yer robe."

She eased off his lap. The sash hung in a loose knot, nearly undone. She pulled it free and pushed the heavy weight of the robe from her shoulders.

It slid off, leaving her in the ill-fitting nightrail.

"I'll assume ye want this off as well?" She fingered the linen, lifting it slightly for him to see the tops of her knees.

A muscle clenched in his jaw. "Aye."

"As ye bid me," she said playfully. She kept her movements measured as she drew it off her, revealing herself one tantalizing inch at a time before letting the garment flutter to the ground. Naked and unabashed, she stood in place, allowing him to look upon her.

His gaze carefully, slowly trailed over her. The place between her legs was still damp from where he'd touched her and thundered with a pulse of lust that made her ache with yearning. His gaze settled on her breasts, and her nipples went hard, eager for the heat of his mouth on them again.

"I believe 'tis yer turn." She propped a hand on her hip.

"Did ye say something?" His brows lifted as he returned his focus to her eyes. "I thought I was the one giving instructions."

She stepped closer to him and pulled his hand to bring him upright. "Mayhap, I have my own demands too."

"Are ye a demanding lass?" he asked in a low, sensual voice. As he rose, he trailed his fingers up her inner thigh and over the slit of her sex.

Her eyes closed briefly, reveling in the wave of bliss that threatened to buckle her knees. "Please me well, and I may become even more demanding," she whispered.

"Do ye promise?" He lifted the leine from over his head, revealing his sculpted torso once more. Now it was her turn to gaze openly at him, over the shadowy valleys and chiseled bands of his powerful body.

He closed the distance between them and pulled her against him as he lowered his mouth to hers. His skin was smooth and warm, the hair sprinkled over his chest rasping just enough to tease at her heightened sensitivity.

Her fingers wandered over his back, his chest, his stomach, sampling his raw strength, reveling in it. His breath sucked in when her fingertips grazed the area beneath his navel. She broke off the kiss and looked to his lower stomach. A line of dark hair trailed from his navel and disappeared beneath the waistband of his trews.

How deliciously tempting.

She traced that line with her fingernail, the pressure intentionally delicate so he would sense it rather than feel it. The massive column of his arousal straining against the leather twitched, and she almost moaned in anticipation.

"I think ye forgot something." She hooked a finger into his waistband.

"Are ye ordering me to remove these?" he asked.

She caught one of the ties of his trews and pulled. "Aye."

He tilted his head in acquiescence. "If my lady commands…" He pulled free the second tie, and his straining arousal burst free.

Faye gasped at the male member, having never seen one before. Thick and swollen with lust, it stuck out from his body like a pole. As much as she didn't want this marriage, she had to admit her husband was not only handsome but finely made. All of him. She stretched her hand toward his sex and curled her fingers around the hot, silky shaft.

He would never have her heart, she knew, but she would gladly be his in body. Again and again and again.

⚜

EWAN ISSUED A TIGHT GROAN AS FAYE WRAPPED HER DELICATE hand around his cock.

"'Tis so hard," she marveled, her eyes bright as they met his.

"Ye do that to me," he ground out as she stroked her touch over him in exploration.

"As ye make me slick with yearning." With one hand on his prick, she slipped the other hand between her legs and brought it back to his cock, swirling her dampness over the spongy head.

Jesu.

Ewan leaned his head back at the extreme pleasure of her touch.

"Do ye like this?" she asked.

When he gazed at her once more, he found a wicked smile curling her lips.

"Aye," he grunted.

He pushed his trews to the ground, so he stood fully nude before her. "Go to the bed," he commanded.

He'd never been one to demand anything of a woman. Certainly, Lara had been biddable, and he would never have ordered her so. But there was a give and take of power between Faye and him that made his prick go hard enough to explore it.

She smiled. "Nay." Her hand traced up and down his cock, her movements tantalizing and teasing all at once. The minx.

He kissed her, using his tongue and lips to play over her mouth, as his touch wandered back down her body to her slick core. He found the nub of her desire and circled it with his thumb until her knees bent slightly.

She panted against his mouth even as she kissed him back. Her body rolled in the rhythm of his caress, eager for more. Meanwhile, her hand moved over him, gliding, squeezing, stroking, driving him nearly mad with need.

"Do ye want this?" he asked.

Her hand tensed around him. "Aye."

"The bed," he growled.

She exhaled and pulled him with her. He touched her body as they walked slowly together, caressing her waist and arse, cupping her breasts. Each new touch elicited a little breathy moan that went straight to his arousal.

When they reached the bed, she arched against him and tugged at the back of his neck in an attempt to drag him down to the mattress. He lowered over her, where he remained, hovering atop her body, his cock straining with the need to thrust inside her.

He nudged the head of his arousal against her wet center and tensed with as much anticipation as dread.

The consummation hadn't gone well with Lara. She'd been

timid, afraid of his aroused state when she'd seen him. Though he'd tried not to hurt her, she'd given him a wounded look when he'd taken her maidenhead and had silently cried. He'd stopped immediately, and it took several more months until they attempted such intimacy again.

He didn't want that again. Not with Faye or any other woman.

He braced himself over her, careful not to allow his weight to settle atop her.

Faye writhed underneath him, arching and squirming. "Is something amiss?" she asked breathlessly. "Or do ye mean to kill me with waiting?"

Her cheeks and lips were flushed with pleasure. Jesu, she was finely made. And lusty. A bonny lass with a sharp tongue he wanted to set to better use.

His stomach curled into a knot as he gently nudged deeper inside her.

Faye's lashes fluttered. "I want ye," she whimpered. "All of ye."

He flexed his pelvis forward, easing in slightly more. The grip of her sheath was impossibly tight, as though trying to squeeze him back out.

His breath came hard and stirred her unbound hair. "It will hurt."

Faye lifted her hips. "Do all of it at once rather than dragging it out."

Still, he hesitated.

Her brow lifted, her eyes flashing with a challenge. "I demand ye take me."

His cock twitched at such a request from her sweet lips. She gasped with pleasure, clearly having felt the movement within her.

"'Tis an order, then?" he confirmed.

She lifted her hips. "Aye."

He balled the bedclothes in his hand and pushed into her,

forcing his way through her delicate barrier until he was fully sheathed. Tight, so damn tight. Sweat prickled on his brow.

She hissed an inhale.

"Forgive me." He began to lift off her when her legs curled around his waist and locked him against her with a delicious squeeze of her core.

"I've waited the whole of my adult life for this moment." Faye's calves crossed over his lower back tensed and drew him down to her. "The pain will pass."

He hesitated despite her certainty.

"Women talk," Faye said with a smile. "The more ye move, the easier I adjust to ye." She wriggled her arse, and a fresh tingle of pleasure rushed through him.

"The more pleasure I will feel," she continued in a throaty whisper. "Ye asked to know what I liked, what I wanted..."

He eased from her carefully, then nudged back in. Her brow furrowed with concentration, and her lips parted.

"Touch me," she said. "Like ye did before." She took his hand and guided it to her sex.

His fingers moved between their bodies as he found the swollen bud and played over it. Almost immediately, the impossible squeeze of her sheath on his cock relaxed. Still tight, but not intense.

Her eyes closed, and she leaned her head back. "Aye."

He moved within her, gliding in and pulling back in slow motions. Each shift sent waves of bliss through him. Every muscle in his body ached with stiffness as he took extra effort to ensure he didn't cause her discomfort.

All at once, the small line at her brow smoothed, and her lips parted around a moan. The forced arch of her body with his became a natural roll, gliding together in the same instinctive rhythm.

She was enjoying their union. His ballocks went tight at the realization, and he was flooded with an eagerness to please her.

He continued to play with the bud of her sex and increased his pace.

Her core clenched around him again. This time, however, it was not pain that made it grip him, but the warning of her impending release. He thrust faster and deeper until she cried out. Her sheath spasmed around his cock, a shudder of pleasure.

His climax exploded through him and roared from his chest like a beast. When at last the final shivers of euphoria drained from his body, he lay on the bed beside Faye, careful to keep his weight from her.

He glanced tentatively toward her, dreading the possibility that she might be upset afterward, as Lara had been. "If I hurt—"

A finger pressed to his lips. "Don't say ye won't touch me again."

He looked to Faye and found her watching him with a languid smile, her eyes half-closed, and her hair mussed from their efforts. The air held the musk of sex and sweat, a perfume that was satisfyingly erotic. His entire body felt as though his bones had melted in his limbs.

Never had he been so thoroughly sated through coupling as with Faye.

"I fully intend to do that again quite soon," she said.

He pressed a kiss to her forehead and stroked a lock of hair behind her ear. "I dinna want to hurt ye."

Something flashed in her eyes, but she said nothing, offering him a simple smile instead.

He pushed up from the bed and cleaned himself before wetting a linen to bring to her. He hated to make a comparison between his wives but couldn't help recalling how Lara had snatched the cloth and curled away from him to wipe at her virgin's blood.

Faye parted her thighs at his approach, revealing herself and the smear of blood for him to clean her. When the cloth touched her, she closed her eyes and sighed with longing.

Ewan moved the linen over her carefully, stroking her clean. His fingertip brushed the little bud at the top, and she gave a quiet gasp.

"Again," she whispered. "Please."

He thought she'd been jesting about indulging this evening. Even if she wished for another bout of coupling, he was not comfortable claiming her again, lest he truly hurt her the next time.

But it didn't mean he couldn't please her. Especially when she was so wonderfully sensitive.

He moved his thumb over the nub as he continued to swipe the linen over her. Her nipples drew taut, and her face relaxed with enjoyment.

"Like that?" he asked.

"Please don't stop," she breathed.

He wouldn't stop for all the coin in Christendom. This time as he plied her pleasure with his hands, he had the good fortune to watch her. Bliss flitted over her face, making her mouth soft and her cheeks flush.

Her whimpers pitched, and he knew she was near release. His thumb flicked faster, and her breasts rose and fell with her quickened breath. Her brows knit together as the sensations overwhelmed her, and her sex clenched beneath the cloth as she climaxed a second time.

He withdrew the linen, and her knees fell to the side, her body limp. Finally drained, or so it appeared.

He set aside the cloth and returned to the bed with her. She rolled toward him and rested her head on his chest.

He settled a hand over her curved hip and swept his fingers over her smooth skin. Lara surfaced in his head again, unbidden. They had never shared passion such as what he'd just experienced with Faye. Nothing even close.

Had that been his fault? Was that part of what had led to the coldness that settled between them?

Guilt clenched his soul. He stroked a hand down Faye's silky, golden hair. "I promise to be a good husband to ye."

"Ye're off to a fine start," she murmured.

He chuckled at her ready response. Faye had a fine wit that paired well with the fire of her spirit.

Beautiful and lusty and brave. It would not be difficult to show a woman like Faye that he cared for her. Indeed, it was far too easy to consider the idea that he might sincerely fall in love.

F aye prolonged waking the following morning. She snuggled against Ewan's side, where she wished to remain for the rest of the day. Well, not simply lying next to him.

She craved Ewan's skilled fingers on her and the hard length of his arousal gliding inside her. He shifted, waking.

She slid one leg over him, the movement slow and sensual. There was no secret in what she needed. She'd spent too long being curious about experiencing what existed between men and women.

Now she knew in body what she'd suspected in mind. And she wanted it again and again and again, like manna for her starved body.

"Faye." His voice was gravelly with sleep.

"Stay with me." She kissed his chest. Her fingers ran down his torso toward his cock, which she found hard and hot.

"I canna." He shifted her hand away gently. "I've got to meet with Monroe this morn." He rolled on to his side and looked down at her. His hair was rumbled from sleep, and his powerful body was carved with muscle where he held himself up.

He stroked her cheek. "Ye're so verra lovely, Faye."

She loved how he said her name—in a single syllable with his rich, rumbled timbre, cut short by his Scottish burr.

She nuzzled into his touch and parted her lips over his blunt thumb.

He uttered a silent curse and drew her to him, his cock hard and insistent as it pressed between her legs where she was already damp with need. They took one another in a quick, desperate passion that left them both gasping for breath after, while their hearts galloped in their chests.

When he finally rose from their shared bed, it was with apparent regret. He washed quickly and slid out the door, promising to have a bath sent up to her chambers. Faye lingered a moment longer in the warm tangle of sheets, then pulled herself from the soft mattress and crossed through the door connecting their chambers together. Her room was the same size as his, with a fine bed of a similar build—four carved posts and heavy, red curtains hanging from the sides. At the base of the bed was a chest for her wardrobe and by the wall near a shuttered window, a table with a comb resting atop it and various bottles. A small wooden tub already sat near the hearth.

This was her chamber and hers alone. How many times had she longed for such luxury?

Yet now, the very thought of Clara and Kinsey tugged at her heart. She would sacrifice the fine room and all the space for the opportunity to be at home with them again.

A red-haired maid entered the room, a woman several years older than Faye. The lines around her eyes crinkled as she smiled. "Good morrow, my lady. I'm Gavina and will be seeing to ye as yer maid. If ye'd take a seat by the fire, I'll have yer bath filled. Would ye like a bowl of porridge as ye wait?"

Faye's stomach gave a growl of hunger in reply. Despite the many miles she'd walked the day before in her bid to escape her grandfather, she'd eaten little more than a few bites of bread and meat. She could have eaten more in the room with Ewan, but then he'd started asking so many questions. Wanting to know her.

What they'd done instead had been far more appealing. Indeed, the recollection made a sensual heat warm between her thighs.

Faye covered her stomach with her hand and gave a little laugh at her apparent hunger. "I think porridge would be fine. Thank ye."

Gavina gave a good-natured grin. "I'll see to that for ye straight away."

Within the hour, Gavina had Faye's stomach filled with food, and she'd been thoroughly bathed and washed in a tub of rose-scented hot water and laced into a fresh kirtle. Unfortunately, the garment Moiré had kindly lent her was as ill-fitting as the nigh-trail had been.

Gavina tsked over the short hem with a frown. "I'll have yer kirtle from yesterday washed and repaired by the morrow. For now, I can let loose the hem and measure ye for some new garments."

She set to work nipping the stitches from the bottom of the kirtle with a pair of sharp-tipped scissors, then took down a number of measurements. She was just finishing when a knock came from the door.

"Mistress Faye," a woman on the opposite side said. "'Tis Moiré."

"Ye may enter," Faye called.

The door opened, and Ewan's cousin stepped in. "Good morrow. I hope ye slept well." A blush crept over her face as she appeared to realize her words and recall how the prior evening had been Faye's wedding night.

"Ewan remains occupied most of his day," Moiré said. "I'm to show ye the castle and the tasks ye'll need to know as mistress here."

Mistress? Of an entire castle? A sliver of trepidation crept over Faye. Never once in all of this had she considered she would be charged with the welfare of so many.

She kept a smile on her face and inclined her head gratefully. "That would be wonderful. Thank ye."

Moiré approached, her eyes sparkling, and took Faye's hands. "I should so like for us to be friends. Ewan is like a brother to me, but I've no' ever had a sister." Her shoulders lifted in excitement. "I've always wanted one."

Faye nodded with a plastered smile, unsure of what to say to this woman she didn't know. She needed no additional sisters. Not when she already had two. And a brother. And a mum. All of whom were most likely beside themselves with worry at her disappearance.

The agony of their fear for her had been a constant companion during her journey to her grandfather's castle, just as it continued to linger in the back of her thoughts even now.

Gavina straightened with a triumphant smile. "It's no' perfect, but it'll do fine for a day."

Faye looked down at her skirt, where the hem had been let out. A folded line showed two inches above the rough edge. It made her remember when Mum had done the same to all their hems when they were girls to make their kirtles last a few months more. When they'd had no food, no coin. Nothing but each other.

And now she had not even that.

"I should like to compose a letter to my family." Her voice caught, but she swallowed down her emotion. She would not cry in front of these strangers. She would yield her control and power to no one. Never again.

"Of course." Moiré's pretty brows turned up with concern. "They must be so worried about ye." She pulled at Faye's hand with the same eagerness Kinsey used to when they were younger. "We'll go to the solar first so that ye can write yer missive."

Faye nodded and tried to keep her melancholy from being so apparent. After all, even if a runner left that afternoon with the message, he would not arrive in Castleton for at least three weeks, if not a month.

A familiar hurt settled in Faye's heart and worked its way up the back of her throat, squeezing until she could scarce breathe. Moiré chattered on as she led Faye through a complicated maze of corridors that would take some time to learn. Faye was grateful for her companion's incessant chatter, for it gave her time to compose herself to speak again without erupting in tears.

She wished Ewan were free to be with her, to kiss her and stroke her. His touch made her lose herself in mindless need, where painful thoughts of her home could not reach her.

Because she could no longer let herself think of the stone manor in Castleton or the people she loved there, for doing so would surely cause her to break.

EWAN SKIMMED THE PEACE NEGOTIATIONS DRAWN UP THAT DAY between the Sutherland and Ross clans. Ewan had kept the bastard from Faye intentionally and was glad for his decision to do so. Faye's grandfather left after they'd both signed it, although only after insisting on being shown the stained sheets from their marital bed.

His hand tightened into a fist now with regret. He should have killed the bastard outright when he'd threatened Faye's sister. They were already on the brink of war anyway.

The door to Ewan's solar pushed open, and Moiré appeared. "Did it go well with the Ross clan?" she asked.

"Well enough," Ewan muttered.

"Do ye think they can be trusted?" She approached the desk and peered down at the document in Ewan's hands.

"We can hope." He pinched the bridge of his nose with his fingers, but it did little to stave off his oncoming headache. "How has yer da taken the news?"

Moiré tilted her head in consideration. "I went to his manor earlier today. He's inclined to put his faith in the Gordons and thinks this turn of events will have them most displeased. But he wasna willing to offer more information than that."

He was right. The Gordons would be unhappy. While nothing had been signed, months of negotiations had finally brought them to the brink of making an agreement that benefited both clans. Though naught close to what the Ross agreement offered to the Sutherlands.

"Do ye think Cruim will do anything rash?" Ewan asked of Moiré's da.

She lifted her shoulder in a slight shrug. "I'll let ye know if I find out."

Were it not for Moiré reporting on her da's behavior, Ewan would have little information on any of his uncle's possible nefarious activities. Suggesting for him to live in a nearby manor had not resulted in any additional trust between him and Uncle Cruim.

Ewan leaned back in his chair and regarded his cousin. For once, his uncle was not the topic that weighed most on his mind throughout the day. "How is Faye?"

Moiré grinned with childlike enthusiasm. Hers was an infectious smile and one of the many reasons Ewan enjoyed her company. "She's so charming, Ewan. I showed her around the castle and gave her some instructions on how to see about running it all. She caught on quickly enough that I expect she'll be doing it all on her own within a fortnight."

Ewan nodded. "Thank ye for instructing her."

"Of course." Moiré put an affectionate hand on his arm. "She wrote a missive to her family, and I sent one of our fastest men to deliver it. I canna imagine what she must be feeling, after all she's gone through." Her expression softened with empathy. "I wish there was more I could do for her."

"Ye've yielded yer position as mistress of the castle to her, taken yer time to introduce her to the staff and even given her yer clothing while hers is being prepared." He got to his feet and settled a hand on Moiré's shoulder. "I think ye've done more than enough, and I thank ye heartily for it."

"I think she'll be good for ye, too," Moiré said. "The way she looks at ye...I could see yer wife falling in love with ye."

Those words put a pleasant warmth in his chest. One he would not allow himself to consider. Not yet.

Moiré tipped her chin as though the sacrifices she made were of little concern. "She's the reason I'm here. She asked to dine with ye in yer chambers rather than at the Great Hall."

Ewan frowned. "Is she unwell?"

Moiré folded her arms over her chest and tapped a forefinger against her sleeve. "She was quiet, but I wouldna say unwell."

"When should I join her?" he asked.

"She's there now."

Ewan nodded his thanks to his cousin and put the contract in his desk drawer, locking it with the small, precious key he'd had made some years back. No doubt, Faye was reeling from the turn of events. Who would not in her circumstances?

She had not said much the prior evening when he'd suggested they get to know one another again. Not that he could blame her. Heat effused his blood at what they'd done instead of talk. He hadn't been able to nudge his mind away from thoughts of her all day. Thoughts and memories.

She'd burned his mind like a brand, and he'd gladly endured its sear. He reveled in it. Craved it.

His cock stirred. "Thank ye, Moiré. I'll go to her now." He bade a good evening to his cousin and went to his chamber.

As Moiré had said, Faye was already waiting for him at a table laden with the evening's meal. What hadn't been mentioned, and most likely had not been known by Moiré, was that Faye wore only a leine.

One of *his* leines.

It rode high on her naked thighs where she sat at the table, her shapely legs crossed over one another. She gave him a coy smile as he approached, then uncrossed and recrossed her legs in a way that made him want to run his fingers up her smooth skin to see if she was as wet as he hoped.

He joined her at the table. From this vantage point, he could make out her open collar parted low on her chest, revealing the round curve of one partially bared breast. His palms ached for the silky weight, the nub of a pert nipple under the pad of his thumb.

He cleared his throat and wished he could clear his lust as easily. "My leine hasna ever looked that fine on me."

"I don't have any clothes that fit me properly," she offered by way of explanation.

"I imagine ye made quite the impression if ye wore that through the castle today." He said it lightly, but the idea of any other man seeing her body on display in such a manner made him tense.

She chuckled, a low, throaty sound. "Nay, I wore one of Moiré's kirtles, but 'tis too small. Gavina is cleaning and repairing mine for the morrow, then will make more for me. Until then..." She swept her hands up her sides, putting herself on display.

"I canna say I mind yer attire."

She ran her fingertips over the delicate line of her collar bone, gently brushing the flap open wider, so just a hint of the rosy pink nipple was visible.

God's teeth, the woman turned him to fire.

"I hope ye enjoy the meal I asked to be made for ye." She glanced down at the trenchers on the table.

His cock was hard as a rock, and his thoughts scattered because of it. Ewan, who had always held a particular fondness for food, hadn't even noticed what laid in front of him. Beyond Faye, that was.

Roasted pheasant stuffed with figs and cinnamon, several rolls and a cabbage stew he'd always enjoyed.

He refocused, putting his attention to her. Where it was needed. "It smells divine. Thank ye." He served her first, offering her a juicy piece of meat and the stuffing with the most chunks of figs, before adding some to his own plate. "Did ye meet everyone ye needed today?"

Faye sliced the bit of pheasant with her slender eating dagger. "Aye, Moiré was so kind to show me about."

Ewan cut a piece of his own food. His gaze wandered down to the shapely calf, resting so close to his own. "Moiré said ye wrote a letter to yer family today."

A smile flashed on her face, so bright, it dulled her eyes. "I did."

"I know what ye've gone through must be difficult." He speared a fig and took a bite.

She looked at her plate and said nothing.

"They're always welcome to visit." He poured some wine into her goblet, which she slowly took and drank. "And ye can travel to see them as well."

"I'd like that." She swallowed and looked away, evidently uncomfortable with the conversation.

"Ye can talk to me," he said. "If ye like."

"We're talking now." She gave him a flirtatious wink. "I was able to see all of the castle today. 'Tis perfect." Despite her happy demeanor, she prodded at the meat on her plate.

"Change anything ye like. Ye're mistress now." He drank from his wine and set the goblet aside. "Did ye find yer chamber to yer liking?"

Faye sank her teeth into the pillowy softness of her lower lip. "I like yer chamber better."

His hard cock lurched at the suggestion in her voice, at the memories of their shared passion. She must have been of a similar mindset, for her nipples pebbled beneath her shirt, making sharp points in the fabric.

"Ye can alter yers," he offered. "To anything ye like."

He wanted to get to know his wife, to be a man she could go to for whatever it was she needed. And yet, she wielded such a powerful sensuality that he could scarcely think around her, let alone carry on a decent conversation. Not when his cock was raging for release.

"How do ye enjoy passing yer evenings?" He asked, forcing the question from the haze of lust crowding his brain. "Needlepoint, mayhap? Or—"

Her naked leg curled around his and slowly slid up his calf. Though she didn't say a word, the way she lowered her head and gazed coquettishly up at him was answer enough. He knew exactly how she planned to at least spend that evening.

❧ 8 ❧

Faye didn't want to go through another round of questioning with Ewan. She didn't care for him to know her any more than she cared to know him.

His strong leg tensed against hers. It was evident in how his stare flicked to the low gap between her breasts in his leine she wore, or how he would look down at her bare leg when she stretched it into his line of sight. He was interested in the same thing as she was.

"Or mayhap if ye dinna like, ehm, needlepoint..." He licked his lips and drank from his wine again, his strong throat flexing around the swallow. "Ye could try...ehm..."

Desire thrummed between her legs. Eager for how he'd made her feel the night before. Desperate to distract her thoughts with lust and passion. While it didn't fill the void in her chest, it at least took her mind from the pain.

"How do ye enjoy passing the night?" She ran the pad of her middle finger down the low neckline of the leine, parting it to share a glimpse of her breast.

His stare settled on her. "I oft remain in the Great Hall after the evening meal to see to the clan."

Faye tilted her head to the side and caressed her skin. Her fingers grazed her nipple, and a sigh of pleasure escaped her lips. "What do ye wish to do this eve?"

His eyes slid up to hers. "Get to know my wife."

She shifted her foot on his leg, gliding upward to where his cock strained at his trews. The heat of his arousal was apparent through the leather. She closed her eyes in anticipation of the pleasure she knew he would bring her.

"I've thought of ye all day," she confessed.

A muscle flexed in his strong jaw. "As I have of ye."

"Is it wanton of me to want ye so?" She gave him a wide-eyed look, intentionally innocent, even as she rubbed her foot over the hard column of his desire.

He gripped the table and issued a low groan.

Faye touched her fingertip to her lower lip. "I want ye, Ewan."

He stood so abruptly that the chair tipped and crashed to the floor. Neither of them paid it any mind. Faye remained where she sat, wanting him to come to her. And come to her, he did.

He drew her up from her seat and took her there against the wall with hard, fast thrusts that left them both crying out in pleasure. After, he'd hauled her into his arms and carried her to the bed where their intimacy was drawn out between tangled sheets, enjoyed to the point of exhaustion.

Ewan fell asleep immediately, an arm thrown protectively over her despite them both being slick with sweat. The previous evening, she'd been so exhausted from walking through the cold for hours that she'd fallen into a deep slumber immediately. This night she was not so fortunate.

The pleasant glow from a night of being thoroughly loved had quickly cooled, bringing with it a hollow emptiness. This was a different world, a different life. It was loneliness and absent familiarity and love.

The chasm widened in her chest, expanding to an agonizing cavern that she could easily fall into and become lost. Her eyes filled with tears and leaked in hot streaks down the sides of her face, silent as they bled into the pillow.

As though sensing her sorrow, the hand on her side tightened. He was turned toward her in his sleep, his face relaxed in a way that made him look younger.

It was so tempting to trust him. He seemed eager to make her happy. He and Moiré both. Even Gavina. She could have love here if she accepted it.

The thought immediately gave way to a memory of when they were in England. Their hearts were still raw from Da's death, their purses weighted with guilt coin from the lord who offered paltry compensation for their loss. The people who had once been neighbors, friends, set cold glares in their direction. No longer were they brethren. Not after their English father, along with many others, had died in a war against Scotland.

They were Scottish. Filth.

The worst had been when a girl Faye had loved like a sister spat on her. Years had passed, and still, Faye could recall her horror as she stared at the foamy puddle of spittle dripping down the sleeve of her kirtle.

It wasn't the only time their trust was betrayed by those they loved. It had happened again in one of the Scottish villages when they'd been forced to leave in the middle of the night after Faye had confessed to a friend they were running from her grandfather. Nay. Faye's trust had been twisted too many times. Love only brought disappointment and hurt.

No one had ever been worthy of such trust, save her family.

And they were now gone.

Faye swallowed hard to clear the lump, but this time it was far too stubborn. The tears came in a stream, and her face stretched with the grief of her silent cries. She turned from Ewan, slipping from his loose hold, and pressed her face to the pillow to allow her tears to pour freely as sorrow shuddered through her.

A strong arm secured around her shoulders. "Ye're shivering, lass." Ewan drew her back against the solid heat of his body, and a blanket came over them both. His lips pressed to her shoulder, and he relaxed once more, evidently asleep.

She hadn't wanted his comfort.

Indeed, she would have declined if he'd offered. But his innocent mistake of her grief for a chill and the gesture to warm her allowed her to remain where she was, reveling in his comfort without sacrificing her pride. There, in the cradle of his arms, with the power of his body at her back and the heat of his skin melting the ice of her loneliness, she found a glimmer of solace.

She remained in his arms thus through the night until the mattress shifted under her, and Ewan slipped away from her. Her body immediately cooled without him near. She turned and found him washing by the basin. Firelight shone off his muscular torso as he scrubbed over his skin, washing away evidence of their passion from the night before.

"I see ye're also awake, my bonny lass." He grinned at her.

Faye gave a little moan and eased a naked leg from the sheets. "Return to bed with me."

He dropped the linen into the basin and approached the bed. But he didn't climb in. Instead, he braced his arms on the mattress and pressed a kiss to her brow. "If I do, I dinna think I'll be able to leave for several hours."

"Do ye promise?" Faye sat up, baring her breasts for his perusal.

And peruse he did, in an appreciative stare. Like a moth lured to a flame, he reached out and slowly cupped her breast as his thumb swept over her nipple.

Before Faye could moan her approval, he pulled his hand away and clenched it into a fist. "Nay, we've plans this morn."

Faye leaned forward, going onto her hands and knees as she looked up at him. She'd seen a farmer's wife being taken thus in the stables once and knew the position to be erotic. "Have we?"

He hesitated as he took her in, his expression sharpening with interest. "Aye." He turned from her and pulled on a fresh pair of trews from the chest at the foot of his bed. "A ride."

"A ride," she echoed.

"Through the Sutherland lands." He threaded his arms into his leine as he drew it on. "I thought ye'd want to see where ye live, meet the tenants. Ye're their mistress now as well."

A horse ride over the lands. Faye slid from the bed to hide her frown. She didn't want to spend the day with him or see how good he was to his people. She wanted, *needed*, their lives to be separate.

She searched her mind for an excuse. Something. Anything.

"I haven't a proper kirtle," she protested.

"Gavina said she'd have it for ye by now, and it will be done." He winked. "Gavina always does as she says."

Faye smiled pleasantly and nodded even as she steeled herself for exploring the lands with her husband. Surely this had to happen at some point. She'd only hoped she might find something displeasing about him to focus on before it did.

As of now, there was nothing to disparage him. In fact, everything recommended him, laid out to pry open her chest and bear her heart.

Except she was not ready to trust and knew she might never be.

Even with a man like Ewan Sutherland.

❧

EWAN WORRIED FAYE MIGHT DECLINE TO ACCOMPANY HIM ON the inspection of their lands after voicing concerns over her garment, but she offered no more protests.

She rode at his side now, the deep red kirtle cleaned and repaired and buried under a thick cloak to ensure her warmth.

"These are the lands we've had for years," Ewan indicated the expanse of the Sutherland territory. Grass-covered hills rolled in the distance beneath an endless blue sky. In the distance, a loch lay nestled like a mirror between two swells of earth. It extended far beyond what they could see, but it would still give her an idea.

She lifted her face into the wind and gazed out at the land with reverence. "It feels like we're the only two people in Scotland."

It was more than she'd said thus far, apparently content to mainly listen.

But then, that seemed to be the way of it with her. She did not offer opinions or share stories of her childhood or family. It did not escape his notice that she often turned toward sexual distraction when he tried to learn more about her. And he'd been too easily led astray by her temptation to stop her.

This journey through the country would give them an opportunity to know one another better. He cared about her already. How could he not when he spent so much time thinking of her?

But he had to let her know he cared for her. An ache squeezed in his chest. She would not end up like Lara, whom he had so egregiously failed.

They slowed their horses to a stop so Faye could take her time studying Sutherland's beauty.

Pride swelled in his chest at the look of awe on her face as she scanned the vast horizon. "Aye, it can feel like that at times. I imagine it seems especially so for ye as ye've lived in villages for most of yer life." He pointed to the west. "Torish is that way."

"Torish?"

"Aye, the lands of yer dowry. Have ye been to them before?"

"Nay," Faye replied.

"Did ye know ye had land as part of yer dowry?" he asked.

She looked in the distance as though she could see it all laid out. "I never even considered that I might have a dowry, though it does make sense..." She spoke so softly that the wind nearly snatched her words.

"'Tis a handsome dowry that came with considerable wealth and fertile land."

"Now yer wealth and yer land." She said the statement in a flat voice.

He edged his horse closer to her and settled a gloved hand over hers. "*Our* land. And I've had Monroe ensure in the event of my death ye receive Torish for yer own keeping."

She started at that. "It would not go back to my grandfather?"

Ewan chuckled. "Only if ye promise no' to kill me."

To his surprise, tears welled in her eyes.

"I dinna intend to die any time soon." He smiled at her by way of reassurance. "But if I do, I want to ensure ye're well cared for."

She nodded, and a tear slid down her cheek. She hastily wiped it away and turned her face from him, as though ashamed of her emotion.

"What is it, lass?" Ewan asked.

She pressed her lips together and shook her head.

Her refusal to share what troubled her did not vex Ewan. The lass had been kidnapped by her own grandfather and forced into a new, strange world. Doubtless, her life had its share of difficulties and such struggles often curled one's true thoughts into a protective shell. Getting her to open up to him would be a slow process, but he was a man of great patience.

Especially when faced with a task so worthy.

"Would ye like to see yer land?" he asked.

She turned her attention back to him and readjusted the reins in her gloved hands. "I'd like that very much."

"As ye wish, my lady." He directed his horse toward Torish and all its surrounding land.

Ewan intentionally kept his pace slow to allow them to speak. When Faye did not offer conversation, he filled the silence with stories of his youth and the many times he'd gone to visit their clan tenants.

"I wasna always my da's choice to accompany him when he saw to his people," he confessed.

"Because of yer older brother?" she surmised.

"Aye, 'twas he who was to be the chieftain and he who received the training for the task." Ewan kept his tone neutral, ensuring the wisp of self-doubt at his role was not discernible. The same as he always did when speaking of his unexpected chieftainship. He'd lacked the formal training other chieftains had benefitted from.

She nodded, more to herself than to him. "Mayhap it was for the best," she replied.

"Why do ye say that?" he asked.

She lifted her shoulder in a shrug. "Ye're a strong chieftain who genuinely cares for his people. Mayhap if ye'd trained for it yer whole life, yer thoughts would be tailored toward a different way of ruling."

He contemplated her statement. He'd never once considered he'd been at an advantage for having not learned the way of a chieftain his entire life.

"My brother wishes to be a knight," she said. "He's far more chivalrous than any English knight I've ever known. He hasna been able to become a knight due to being English and Scottish. I believe because he was not able to attend such formal education, he's remained uncorrupted."

"Drake," Ewan recalled.

She nodded, and her silence resumed. But what she'd told him said more about her than if she'd chatted on extensively. She was an astute woman who was keenly aware of what transpired around her. What was more, her brother's restrictions with the English no doubt were a shared burden.

Ewan didn't remark further on what she'd said. Rather, he pointed out the village of Torish as they approached. The land appeared much the same as his own, save that it was dotted with sheep who milled about with their thick, billowing coats. As they neared, he could make out the shoddy thatching in the roofs and the general disrepair of the huts.

He'd anticipated Ross had not properly cared for the people in some time, especially in light of having it soon belong to someone else. But it was far worse than Ewan had expected.

"Is something amiss?" Faye asked.

"The homes need mending." He directed them toward the edge of the village and dismounted. "We've wedding gifts for the people." He offered her hand to her to assist her from her horse.

She put her fingers to his palm and slid from her steed. "For the people?"

"I thought they'd have need of it." Sutherland untied a purse from his saddle. The coins within clinked.

Several villagers nearby glanced toward them, their faces guarded, but curious. Doubtless, it had been some time since they'd seen a chieftain. A considerable time if the state of their homes was any indication.

"Ye're giving the people money?" she whispered incredulously at his side.

"They have need of it," he responded again, quietly.

She stared at him for a long moment, her expression one he could not quite make out.

He handed the purse to her. "I'll announce who we are. Would ye like to distribute the coins?"

She accepted the bag and nodded.

"Good morrow," Ewan said to those who had gathered. "I'm Ewan Sutherland, Chieftain of the Sutherland clan and yer new chieftain as well. This bonny lass is the granddaughter of the Chieftain of the Ross clan and saw fit to wed a man like me, thanks be to God."

Several people chuckled.

"And though I dinna deserve her or any of ye, I promise to care for ye to the best of my ability." He looked about at the upturned faces as he spoke, conveying the earnestness of his words. "I'll see to coordinating the repair of yer homes upon my return to Dunrobin Castle. Until then, my bonny wife has offered to share part of her dowry with all of ye to welcome ye to the Sutherland clan."

Faye opened the purse and took out a coin. The villagers stepped forward but held a respectful distance. First, she approached a little boy whose grubby hand was extended with anticipation. Her hand trembled slightly as she settled the bit of metal into the boy's palm. The coin disappeared in his fist, and he ran off as she approached the second villager.

On and on she went through the people of the village, smiling shyly at their gratitude, stopping only when the bag was empty.

She handed the empty purse to Ewan and accepted his proffered arm. She remained quiet as he led her back to their horses, and they left the village of Torish behind them.

"I hope ye are no' displeased with me," he said. "Mayhap, I ought to have told ye my intentions for Torish."

"'Tis fine," she replied.

A catch to her voice pulled his attention back to her, where he found her eyes swimming with tears. She looked away, but not swiftly enough to hide the fact that she was crying.

9

F aye tried to restrain her tears. Even now, she swallowed hard at the ache in her throat, but still, the knot did not abate.

Never in her life had she seen as much coin as was nestled inside the fine leather purse. To think that all this time, all these years, she had wealth at her fingertips. Land!

So many times, she'd flirted to get an extra bit of grain for her family, or a lower price on meat. Or how they'd worn clothes that pinched at their elbows and squeezed at their waists when there'd been no money for new clothes. Or how Drake had to sacrifice his attempts to become a knight in order to help them survive.

Never had she dreamed there had been any other way. Never had she suspected that in the Highlands of Scotland, they could be wealthy, that there was a life available to them where every day was not a struggle.

Why had her mother not told them? How had she let them all suffer when they could have lived in comfort?

A sob choked from Faye's throat.

"Faye." Ewan drew his horse to a stop. "What is it? Are ye hurt?"

She shook her head again, not even certain where to start. "I had no idea..." Her voice trembled, but she cleared her throat and tried again. "I had no idea we had such wealth. And I've never seen a lord give his tenants coin."

She remembered meeting the lord of the village once when they lived in England, back when her da had still been alive. Lord and Lady Astair. They'd come to the village in matching yellow silk so fine that it reflected the sun like gilt. Or at least, what Faye assumed gilt looked like.

She'd looked up to them as if they were gods emerged from the heavens above. Indeed, they might as well have been, with their fine clothes and clean, friendly faces. She'd been awed into silence by them. As some had been with her in the village of Torish.

But though the experience had been memorable enough to settle into Faye's memory, Lord and Lady Astair never gave out coin, with the exception of the final pay they offered when Da died. But nothing after that small stipend, when they were in such sore need, when everyone else had turned cold with hate.

Ewan watched her with a sympathetic gaze. She didn't want his sympathy or his kindness. She didn't want to see how easily and confidently he spoke to his people or how affectionately they responded to him.

Oh, how she longed to be back in Castleton with people she knew she could trust, where she didn't have to be so guarded.

"Faye," Ewan said in a gentle voice. "Ye can tell me."

She looked away, ashamed of her outburst. If they were at Dunrobin Castle, she might have given him a coy look, or suggestively trailed her fingers over the neckline of her kirtle. But they were on horseback in the middle of a land she didn't know. She couldn't spare herself by turning her emotions to passion or swaying the conversation toward sexual teasing.

And yet, part of her felt ridiculous for staying so quiet when he was so willing to listen. He had vowed to protect her.

Tell him.

She rubbed the thick leather rein between her thumb and forefinger, giving it her focus as she spoke. "We grew up with very little. There were so many times we went to bed with our stomachs so empty that our navels felt as though they were grinding against our spines. There was never enough. Not food or wood to burn or cloth for kirtles."

Tears clogged her throat, and she stopped her horse, unable to focus. "When I think of what we've had to do to survive...and when all this time, we had wealth. I had this dowry..." She covered her face with her palms to keep him from seeing her cry. "We never had a lord give us coin in celebration as ye just gave those people."

"I wish I'd known," he said in a gruff voice. She uncovered her face to find he'd dismounted and was standing beside her horse. He held his palm up to her to assist her down. She accepted his offer and slid off her steed and into his arms.

He was strong and warm, exquisite comfort. He enveloped her in all those wonderful sensations and held her to him as he stroked her back, which only made her sobs come harder.

When the better part of her sorrow had quelled, she swiped at her tears and pushed back to gaze up at him. "Forgive me. I should not have reacted so."

"Ye dinna need to apologize." He stroked her cheek, his expression pained. "'Tis I who owe the apology. I should have pressed to know more about ye when ye dinna return to Scotland. I should have known this was what ye'd endured. I would have done everything in my power to see ye and yer family safe."

Though she was hesitant to trust him, the truth of his words lodged in her chest. He *would* have done everything in his power to ensure she and her family had remained safe.

"We managed," she replied.

"Ye shouldna have had to." He swept her hair back from her face. "I vow to ye, ye'll no' ever suffer again in yer life."

She stared up into his hazel eyes, mesmerized by the flecks of green and amber and black within. "Ye needn't do that," she protested.

He drew off his gloves and tenderly put his hands on either side of her face. "Let me care for ye, Faye." He smoothed his hands downward in a caress that stopped under her chin. "Open yer heart to me."

Her heart?

How could she possibly open her heart to anyone when it was bound with iron and locked with a key that went missing long ago?

She stared up into his beautiful eyes and felt the stirrings of lust pulse to life. Though she knew her attraction to him to be strong, she understood her desire for what it was: a distraction.

One she would not indulge.

She opened her mouth, uncertain what to say when the thundering of approaching horse hooves rumbled in the distance. Together, she and Ewan turned toward the sound as riders crested a nearby hill.

"Get on yer horse and head back to Dunrobin," Ewan said in a low voice. "I'll handle this."

Even if Faye had known the way back to the castle, she wouldn't leave his side. Not when there were so many warriors, and only one of him.

"I can fight." She pulled her eating dagger from her belt. It was nowhere near as fine as the sharpened weapon Drake had given her when she'd turned fourteen, the one her grandfather had confiscated. But it would do.

Ewan gave her a hard look. "Go now, lass. I dinna want ye to be injured."

She tightened her grip on her weapon. "I won't be."

He eyed the blade. "Is that an eating dagger?"

"Who are they and what do they want?"

Ewan squared his shoulders, shielding her from the onslaught of men approaching. "They're from the Gordon clan. And they're here because I was in negotiations to wed their Chieftain's daughter before I was approached by Ross."

Faye's stomach clenched as the mass of stony-faced riders approached. "Do ye mean...?"

"Aye," Ewan said. "I married ye instead of Mistress Blair. And they're no' pleased."

⚜

EWAN PULLED HIS SWORD FREE OF ITS SHEATH AND ENSURED HE was directly in front of Faye. She was a spirited lass, one who only obeyed when she wished to. And while he appreciated such fire in her, he did not like that it now put her in danger.

The Gordons were never predictable. They could be coming to demand a meeting with him as much as they might be coming to slay him. Or the woman he'd wed.

Outrunning them would be pointless. They would meet him at Dunrobin, and the act of trying to flee would label him a coward. Nay, he was best left facing them with his stubborn wife safely tucked behind his back.

With her paltry eating dagger.

Once they were back at Dunrobin, he'd ensure she had a proper blade.

The bald chieftain led his group of a dozen Gordon warriors, his scalp red with rage. Gordon held up his fist to stop his men and glared at Ewan. "Sutherland." Both rows of teeth showed as he spoke, biting out each word. "We had an agreement."

Ewan squared his shoulders and faced the other chieftain head-on. "What is it ye want?"

He peered around Ewan to Faye and sneered. "Is that her? The Ross whore?"

"Ye're lucky I dinna smite yer head from yer body," Ewan growled. "Mind yer tongue around my wife."

"Ross says ye had a betrothal since ye were bairns," Gordon glared at him.

Damn Ross and his determination with the unsigned agreement. "The betrothal wasna valid. Are ye here to fight or to talk?"

Gordon had always been the straightforward sort. Whatever path he set his mind to, he made known. He studied Ewan and grunted. "Talk."

Ewan sighed and eased the sword into its sheath. "Come to the castle where we can speak properly."

"Ach, aye, we're on our way there now." Gordon scoffed. "It appears yer uncle is willing to be the man ye dinna have the ballocks to be."

Ewan maintained his relaxed demeanor even as dread tightened in his gut. Not only was Cruim claiming to wish to wed Mistress Blair, but he was also negotiating the arrangement at Dunrobin rather than his own manor. Meaning he wanted Ewan to be aware of the dealings. But why?

To make his desire for the chieftainship publicly known among the clan?

And why had Moiré not told him?

"I'll meet ye there," Ewan said with finality.

The Gordons didn't wait for him before they rode off toward the castle. Ewan turned to aid Faye onto her steed and found her already mounted.

"Are we going to let them arrive before us?" She took up her reins and raised a brow at him.

Ewan grinned at her temerity. Without another word, he leapt into his saddle, and together they streaked across the countryside in their determination to reach Dunrobin before the Gordon clan. They had the benefit of only two riders and steeds who were not exhausted from the sennight-long journey from Huntly Castle, where the Gordons had traveled from.

Ewan and Faye arrived at the castle with enough time to prepare themselves at the Great Hall and summon his uncle,

Cruim. Any attempts to encourage Faye to adjourn to their rooms while Ewan handled the Gordons was met with her obdurate insistence that she attend. After a heated exchange, she finally conceded to wait in the hall as she had done when her grandfather had come for her.

With Faye securely out of sight from the already irate Gordons, Ewan waited with barely tethered patience for Cruim. Monroe arrived first with a rushed pace to be at Ewan's side and eventually, Cruim joined them in his usual way, his lope unhurried, unfettered. His expression was placid as ever, his bushy gray eyebrows lifted in question as though he couldn't possibly wager to guess why he'd been summoned.

Ewan narrowed his eyes at his uncle. "I hear ye've made an alliance with the Gordons."

"I'm protecting the agreement ye negotiated with them," Cruim replied simply.

There appeared to be no malice in his expression. As though he'd truly meant to help. He'd always been so good at playing innocent, hiding his cleverness behind the eyes of a dullard. It was why Ewan couldn't cast him from the clan for what he'd done, not when Cruim was so adept at having his actions appear to be for the good of the clan.

Ewan looked to Monroe and found his friend's expression to be one of resignation. Which meant Monroe agreed with the idea of the alliance with the Gordons. Damn.

"Ye negotiated this without my authority," Ewan said to his uncle between clenched teeth.

"It had already been negotiated," Cruim argued. "By ye. We need the alliance from the Gordons."

"We have an alliance with the Ross clan." Anger simmered at the edge of Ewan's patience, singeing it with red hot intensity. "We needed the aid from the Gordons to prevent the Ross attacks. That isna required any longer."

"Nor is a new feud with the Gordons." Cruim's cheeks puffed

out with an unexpected cough. He cleared his throat and straightened. "My marriage will ensure—"

The door to the Great Hall banged open, and the Gordon chieftain entered with the authority of a man set on getting his way. "Cruim," he cried out to Ewan's uncle as if they were old friends. The two locked forearms and patted one another affectionately on the back.

Ewan narrowed his eyes as he observed the comfortable interaction between the two. They had been well acquainted for some time based on their camaraderie. How much of Ewan's prior negotiations with the Gordons had been moved by his uncle's hand?

Never had Ewan questioned it until that moment. But now...

Gordon turned his attention to Ewan and scowled. "I want the marriage terms drawn up to include Cruim rather than yerself."

Ewan shook his head. "I dinna sanction this union."

"Ye will," Gordon stepped forward. "Ye've had us as tentative allies for years. We've helped ye in yer time of need—"

"As we've done for ye." Ewan matched the other chieftain's step with one of his own, so they stood in front of one another.

Gordon's mouth pinched together at the nudging reminder of how Huntly would have been taken were it not for the efforts of Sutherland warriors coming to their aid.

"I'd like to keep our alliance." Gordon lifted his head, so the furrow of his brow hid the gleam of his bald head. "Much more than ye being an enemy."

Ewan cocked his chin upward. "What are ye saying?"

Gordon stared; his gray eyes unblinking. "Either ye give us this marriage, or ye'll have a war on yer hands."

Ewan glanced to his uncle but did not find triumph on his face. Instead, there was the same expressionless set to his features. As if none of it mattered to him, as though he had not acted as a traitor to his own people.

"When would this occur?" Ewan demanded.

"Two days' time." Gordon grinned, revealing a mouthful of crooked teeth. "'Tis when my Blair will be arriving. Ye know lasses always take a goodly amount of time with travel."

"'Tis hardly time to prepare a feast," Ewan protested. Mayhap if he could buy more time—

"We dinna need a feast," Gordon replied. "Simply a marriage."

Ewan looked once more to Monroe in the hopes he might offer a protest, some form of a hole in the contract that could be exploited to their benefit. Ewan's advisor gave an almost indiscernible shake of his head.

Ewan wanted to rage against the other chieftain, to throw the contract in his smirking face. But that would solve nothing. He had always been the calm one. It had been his brother, Ragnall, whose temper had run hot.

An alliance with the Gordons would benefit the Sutherland clan overall. Why then was Ewan so against it?

He was ashamed of the answer as it pushed to the forefront in his mind.

Pride.

And where there was pride, there was failure. Ewan knew his answer regardless of how little he liked it.

He only hoped Faye could get with child quickly and that their child would indeed be a boy, for it could very well mean the future of the clan.

❧ 1 0 ❧

Faye remained pressed up to the doorframe, her ear locked against the narrow gap to catch the low rumble of Ewan's voice.

She hated being pushed behind a door again, set back from the action, but she understood Ewan's reasoning. She was who he had married instead of the one named Blair. Surely, her presence would be a slap in the face.

But who was Blair, and why had Ewan not mentioned her? Apparently, he would have wed her had Faye not been dragged to the highlands. The idea of another woman crowded into Faye's thoughts.

She strained to listen, her heart caught in her chest for the man who had so bravely saved her several times over, who cared for her and protected her. The man who was slowly chipping at the stone surrounding her heart.

The man who might want someone else.

"What is amiss?" a familiar feminine voice asked. "Why are ye listening?"

Faye spun around, grateful for the interruption of her thoughts. She didn't need to consider her feelings for her husband or his for another. Especially when she ought not to have feelings for him at all.

"The Chieftain of the Gordon clan claims Ewan shouldn't have wed me due to a contract negotiated between them for Ewan's marriage to Mistress Blair." Faye tried to ignore the pinch of guilt in her chest that her union to Ewan had caused so much difficulty.

When she'd wed him, she'd never once considered what he'd given up. She'd only thought of her own loss. Now, she realized the depth of his sacrifice.

Moiré pressed her ear to the other side of the doorframe. "I feared the Gordons might be displeased."

"Verra well," Ewan's low timbre sounded in the Great Hall, silencing the two women. "I'll allow marriage between Cruim and Mistress Blair."

Moiré gave a sharp gasp. She slapped her hand over her mouth, her eyes wide with shock.

"When the lass arrives, they'll be wed," Ewan said. There was an unmistakable tension to his usually smooth voice. "Until then, ye may stay in the castle as my guest."

Servants were summoned to escort the Gordon men to rooms in the castle and see to their comfort. Faye glanced at Moiré, who dropped her hand and shook her head. Before either could speak, the heavy fall of footsteps came toward them. Both women leapt back from the door as it swung inward and brought Ewan standing before them, his expression tense.

"What happened?" Faye asked innocently.

He scowled. "Dinna act as though ye were no' listening at the door."

Heat touched her cheeks at having been caught.

He directed his ire toward Moiré. "Did ye know about this?"

She shook her head so vigorously, her hair brushed across her rose-colored kirtle. Admittedly, the color was fine on her. It complimented the rich brown of her eyes and made her lips and cheeks pink against her fair skin.

"Do ye think...mayhap..." Moiré linked her hands together and stared at her interlaced fingers. "Was anything said about a union between Finn and me? Mayhap my union could..."

The ferocity on Ewan's face dissolved into compassion. "There wasna any mention of Finn."

"Oh." Moiré tucked her chin lower, hiding her face. "Of course, thank ye for informing me," she mumbled.

Her disappointment cut into Faye.

Ewan must have understood his cousin's pain as well, for he put a hand to her shoulder. "I'm sorry, Moiré."

She stepped back with a mumbled apology and practically ran down the hall.

Faye looked questioningly at Ewan, seeking answers not only about Moiré but about Ewan's uncle and the woman he was supposed to marry before she was pushed in his path.

He indicated she should follow him and led her to his chamber. "I dinna wish to risk being overhead," he said once the door was closed. "Especially with the Gordon clan about."

"Ye were betrothed before me?" Faye asked, addressing her most pressing concern first.

Ewan rubbed the back of his neck. "The contract wasna signed, but aye, I was to be betrothed to Mistress Blair."

His reply nipped at Faye's heart; a foreign hurt she didn't want to think too hard upon. And yet, she had to know... "Did ye love her?"

He offered an affectionate smile. "Nay, 'twas simply to secure an alliance."

"And ye're displeased that now yer uncle is wedding her?" Faye frowned. If Ewan did not care for the woman, why was he so flustered?

Ewan tugged off his doublet, so he wore only his leine and

trews. "My uncle, Cruim, has always had his eye on the chief-tainship."

Faye had not met the man yet. He'd not been to the castle in her time there, at least not that she'd been aware of. Nor had he attended her rushed wedding.

"The man is surprisingly clever," Ewan continued. "While I was considering arranging for a union with Mistress Blair, Cruim began negotiations for a marriage between Moiré and Gordon's eldest son, Finn. Apparently, Moiré has had her heart set on him for some time."

Faye poured a goblet of wine from a flagon on a nearby table and brought it to her husband, who accepted it with a grateful nod. "I take it the betrothal did not work out," Faye said.

Ewan shook his head. "We couldna come to terms that we both agreed on for Moiré to wed. But I have my suspicions that no matter what I offered, they would deem it insufficient."

Faye directed Ewan to a chair by the fire, intent on making him feel better. As he had done for her earlier that day after Torish.

"Why is that?" She asked.

Ewan sank into the chair with a grateful sigh. "Finn dinna want to marry her. I kept it from Moiré, of course, but I suspect she knows."

Faye winced for the other woman as her suspicions at Moiré's hurt were confirmed.

"And now yer uncle is seeking an alliance with the Gordons once more, but for his own benefit." Faye slid her hands down the back of Ewan's neck, kneading the tense muscles there.

She did the same ministrations for her mother often, when she suffered from overwhelming moments of grief at Da's loss. It didn't matter what form of tincture or tea Clara made for their mother, nothing had worked as well as massaging the tension from Mum's wiry body.

Ewan sighed in pleasure, and his shoulders relaxed somewhat.

"He passes his intent to marry Mistress Blair as placating the Gordons, but 'tis deeper than all that. I know it."

"Might he take yer position by force with their aid?" Faye glided her hands down the sides of his spine, slowly working through the bands of powerful muscle.

Ewan dropped his head forward to allow her better access. "If he attacks outright, 'tis possible. But it would be difficult considering my alliance with yer grandda's clan. But if I die, Cruim would inherit my chieftainship. I worry what might happen to the clan if such a thing occurred."

"Unless we have a son," Faye surmised.

Ewan leaned his head back and took her hand. With a wicked grin, he dragged it down his chest and stomach to where his arousal strained eagerly against his trews.

Desire dampened her center and left her hot with immediate lust.

"We should ensure I get with child soon." Faye cupped her hand around the hard column.

"We can start now." He caught her wrist and gently drew her around the chair as his fingers worked to free his cock. "Come to me, wife."

She climbed atop his lap and sunk down onto his length with a sigh of pleasure. They gripped one another with desperate passion, arching and thrusting as she rode him until they both cried out in shared pleasure. Later, as their hearts calmed from the intensity of their coupling, Faye considered the possibility of a bairn in earnest.

It was a strange thing to ponder, as it was nothing she'd ever wanted before. Quite the opposite, rather. Children were loud, time-consuming and filthy.

An image popped in her mind of Ewan holding their babe, his face sweet and tender as it often was when he spoke to her. An unwanted warmth filled her chest.

It was more than a bairn with Ewan that appealed to her—it

was the man himself. And that held the strong possibility of leading to love, which Faye knew could hurt her worse than anything else.

❦

Having the Gordons stay at Dunrobin disrupted the easy comfort of daily life. Especially when Ewan felt he could not leave the castle. Not when another clan occupied a good portion of it.

More than anything, he most regretted the discomfort Moiré clearly felt in the presence of Finn. She often disappeared, feigning excuses so that she might go to her chamber.

As Gordon had predicted, his daughter arrived two mornings later with her maid and several warriors in tow. Which meant the wedding would be held the following day, thanks be to God. Then the Gordons would finally leave, and Cruim would remove himself to his manor with his new wife.

It was an awkward thing, however, to have a woman nearby whom Ewan had intended to wed. Mistress Blair's gray-blue eyes lingered upon him, often like a weight he could feel in his soul.

As the castle bustled with activity for the upcoming nuptials, Ewan often escaped into his solar. It was truly bad indeed if he was willing to lose himself in the transfer of Berwick to Ross rather than hear one more question about food preparations or minstrels for hire. He didn't give a goat's arse about any of it.

The door to his solar creaked open, and he glanced up to find Mistress Blair peeking in his room. Her curly red hair was bound up, revealing her long, slender neck. "May I speak with ye?" she asked in her husky voice.

He intentionally looked behind her. "Where is yer maid?"

"I dinna want anyone to know I've come to see ye," she replied. "I wanted to speak privately."

Ewan swallowed down his displeasure. After all, he had rejected her as his wife. He knew what that had done to Moiré.

The least he could do was talk to Mistress Blair and keep her confidence.

Ewan nodded and indicated the seat opposite him. She closed the door behind her and strolled past the chair, her hands tucked behind her back as she explored the solar.

"I apologize for having so abruptly ended our marriage negotiations," Ewan said.

She faced him abruptly. "What is it about me ye find so detestable?" She lifted her small, pointed chin. "Am I unpleasing to the eye?"

He stifled a swell of irritation. After all, he had decided to wed another. The least he could do was explain his reasonings. "Nay. Ye're bonny. Ye always have been. 'Tis never been ye, but negotiations between clans with dowries and threats."

The stiff set of Mistress Blair's shoulders relaxed. "I see. Then it wasna me?"

He shook his head.

She twisted her fingers in front of her waist. She wore a gray kirtle that made her gleam like silver. "I believe yer uncle intends to set my family against ye, Ewan."

He started at the use of his Christian name. He'd met her only a handful of times in the course of the negotiations with her father.

"What has he done?" Ewan asked.

"Ye mean, what will he do?" She stepped closer, and the weight of her silk skirt nudged at his shins. Too close.

Ewan edged back slightly. "What do ye know?"

Mistress Blair leaned toward him and rested her hand boldly on his chest. "We'd be good bedfellows, ye and I."

Ewan gently lifted her hand from his chest. "I am faithful to my wife."

"We would be a perfect fit." Her gaze slid down his body and back up to his face. "Passionate, eager."

"I'm faithful to my wife," Ewan repeated. "I believe this conversation is—"

"I could report to ye what it is yer uncle does," Mistress Blair rushed. "Ye need only take me into yer bed."

Ewan shook his head. "I'm loyal to the woman I married. I think it best ye leave."

"Ye'll grow tired of her," Mistress Blair said. "Men always do." She tilted her face confidently up as if she meant to kiss him or be kissed in return. "When ye grow weary of her, ye'll find my bed warm for ye and my tongue loosened with secrets."

With that, she swept away from him and quit the room, leaving the air scented with a cloying powder scent that stuck in the back of his throat.

Ewan clenched his hand into a fist. Clearly, his uncle did have a plan. There were secrets about, and he would find a way to learn them, something that had nothing to do with Mistress Blair.

The door to his solar pushed open again, this time revealing Faye. "What did she want?" There was a feigned sweetness to the way she asked him that told him she did not care for the idea of the other woman being in a room alone with her husband.

"She wanted me to lay with her," Ewan said honestly.

Faye blinked as the color rose in her cheeks. She glared over her shoulder at the closed door, as though she meant to shoot the spear of her gaze like a weapon at Mistress Blair.

Faye's ire snapped back to Ewan. "Ye didn't—"

He had to laugh at that. "I'm faithful to ye, lass. I always will be." He came around the desk and pulled her into his arms.

She turned her face from his.

"Are ye jealous?" he teased. "Even as I tell ye ye've no need to worry?"

"Nay." It was a lie, evident in the flash in her blue eyes. "Though she is lovely."

"No' nearly as lovely as ye." Ewan eased Faye's face toward

him, her skin soft under his fingertips. "Besides, ye leave me depleted, lass. How would I ever have the energy for a leman?"

"Mind yerself." She playfully poked his chest.

"I do need yer help though," he said in all seriousness.

She lifted her brow with apparent skepticism. "I'll no' do anything to help that woman."

Ewan shook his head. "Me. And the clan. Mistress Blair alluded to something my uncle planned. She wouldna tell me after I refused her."

Faye smirked. "And ye want me to find what it could be," she surmised.

"Aye. I believe plans are afoot, and we need to ensure we listen at the wedding for what we can learn." Ewan gritted his back teeth. If he could catch Cruim in a plot to try to kill him, he would have justification to banish him from the clan.

As careful as Cruim was, he would have to slip up sometime. When he did, Ewan would be there to see him stumble and ensure he paid the price for his treachery.

❧ 11 ❧

It was easy for Faye to dislike Mistress Blair Gordon. Even as she sat at the other woman's wedding feast the following day, the bitterness hung between them. But then, such animosity had started the night before when Blair passed Faye as she was leaving Ewan's solar. After she'd propositioned him.

Faye hadn't missed the way the other woman's gaze had slid over her in apparent assessment, followed by an overconfident smirk. As though finding Faye to no longer be a threat.

Not that Faye was so easily put off. On the morning of the wedding, Gavina had presented her with an exquisite new kirtle. It was a rich, vivid blue that made Faye stand out like a sparkling sapphire. Her blonde hair had been combed to shining and bound back in a gold caul adorned with pearls.

If she had any doubt at how she looked in the new attire, she need only take note of the bride's attitude toward her. For Blair was simmering with barely contained jealousy.

Faye might have felt her own twinge, for Blair was a stunning bride in a green silk dress that made her hair glow like burnished copper. She tapped her fingertips in time to the music in a graceful movement her new husband seemed oblivious to.

Cruim was not as Faye had expected. She knew he'd be older but had not expected someone so...withered. His hair was leeched of color, the strands white and flimsy as cotton fibers where it circled his balding pate. There was a gray pallor about his skin, and he continued to cough into his fist.

The man was so archaic and frail, Faye almost felt sorry for the other woman.

Almost.

It did not escape Faye's notice that when Ewan strode past Blair at the wedding feast, he didn't turn toward his former betrothed once. Nay, his eyes had remained fixed on Faye with interest.

"He loves ye." Moiré nudged Faye gently with her elbow.

Faye's cheeks warmed at such words. "Why do ye say that?" She shouldn't be so pleased by what Moiré had said. Nay, she ought to be upset. She shouldn't want Ewan's love, and yet she found herself nearly holding her breath as she waited for his cousin to answer.

"I've no' ever seen Ewan look at a woman the way he looks at ye." Moiré followed her cousin with her eyes, a smile pulling at her lips.

"No' even with Lara," Moiré said.

"Lara?" Faye looked sharply at Ewan's cousin.

Moiré lifted her goblet and took a sip of wine. "Aye, she was his first wife. She couldna bear him a child and never got over the shame of it. 'Twas so verra sad."

Faye's stomach tightened. Ewan had been married before? Why had he never mentioned it? Why had *no one* ever mentioned it?

"I've upset ye." Moiré put a hand over Faye's. "I shouldn't have brought it up at all."

Faye shook her head, unsure how to sift through the sudden torrent of emotions. "What happened to her?"

Moiré's eyes went large and gentle with sorrow. "I shouldna say."

"Please," Faye pushed. "I would prefer not to ask Ewan."

Moiré shifted her focus to her lap and nodded, resigned. "She took her own life," she whispered. When she looked up again, her eyes glistened with tears. She sniffled and brushed her fingers beneath her right eye. "Forgive me."

Before Faye could apologize for pressing her, Moiré slipped from her chair and away from the Great Hall. Faye stared after her in horror. She hadn't meant to cause the other woman such distress, especially after all of her kindness.

"May I join the bonniest lass in Scotland?" Ewan's voice interrupted her thoughts.

Faye glanced up at her husband, and the charming smile on his face wilted. "Is something amiss?"

"Ye were married before," Faye said.

"Aye," he replied casually as he settled into his chair beside her.

His confirmation dug into a tender spot in her chest. She was getting too close. Caring too much. Being too vulnerable.

"Why didn't ye tell me?" she asked.

Ewan shrugged. "It dinna come up." He searched her face, and his forehead crinkled. He gave a little grunt of acknowledgement. "This should have been mentioned, I take it?"

Faye lifted her brows.

He cleared his throat. He shifted in his seat uncomfortably as though what he wished to say might not be something easily discussed in such a setting. And, of course, it would not be when Lara had taken her own life.

"Moiré told me," Faye said in a softer voice. "I imagine it must have been hard." She intentionally looked around the room as well to indicate she understood his hesitation.

The tension eased from his shoulders somewhat. "Mayhap we can speak more on it later?"

She nodded.

"I wasna keeping it from ye." He paused as if collecting his thoughts. "It isna something I discuss."

Awareness tingled at the back of Faye's neck—the distinct sensation of being watched. She lifted her gaze and found Blair watching her with smoldering hatred.

Cruim sat beside Blair, a grin on his thin lips as one hand locked possessively around hers. Again, Faye experienced a flicker of pity for the other woman.

It was a strange thing indeed, disorienting and foreign, to be pushed into a marriage with a man one didn't know, especially when forced from one's own home. It had been difficult enough with Ewan who was a fine, fit man...

A man Blair thought similarly of. Any sense of pity was once more washed away by the reminder of what Blair had offered Ewan.

"Have ye overhead anything?" He asked quietly.

Faye glanced at him and shook her head, knowing he referred to the Gordons and their potential threat. "Nay. They go quiet when I approach."

"In awe of yer beauty." Ewan winked.

Her cheeks heated at his compliment.

"'Tis true." He leaned closer. "There's no' a man in the room who can take his eyes off ye." He swept his fingers over her thigh beneath the cover of the table. "Including me."

Her body's reaction was instantaneous, hot and eager with desire. "Ye're the only one that matters." She glanced at him through her lashes.

"Sutherland," someone shouted from across the room.

Ewan sighed. "I must go." He touched his fingers to the underside of her chin, lifting it toward him. "Ye're beautiful, Faye. So verra beautiful." His mouth brushed hers in a chaste kiss that made her long for so much more.

And then he was gone, striding confidently toward a group of his men who in their intoxicated state cheered his arrival. She knew she was not the only one who watched her husband. Blair's focus had shifted from glaring her hatred at Faye to feasting her eyes upon Ewan with blatant appreciation.

Ire boiled in Faye's blood. She'd had enough. The hour was growing late, and she was ready to retire for the evening. After all, the following day would be busy with her new duties as mistress of the castle. Moiré had spent the past sennight explaining what was required, and Faye was ready to take ownership of her new role.

Faye exited the Great Hall, shutting the noise of revelry away with the sweep of the heavy door. In the hall, the sconces cast meager light and almost no heat. The chilled darkness was a wonderful reprieve after the chaos of noise in the Great Hall.

She took her time making her way to her chambers. She was nearly to her suite of rooms when a door opened at the opposite end of the hall. The idea of seeing another person, of engaging in yet another tedious discussion, made exhaustion sink deep into her very bones. It was in that moment of longing for solitude that Faye slipped into an alcove to avoid being seen.

A woman's throaty chuckle echoed down the otherwise empty corridor. A man's murmured reply followed, indiscernible save for the masculine timbre. Another titter of amusement followed by the wet sounds of kissing.

A door clicked closed and footsteps padded to where Faye hid. She pressed herself back against the wall to ensure the shadows fully concealed her, now not wishing to be seen for an entirely different reason.

A woman walked by with tousled light brown hair and a languid smile spread on her lips, clearly having been recently well-loved.

Not just any woman.

Moiré.

⚜

EWAN NEEDED TO TELL FAYE ABOUT LARA. BUT THERE HAD been too much ale, too much whisky, too many rounds of cheers and filled tankards.

He should have declined them all and left when Faye departed the Great Hall. He paused in front of the chamber door and braced himself on the frame.

Lara.

Her memory lodged like a burr in his chest. He hadn't wanted to discuss her with anyone, let alone Faye. As though keeping her name from being spoken would keep the manner of her death from casting the same darkness upon his current marriage.

She had taken her own life because she couldn't tolerate the idea of him not loving her. Her death had been his fault. Such a weight would never lift from his soul.

He unlatched the door to his bedchamber as quietly as he could because of the late hour. This was the first night they had retired to bed separately. He hoped she had not gone to her own chamber and might instead be waiting for him in his bed, sleep warm and silky to curl against.

His gaze fell on the bed, followed by the sting of disappointment. It was still made and absent his wife. He entered the room and drew up short at a figure sitting before the hearth, staring into the dancing flames.

Faye.

She still wore the blue kirtle her maid had sewn for her. The one that fit her body perfectly, contouring the sensual dip of her waist and flare of her hips, hugging the firm roundness of her breasts in a way that made him want to cup his hands around them. She'd taken her hair down from the caul, and the rich, golden waves tumbled down her shoulders.

She was beautiful. Achingly so. And she was his.

He closed the door, and she started. Her gaze darted to him, and an embarrassed smile flicked over her lips. "Forgive me. I was lost in my own thoughts."

"God, ye're bonny, Faye." He slowly walked toward her through a room that seemed to dip and spin.

She laughed softly. "And ye're quite drunk."

She was at his side in an instant, her floral perfume a balm and an aphrodisiac all at once. "Come, I'll help ye to bed."

He shook his head and regretted it almost as soon as he'd done it for how it made the room twirl faster. "I need to talk to ye. About Lara."

She stilled. "That isn't necessary if ye don't want to discuss it."

"Ye deserve to know." He reached out for the chair and settled heavily into it. "Mayhap, it makes me a coward, but it will be easier to say if I'm daft with drink."

She put her hand over his, her expression so tender it nearly made his heart wince.

"I should have told ye sooner." He turned his hand over to wrap around hers. "'Tis no' an easy thing to bring up."

She regarded him with concern. How he wanted to draw her toward him and kiss her. But maybe not for too long or he might tip over. Nay, just long enough to draw her to the bed and nuzzle against her before they fell asleep.

But now was not the time. Not yet.

"Our marriage was arranged by a member of my mother's clan after it was confirmed ye werena able to be found." Ewan offered her an apologetic look. "Or I'm certain yer grandda would have pushed for our union sooner."

She shook her head. "Ye needn't explain yerself."

Ewan squeezed her hand in appreciation for her understanding. "I dinna know her before we wed, but we got on well enough. She was a fine wife and a good woman who ran the keep smoothly." He paused, uncertain what else to say to recommend Lara. She had not caused any problems. She'd been quiet and biddable, but outside of that, he could think of little else. Was it any wonder she had taken her own life when he'd been so reluctant to see her as more?

He winced at how bad his words sounded, even as he spoke. "We were wed only three short years and, in that time, she never once ripened with child. One morning, I went to meet with several tenants, and when I returned, I was informed she had thrown herself from the cliffs."

His throat was suddenly dry and the memory sat like a jagged stone in his chest. "Moiré was there when it happened and tried to stop her."

Faye touched her fingertips to her mouth. "How horrible."

Ewan drew in a deep sigh, but it didn't alleviate the grip of his grief, his regret. "'Tis worse than even that." He pulled his hand from Faye's and stared at his creased palms. For how could he possibly look at her when making such a confession?

"All this time, I thought she'd done it because of her inability to conceive." Ewan gave a mirthless laugh. "What a selfish fool I was. She did it..." He swallowed, hating the words before they even left his mouth. "Because I dinna show her that I cared for her. She felt unloved. Unwanted." He gritted his teeth. "And she was unloved. By me. I dinna love her. I dinna ever take the time to."

He lifted his gaze up hesitantly to gauge Faye's reaction. She continued to gaze upon with him compassion and tenderness.

He couldn't stand it and put his face into his hands. "I never loved her, and she took her own life because of it."

Faye rose from her chair and came to him, setting her hands on his shoulders. "Most marriages do not have love. 'Tis not uncommon."

"Most marriages dinna end in one person taking their own life," he replied miserably, keenly aware of how his words slurred slightly. "I dinna want it to happen to ye."

She knelt down in front of him so he could see her face. The fire in the hearth played shadows over her skin. "It won't happen to me."

He touched the petal softness of her skin. "I care for ye, Faye. Already so much more than I ever did for Lara, may both she and God forgive me."

A flash of pain showed in her eyes. As soon as it was there, it was gone, blinked away and replaced with the coquettish smile that set his blood on fire. "Come to bed, lover. The hour is late."

"Nay."

She paused and tilted her head.

"Ye do this often." He pointed an unsteady finger at her.

She blinked innocently. He knew better.

"Ye dinna trust me, Faye." Saying the accusation aloud was more striking than he'd anticipated. He hadn't planned to speak his mind on it at all, but the drink guided his words with no care for fault. "Ye choose passion over conversation."

"Are ye truly complaining?" Her fingers crept up his thighs and brushed at his cock, which still stirred even in his foggy state.

He shifted in this seat, away from her touch. "I want to get to know ye, Faye. I want ye to trust me the way I've trusted ye with this painful admission tonight." He ran the back of his thumb over the hand she'd tried to entice him with. "I want to love ye."

Her eyes filled with tears. A single one spilled down her cheek like a dropped diamond. "I don't want that." She wiped at the moisture on her face. "I'm not like yer first wife, Ewan."

He frowned, his thoughts sloshing in his mind. "What do ye mean?"

She stared up at him, resolve glittering in her eyes. "I don't want to be loved."

$$ \text{꙰} \quad 1\,2 \quad \text{꙰} $$

F aye woke alone in the large bed she had shared with Ewan since they were married. And for the first time, they had not spent the night coupling.

After she'd confessed her lack of desire to be loved, Ewan had refused to leave his chair, and she'd been forced to go to bed. Alone.

He had consumed a good bit of alcohol. That much had been evident in the slight slur of his words and the completeness of his confession.

She eased quietly from her bed to dress and found the chair empty. Her reply had disappointed him. She shouldn't care, of course. She should have put enough distance between them to prevent herself from becoming emotionally involved.

But the burning ache in her chest told a different story than the one she tried to tell herself. It bespoke of a man who had opened his heart even as she closed hers off, one who was inclined to get to know her despite her determination to remain aloof.

And through the silent battle she'd waged against him, he'd somehow begun to find cracks in the wall she hid behind.

She crossed the connecting doors into her own chamber as a soft knock sounded. Gavina entered with a new kirtle in her arms, this one a sumptuous crimson red with a gold circlet and veil. Faye tried to maintain a friendly demeanor as the maid dressed her, but the smile continued to slide from her face, and the painful clutch of emotion remained locked around her chest.

When Gavina was done, and Faye had thanked her for her talents with a needle, Faye made her way down to the kitchen to first speak with the cook to prepare the midday and evening meals. Then she went to the chatelaine to ensure the essential household duties had been properly carried out.

She had dreaded becoming the mistress of the keep when she'd first learned of the task. After all, it had taken her mother and sisters to ensure the manor remained clean and their stores well-stocked. But now that she was heading a well-trained staff, it was entirely manageable. More than that, it was enjoyable. At least she never had to wrestle wet laundry onto a line again or pluck a chicken. The latter of which was the most deplorable task in the entire world.

And the work required of the mistress of the castle was a glorious distraction from the heavy ache in her soul.

Faye had only just finished scheduling the laundry pressing with the chatelaine when Moiré approached. She wore a fine yellow kirtle with her long chestnut hair plaited back in a braid. Whatever glimmers of lust that had lingered on her face the night before had been scrubbed away to reveal her usual sweet, pleasant expression.

What Faye had seen the night before had skittered about in her mind in the brief moments she wasn't fretting about Ewan. She still hadn't recovered from her shock at seeing gentle Moiré leaving a man's room. And not just any man's. After all, discovering the chamber's occupant was a simple task for a mistress traversing the castle with her chatelaine earlier that morning.

Finn Gordon. The very man who had rejected Moiré as a wife.

"Good morrow," Faye said to Ewan's cousin.

Moiré smiled. "Good morrow. I trust all has gone accordingly this morn?"

"Quite well, thank ye." Faye studied the other woman. There was still an innocence about her wide brown eyes that was entirely opposite what Faye had seen in the sexually confident grin the night before. Had it truly been Moiré?

And yet, Faye trusted no one better than herself. Indeed, it *had* been her.

"I'm grateful for yer instruction," Faye said. "'Tis been most helpful."

Moiré beamed. "I'm so pleased to hear it."

There was such a genuine benevolence to Moiré that it tugged at a tender spot in Faye's chest. If Finn had used Ewan's cousin, Faye had to know, to plan out how to make reparations. Or, at the very least, to prevent Moiré from getting hurt again.

But how did one go about bringing up such a topic?

"I wonder..." Faye began, then thought better of her approach, and the words died on her tongue.

"What is it?" Moiré leaned closer. "Is it about Lara? I shouldna have ever mentioned it at the feast." Her large eyes filled with regret. "It was no' my place to do so."

"Please put it from yer thoughts." Faye meant to reach for Moiré's hand but stopped short. Black ink stained her forefinger as though she had been writing recently. "I confess," Faye said. "'Tis ye who most occupies my concern."

"Me?" Moiré chuckled. "Dear Faye, ye need no' worry after me."

Faye bit the inside of her cheek to keep from outwardly wincing at Moiré's words. What Faye had witnessed was indeed cause for concern. She took Moiré's slender arm in her hand and gently drew her toward an alcove. A quick scan of the hall confirmed they were alone.

"I saw ye last night," Faye whispered.

Moiré said nothing. Her expression remained blank, as though Faye had not spoken at all.

"In the hall," Faye pressed. "After ye left the feast."

Moiré swallowed. "Mayhap, we can speak in yer chamber?"

It was a reasonable enough request, especially regarding the topic of their discussion. They were already near Faye's rooms, and the two quickly hurried there together. Faye secured the door behind her. Moiré perched herself on the edge of the seat by the dressing table, her expression pinched.

"Was it Finn Gordon?" Faye asked.

Moiré folded her arms around herself and gave a sullen nod.

"Did ye..." Faye glanced around the room, terribly uncomfortable with the question she knew she needed to ask the other woman. "Did he have ye?"

Moiré's cheeks blossomed with a brilliant red, and her eyes lowered to where her leather shoes peeked out from beneath the sunny yellow hem of her kirtle.

"Has he promised himself to ye then?" Faye's heart clenched with hope. A hope that was met with silence.

Jesu.

"Moiré, does he plan to wed ye?" Faye asked.

The other woman shook her head, tears bright in her eyes.

"Moiré." Faye approached her and smoothed her hand over the other woman's hair. "Why?"

Moiré looked up; her lashes spiked with moisture. "Do ye ever get tired of all the rules we have as women?" she asked abruptly. "We're to flirt, but no' too much. We should be bonny at bed and at board, but only after we're wed. We should marry, but only to whom men agree we can." Her brows lifted with emphasis. "No matter how it happens."

An ember of anger glowed to life in Faye's chest. Aye, she knew well the unfairness of a woman's lot.

"I grew weary of the rules." Moiré sucked in a breath and

shook her head. "I made my own choice. I know he doesna want me as a wife. I understood that when I went to him and I dinna expect anything from him, above what we shared last night."

Faye had heard other women claim such and had seen their hearts broken regardless.

"Ye know this will impact yer options for marriage," Faye said gently. "Unless ye are certain he will keep yer secret."

Moiré lifted her chin with a flash of spirit Faye had not yet seen. "Mayhap, that was the point."

Faye opened her mouth, unsure what to say to such defiance. Part of her cheered the other woman on, for taking a stand for her own path. But the other part of Faye feared Moiré would come to regret such a decision, especially with so much of her life still ahead of her. She was young and attractive. Someone may steal her heart yet. And a secret such as Moiré's could be an impossible wall between herself and happiness.

"I dinna..." Moiré pressed her lips together.

"Ye didn't what?" Faye pressed.

"I saw how ye were forced to wed Ewan." Moiré shook her head, her face set. "I dinna want to ever be in such a position."

"Ewan would never do that to ye," Faye gasped.

"He wouldna," Moiré conceded. "But my da has the support of the Gordons now. I wouldna put it past him to do as yer grandda did to ye." She caught Faye's hand in her hot grip. "Dinna tell Ewan about Finn, please. Or anyone else."

Ewan.

Even the mention of his name fanned the flame of hurt within her. She was not a good wife to Ewan, most assuredly not what he deserved. She didn't want to be loved, and now she was considering holding back such a large secret...

"We women who have been so wronged by men must stick together." Moiré's gaze pleaded silently with Faye.

Uncertainty twisted in Faye's gut, but still, she found herself nodding in reassurance to Ewan's cousin. "Aye," she said at last. "I will keep yer counsel."

But even as she vowed to keep such secrets, she already knew to do so was a grave mistake.

⚜

EWAN HAD YET TO DEED BERWICK TO THE ROSS CHIEFTAIN. The parchment with the terms written out in a neat, slanting hand lay out on his desk, weighted down with stones on either corner to keep it from rolling up.

Giving Ross what he wanted did not sit well with Ewan. Dealing with a man such as him never did.

The ghost of a lingering headache pounded in the background of Ewan's brain, punishment for having consumed far too much alcohol the night before.

Thoughts of Faye drifted into Ewan's mind, but he tried to shove them away. There was too much in the forefront that required his concentration. He had ensured the Gordons left that morning without issue and that his uncle and his new bride were on their way to Cruim's manor on the outskirts of the village.

In all the revelry the night before, the Gordons had not once mentioned an intent to overthrow Ewan. They had, however, indicated Cruim's decision to negotiate a union between Moiré and one of the Murray Chieftain's sons, a clan the Gordons sought to align with. If Moiré was not amenable to the idea, Ewan would do what he could to aid her.

Ewan skimmed the contract for the land to Ross once more, and his gut twisted with dislike. After all the years of constant attacks from the Ross clan and what Ross had done to his own granddaughter, the idea of deeding over the land felt like a reward for nefarious deeds.

The savory scent of a meal tugged at Ewan's awareness, and

his stomach issued a low, hungry rumble. He lifted the stones, so the parchment curled in on itself, and tucked the document into his drawer. He would consider it tomorrow. Again.

Ross's patience would only last so long. Ewan needed to come up with a solution, and soon.

He arrived in the Great Hall as everyone else was taking their seats for the evening meal. His gaze found Faye, and his heart gave a solid kick against his ribs.

"I don't want to be loved."

Such words were hard to absorb.

He settled into the large, ornate chair on the dais beside her. She was resplendent in a red kirtle with a gleam of gold glinting from her circlet.

She cast him an anxious glance. "Ye're displeased with me."

He considered her words. She hadn't made him discontented; it was her determination to not fall in love that vexed him.

"I canna force ye to want anything," he replied in a quiet voice for her ears only. "Especially no' love."

She nodded and nervously touched the metal stem of her goblet. Her fingers were elegant, graceful as they stroked over the metal.

"'Tis no' because of ye." She paused until the maid delivering bowls of bread walked away. "I..." She released the goblet, and her fingers twisted against one another in her lap. "There has been much betrayal in my life."

"And it's made ye hesitant to trust," Ewan surmised.

She nodded slowly.

Understanding dawned on Ewan then. It wasn't that Faye didn't want love. It was that she was afraid.

That, at least, was something he could manage.

But now was not the time for platitudes or trying to sway her with words. Not when actions worked so much better.

"I'd like to know what happened, but only as ye feel comfortable telling me," Ewan said. "I'll no' force anything from ye. Especially no' a feeling."

Her rigid demeanor relaxed somewhat.

"Ye assumed the role of mistress of the castle today, aye?" He inspected the table, set with fresh linen and dotted with sprigs of heather.

Color flushed at her cheeks. "Aye. And I had the cook prepare one of yer favorite meals."

"Ye know my favorite meal?" Pleasure rushed through him that she would be mindful of what he'd eaten to try to accommodate his tastes. It was a considerate gesture. Especially from a woman who claimed not to want to be loved.

She grinned at him. "I believe I am correct in what ye like."

A servant carried over a platter and settled it before Ewan. He peered at it and froze. Coils of cooked eel snaked around one another, their dull eyes staring at nothing. A shiver of disgust crept up his spine.

He'd never cared for the wicked looking creatures. Not when they were alive with their serpentine bodies and sharp teeth. And even less when they were dead and set on a plate before him.

Mindful of her stare upon him, he pressed his lips together to stifle his expression.

She looked at the platter and gasped—no doubt in delight.

He steeled himself to force the meal down in an effort to please her. Not just one bite, but many. Enough to fill his belly. He stared down at the glossy, baked skin and bile burned up the back of his throat. Mayhap he'd need to eat an entire one.

"That isn't what I asked Cook to make." Faye glanced around the room, as though seeking the man out to speak with him then and there.

Ewan eyed the unappetizing meal before him. "What did ye ask for?"

"Venison," she replied.

"So, ye dinna order eel intentionally?" Relief eased his tense shoulders.

She shook her head, her expression wounded. "I don't know what I did wrong. How could I possibly confuse so simple an order?"

"May I confess something to ye?" Ewan nudged his elbow against hers.

She turned her worried gaze up to him and nodded.

"I'm glad ye dinna think I liked this." He didn't bother to hide his revulsion for the meal. "I canna stand eel."

Her mouth curled up with mirth. "Nor can I." She turned her face away from the platter. "I could go the rest of my life without ever having another."

"My mum gave up with me when I was a lad." Ewan chuckled. "I made such a show of it every time it was set before me."

"It was all my mum could afford after my da died when we were in England," Faye said. "We ate it for years." A shiver of revulsion wracked through her, and they both laughed.

Their eyes caught with their shared distaste for the food, and a pleasant warmth hummed in Ewan's chest. He reached for the bread, his hand hovering. "May I select the finest piece of bread for yer supper this evening, my lady?"

Faye smiled at him and made a show of perusing the small rolls. "That would be most kind of ye."

He plucked one from the top. "This appears to be the bonniest in the bunch."

She nodded her thanks as he took one for himself. Together, they split their bread and spread a glossy smear of salted butter over it, while the rest of the castle dined on eel for the first time in nearly a decade.

One of Ewan's warriors entered the Great Hall at a clipped pace and approached the dais. "Forgive the interruption, sir, but there are several visitors who insist on seeing ye."

"Several visitors" was vague enough to imply any number of

people. Including the Gordon clan, which was the last thing Ewan wanted now that he'd finally removed them all from his home.

"Visitors?" Ewan set his bread on the plate in front of him, no longer plagued with hunger. "Who are they?"

The young man glanced toward Faye. "They claim to be Lady Sutherland's family."

❧ 13 ❧

Faye sat forward in her chair. "I beg yer pardon?"

The young man ducked his head, revealing the top of his bushy blond head. "They claim to be yer family, my lady. They're in the bailey and insist on seeing ye both."

Ewan nodded toward the large entryway. "Go to them. I'll join ye in a moment."

Faye leapt to her feet and raced through the Great Hall, heedless of so many eyes set upon her. She would have gone with or without Ewan's permission, though she hadn't anticipated he would deny her the opportunity to see her family.

They'd come for her.

All this time she'd worried they would think she was dead, or that they might not ever see her again. Drake, so strong and determined. Kinsey, all fire and driven with purpose. Clara, with her exquisite kindness. And Mum...

Tears blurred Faye's vision, but she'd ventured through the castle enough times by now to know its layout. The missive she'd sent her family would not have reached them yet. They hadn't come because she'd summoned them.

They'd come because they'd sought her out.

Such a realization made her tears spill over. She ran faster, erupting from the entrance to the castle and out into the cold night air.

All at once, there they were. Her mother with Kinsey on one side and Clara on the other.

"Faye!" Kinsey's voice pierced the quiet with excitement, and the trio ran toward her.

They met halfway in a fiercely clashing hug. Arms curled around Faye, bringing with them the familiar sweet scent. Faye closed her eyes, welcoming the torrent of memories of her home and family, ones she'd turned away from previously in an attempt to stay sane.

They rushed back now, brought on by the familiarity of her sisters' and mother's voices and the clean perfume of lavender. Clara sewed the little sachets every time she harvested her herbs, setting aside a batch of buds specifically to perfume the kirtles stored at the foot of their beds. It was such a small, simple thing that Faye had always thought foolish.

Now, it was the smell of home. Of love.

"Thanks be to God ye're here," her mother whispered.

"Where's Drake?" Faye hoped he hadn't left his post at Werrick Castle, not when it meant so much to him.

"Two or three days behind us." Clara glanced at the horizon as if she might be able to see him making his way to Dunrobin already. "We had a missive sent to him."

"Are ye hurt?" Mum held Faye by the shoulders and looked at her, examining her with a sharp gaze from her head to the scuffed toes of her shoes.

"I'm fine, Mum," Faye reassured her.

"We were so worried." Clara caught Faye's hand and clung to it as tears filled her crystal blue eyes.

"How did ye know to come here?" Faye asked.

"Yer grandda approached me a day before ye disappeared asking about yer betrothal," her mother replied. "When ye dinna come home, it was too easy to guess what that arse of a man had done." The anger on her face deepened to sorrow. "I worried about ye every day, hoping ye were safe and healthy. At the verra least, well cared for."

Memories of the journey to the Highlands flooded Faye's thoughts as the reality of everything that had transpired overwhelmed her. The forceful way she'd been stolen from her home. How she'd spent so much of that journey bound in chains like a prisoner, shoved in that damn box. Then left in a room to wait for a man she could barely remember to claim her as his wife.

A sob burst from her, and her mother pulled her into an embrace. "I swear that if he hurt ye, I'll kill him."

"He didn't," Faye lied. Her mother couldn't know the truth of it. Faye wouldn't have her mother embroiled in any of this, or her sisters for that matter. She wanted her family as far from her grandfather as was possible.

Faye burrowed into her mother's embrace even as a voice in the back of her head told her a grown woman shouldn't need such comfort from her mum. But she couldn't bring herself to pull away. Not when her mother provided such solace.

"I'm too old for this, Mum," she offered weakly.

Her mother exhaled a hard breath and finally released her. "It doesna matter how old ye are, lass. Ye'll always be my bairn. Ye and all yer siblings." Tears shone brightly in her eyes, but her voice remained clear.

"We're here to bring ye home." Kinsey puffed out her chest and glared around them. "And if anyone tries to stop us, I'll put an arrow through their eye."

"Ye needn't be so violent," Clara chastised before their mother could.

Kinsey nudged Faye with her elbow. "Says the one of us with perfect aim. Even *she* brought her daggers with her."

Of all of them, Clara had the most skill when it came to weaponry. She could pin a fly against a tree with the point of a dagger from seventy paces away. All without so much as hesitating to aim. Were it not for her impossibly gentle nature, she could have possibly been the best mercenary Scotland had ever seen. England, too, at that.

"Did ye actually bring yer daggers?" Faye asked in surprise.

Clara simply shrugged, as if it were of no concern. "We want ye home and will stop at nothing to see ye safe." She smiled tenderly at Faye. "We love ye."

Love.

If it were a tangible thing, it would be in Faye's hands right now, as thick and warm as a coverlet filled with down, something she could wrap around her shoulders.

Ewan rose forefront in her mind.

Could I love him?

"We must go." Kinsey pulled at her arm, dragging her a step forward.

Faye shook her head. "I can't go."

"Have they threatened ye?" Kinsey demanded.

"Whatever it is, ye need not worry about it," Clara confirmed. "We're here." She settled one small hand on a dagger at her belt.

The show of intent from someone as soft-hearted as Clara tugged anew at Faye.

"I'm not leaving," Faye protested.

If she allowed herself to be taken away now, her grandfather would most likely be back for Clara. To force her into another marriage with some other neighboring clan whose favor he sought. Faye's presence at Dunrobin meant he would keep his word and leave her family be.

"Let us get ye gone from this place." Kinsey tugged at Faye's arm again.

A figure appeared in the doorway of the castle.

Ewan.

Faye's pulse quickened.

"I canna go," she said again.

Her mother and sisters looked toward the doorway as Ewan descended the stairs, his handsome face set with an intense expression Faye couldn't make out.

Kinsey slid her gaze cautiously from Ewan to Faye. "Who is this?"

"This is Ewan Sutherland, Chieftain of the Sutherland clan," Faye said by way of introduction. "My husband."

⚜

SILENCE FOLLOWED EWAN'S INTRODUCTION TO FAYE'S FAMILY as they stared up at him with apparent wariness.

While Faye's sisters all had the same slender nose and large eyes, taking after their mother by the look of it, they did not share her fair hair. The one with wavy red tresses put herself in front of Faye. "She's returning home with us."

"We've been wed for nearly a fortnight." Faye shifted around her sister and came to his side. "Ewan is a good man."

Kinsey's mouth fell open. "He forced ye to marry—"

"He didn't," Faye said vehemently. "I made my own decision."

Under the fear of a threat.

Ewan kept the words to himself. This was Faye's family. It was her decision what she wished to tell them on the matter of their marriage. And what she wished to keep secret.

Faye's dark-haired sister glanced first to her, then to him, before cautiously stepping forward. Her smile was kind and genuine as she offered a small curtsey. "I'm Clara."

Faye's mother approached tentatively, also looking to Faye as though weighing the truth of her words. "I'm her Mum, Cait."

They all looked to the red-haired sister, who scowled back at them. She folded her arms forcefully over her chest. The bow slung over her back awkwardly tipped to the side, making her have to uncross her arms to toss it back into place, which made her scowl all the more.

"That's Kinsey," Faye said with a sigh.

"Welcome to Dunrobin Castle," he said. "The evening meal was just served. We'd be honored if ye'd join us."

Faye put her hand around his arm. "Please join us. We can speak on this more later."

"Of course." Cait approached her and pressed a kiss to her brow. "Ye do look well, daughter."

Faye smiled at her mother. "I am well cared for here."

Ewan offered Cait his other arm, which she took with a careful smile.

Clara joined them next, followed by a reluctant Kinsey. Together, the four of them returned to the Great Hall, where Ewan had them sit at the dais with Faye and himself as their honored guests. After a quick introduction to Moiré and Monroe, they all settled down to eat.

Kinsey glanced at the platter of food and groaned. "Eel?" She turned an accusatory look at Faye.

"Shush now." Cait shot her daughter a stern look.

"It isn't what I ordered to be served tonight," Faye said apologetically.

Clara took a piece, then did little more than stare at it.

"Ye don't have to eat that, Clara," Faye said.

Clara lifted her gaze, her face bright with relief. "I didn't want to be rude."

Faye laughed. "Oh, Clara, ye're too kind. We spent far too long eating this when we were children to ever have to endure it again."

"And we ate so much." Kinsey grimaced.

"It wasna that terrible," Cait protested.

All three of her daughters stared at her, skeptical.

"Well," she conceded, "mayhap it was."

They all laughed this time, including Ewan, who promptly ordered more bread to be brought to the dais.

"Do ye remember the time Faye managed to bring home that old chicken?" Kinsey asked. "I've never seen such a pathetic bird in my life, but we ate it as if we were kings being served the greatest feast."

Faye's cheeks darkened with a blush, and she glanced at Ewan with apparent discomfort. "We don't need to speak of such things," she said to her sisters.

"I've had my fair share of eel." Ewan made a face of disgust that made Kinsey laughed. "My da loved it, but I could never stand it. 'Tis mayhap the first time it's been served here since his death."

"I don't understand what happened to the venison." Faye shook her head. "Tomorrow should be a pigeon pie. I fear what may come out instead."

"It happens sometimes," Moiré offered politely. "'Twas yer first day running the keep."

"And ye did a fine job of it." Ewan beamed proudly at Faye.

"Except for the eel." Faye frowned at the food that had caused so much offense.

"Talk to cook on the morrow." Ewan reached for a plate of vegetables. "'Tis no great concern. Regardless of what we're eating, 'tis among good company."

And it was. He hoped Faye's family might be what finally set her at ease, allowing her to be herself truly and mayhap open up to him.

She smiled so much more among them. A bright, unfettered grin that lit the room with her joy. He'd never seen her so happy, and it made him realize how all this time, she must have been miserable.

Aye, she had been the one to make the decision to wed him. But after witnessing what she regained with her family, what she had been forced to give up marrying him, he couldn't allow her to keep making such a sacrifice. Even though the threat had not been his doing, she had still been coerced into their union. He could overlook it no more.

Though it twisted an ugly knot in his chest, he knew what he needed to do.

❦ 14 ❦

Faye finally departed the Great Hall with reluctance. The hour had grown too late to keep her sisters and mother at the dais after such a long journey.

After all, they would speak again on the morrow.

But it was still so hard to leave. For the first time since she had arrived in the Highlands, she felt a sense of completeness. Having them appear was like a dream, a mirage of happiness she feared might disappear if she let it go for even a moment.

"'Twas good to meet yer family," Ewan said as they made their way up to their chambers.

"I think ye even won Kinsey over in the end." She smiled at him, though the action felt forced.

Exhaustion pressed in on her as if her energy had been fed by her family, and now without them, she was nothing but a husk once more.

In the past evenings, Ewan had always brought her to his chamber without passing by her door. Tonight, however, he hesitated in front of her chamber. "If ye'd rather be alone tonight..."

She shook her head. Of all nights, she did not want to be alone on this one. Except this time, the strange hollowness ringing out within her could not be burned away by desire. She didn't want Ewan in the way a woman wanted a lover, but in the way that a wife needed her husband. She longed for his arms around her, cradling her to his powerful body and shielding her from everything hurting in her heart.

They entered his chamber together, but neither reached for the other, not like they'd done previously when an insatiable lust had spurred their actions.

Instead, Ewan watched her with tenderness. "Was it difficult to see them again?"

Tears immediately filled Faye's eyes. She'd spent the night controlling them, wrangling her feelings with the force it would take to contain lightning.

Ewan said nothing. He simply opened his arms, and she ran to him, collapsing against him as the tears came. His head bowed over her, enveloping her in his warmth, his strength and the wonderful spicy scent of him.

"I know ye've missed them," he said gently.

She nodded against his chest.

He pressed a kiss to the top of her head. "This isna fair to ye."

She leaned back to look at him better. "What do ye mean?"

"For ye to stay here."

An indiscernible emotion flickered in her chest. "'Twas my decision to make."

"One ye were pressed into in order to keep yer family safe." He tucked a lock of hair behind her ear. The gesture was affectionate, as though trying to soften an impending blow.

"Just as ye wed me to keep yer people safe," she replied slowly, warily. "We are both protecting those we love."

He shook his head, and a muscle flexed against the sharp edge of his jaw. "It was worse for ye, being taken from yer home." The firelight caught in his eyes and revealed a troubling flash in the hazel depths.

He gently took her hand in his and pulled back her sleeve to reveal the red bands around her wrists where her shackle wounds had recently healed. "Ye dinna talk about it, but I know what ye went through was terrible."

She turned her face away so he couldn't see her expression as she recalled exactly how bad it had been. Aye, she didn't talk about it. She hadn't even wanted to think about it. Not when the memories were even more painful than the abuse.

"I thought I could make it better, that I could protect ye. But seeing ye tonight..." His voice caught and drew her attention back to him.

"Faye, ye were happy." He ran a finger down her cheek in a delicate caress. "Truly happy. And ye've no' been that way once since ye've been here. I'll no' commit ye to a life of misery."

"I haven't been miserable," she protested.

"But nor have ye been happy."

His statement plunged into her heart like a dagger. The impact carried so much pain, she almost gasped.

"I cannot leave," she whispered. "If my grandda found out..."

"He won't," Ewan said so vehemently, she almost believed him.

"He would," she replied. "If I left and never came back, he would know."

Ewan went silent suddenly, and the impact of her own words hit Faye liked a punch.

If I left and never came back.

If she never saw him again. A fresh fission of pain ripped inside of her and warred with the ache of being away from her family. The sensation was new and unexpected.

And it had everything to do with the thought of losing Ewan.

She didn't want to think of what the new tendril of emotion meant to her. Not when doing so might pry open her heart more than it had already been.

"Ye need a son," she whispered.

He swallowed. "No' at the expense of keeping ye here like a

prisoner. I care for ye too much to have ye sacrifice everything for me."

She studied him for a long, quiet moment. His expression confirmed the sincerity of his words, though she needed no proof. Somewhere along the way, she had begun to trust him. She knew how urgently he needed a son, another barrier between the chieftainship and Cruim.

And he was willing to give up that prospect for her happiness.

"I can't." She shook her head. "I can't do this. It isn't possible. I couldn't deprive ye of a son. Not when the safety of the clan is at stake."

His jaw clenched. "Ye could come back for visits as ye used to when ye were a bairn. Eventually, we would have a son and ensure Ross knew ye were here so he wouldna question our marriage."

"Ewan..." She searched for words but found none when she couldn't even sort through the clutter of her own thoughts. What he offered was more generous than any man in his position would.

It was a chance for her to return home. To be happy. And at great cost to himself.

"Dinna answer now," he added quickly. "Think about it."

She nodded, unable to tear her gaze from her husband. How could such a large man who appeared cut from stone have such tenderness in his heart? He was not only good to his people; he was good to her, putting her happiness before his own needs.

He drew her toward him and curled his strong arms around her once more, wrapping her in comfort she lost herself in. Yet it only made the agony in her chest twist tighter. This time, however, she understood the reason.

The wall she'd built around her heart, erected by a lifetime of pain and betrayal, had finally begun to crack.

EWAN WASN'T CERTAIN WHEN TO EXPECT AN ANSWER FROM

Faye. He hadn't given her a date to reply, not when he wanted her to think it through and come to her own decision. Still, he could not clear it from his mind, alternating between fear at the certainty of losing her and hope that she would stay. In the end, he was proud of himself for having the courage to do what was right for her to ensure her happiness.

She was correct that he needed an heir, especially with Cruim having married Mistress Blair. The union did not sit well with him and continued to rankle him. He'd learned long ago not to ignore the feeling in his gut, and this one sat there like a boulder.

He reviewed the contract in front of him once more, the one that would deed Berwick to Ross. Only this time, Ewan had a plan.

A gentle knock sounded at the door.

He bade his guest enter and stood as Cait stepped in. "Thank ye for coming." He bowed to her.

"Ye need no' put on airs for me." She waved her hand at him dismissively.

He indicated she have a seat while he came around his desk. "Ross claims to want a bit of land we own between the English and Scottish border. Do ye know why?"

She glanced down at the parchment, and her eyes flicked over the agreement, then rolled heavenward. "Ach, he'd be still after Berwick." She sighed. "'Twas Ross land several ages ago but was taken from them by the English. 'Twas a sore spot for years that they were so soundly defeated, and they resolved to get it back. Except the English had fortified it so well, it wasna possible. Until Lady Isolde."

"Lady Isolde?" Ewan sank into his chair.

"Aye, the land was part of her dowry," Cait said. "But rather than wed a member of the Ross clan as she was supposed to, the Chieftain of the Sutherland clan swept her off her feet, killed the Ross clansman she was meant to wed and took the land for himself." She shrugged. "It happened far before my time, but we've been fighting since, and my da has wanted the land back for as long as I can remember. As every chieftain before him has."

Bits of the tale was familiar to Ewan from his own boyhood. But then, it had been Ragnall who would have been told the full details in his training to become chieftain.

Ewan framed his hand over the document and tapped it with his fingertips. "I dinna want to give this land to Ross. I'd prefer to deed it to yer eldest son, Drake."

"It will anger Ross." Cait's brows furrowed, and a small line appeared on the skin between them, the same as Faye when she was in deep concentration.

"But it willna breach the marriage contract I signed with Ross the night I wed Faye."

Cait's mouth curled up at the edges. "Nay, it willna."

"Then, it will be done." Ewan pulled the stones from the corners and let the parchment roll up. But he hesitated to send Cait on her way.

He cleared his throat. "I want ye to know, I dinna have any part in forcing Faye to marry me."

"I know." Cait cast him a sympathetic look. "I spoke with her this morn while we were breaking our fast." She leaned forward in her seat and put a slender hand on his forearm. "Faye told me how ye tried to help her. Thank ye for that."

Ewan simply nodded in acknowledgement. After all, his efforts hadn't been helpful.

Cait released him and drew her arm back. "Why did she agree to her grandda's wishes?"

"I take it she dinna tell ye?" Ewan secured the rolled parchment with a string and placed it into the drawer at his side.

Cait shook her head. "Nay. And she's no' ever been one to desire marriage, so ye understand my confusion."

Ewan remembered how Faye had stood proudly at his side when they met her family as if she were a woman who had wanted to wed rather than a captive forced into marriage. No doubt, she did not want her sisters to know she had done so to save them. "If she wishes to tell ye, she will," he replied.

She smiled. "Aye, I'm sure."

The fire crackling in the hearth filled the gap of silence while Ewan warred with indecision on whether to tell Cait about the option he'd presented to Faye. Her mother would most likely ensure Faye genuinely considered the choice. Regardless of what Faye decided, he wanted to ensure it was one she had thought through.

He tapped a finger on the glossy surface of his desk. "Did she mention anything else to ye this morn?"

Cait lifted her chin. "Do ye mean how ye have given her the option to come home with us and return once a year to ye?"

Ewan tensed, unsure if he was relieved Faye had shared the information with her mother, or fearful. "Aye. She's no' happy here. I dinna realize how much until I saw her with all of ye."

Cait glanced at her lap. "Faye doesna share her thoughts readily." She spoke slowly, as though considering her words before speaking. "I dinna know if ye remember her as a lass, but she wasna always this way. When my husband died, it was difficult for us all. But when our neighbors turned on us, that was what hurt Faye the most. It wasna her da's death that changed her; it was the people's betrayal."

Ewan settled back in his chair. It made sense how she had tried to keep him at arm's length, how she was so slow to share parts of herself. How she turned to lust and pleasure rather than conversations about who she was and what she wanted.

Cait got to her feet. "If ye asked if I knew about yer proposal to Faye in the hope I would sway her decision, I'll tell ye 'tis a waste of time. The lass is too stubborn to be moved whatever way she doesn't want to go."

Ewan quickly stood as well, and Cait regarded him affectionately. "But if I had a choice myself, I would want her to stay here," she said.

"Ye would?"

"She has happiness at Castleton, but it's precarious," Cait replied. "Here, I believe she can have happiness, security and love. She's lucky to have a man such as ye in her life." She inclined her head and swept from the solar, quietly closing the door behind her.

Ewan lowered himself to his chair and studied the closed door as Cait's words played through his mind, warring once more with the indecision of what Faye would choose. And how it would impact both their lives.

Only time would tell.

🦋 15 🦋

The sun bathed over Faye's face as her thoughts flitted once more to Ewan. In the distance, Kinsey fired arrows into the tree as Clara offered advice on her aim. Mayhap Faye ought to be listening to the instruction as well, but it was too difficult to do when the choice he'd given her weighed on her mind so heavily.

It should have been an easy decision to make. After all, she'd had no choice in coming to the Highlands. But every time she recalled her small bed at the manor in Castleton, tucked in the corner of a room she shared with her sisters, her chest rang with hollowness.

Mayhap she'd gotten too used to Ewan's arms around her, his warmth drawing her into the cradle of sleep, his scent all around her, familiar and comfortable. She'd begun to enjoy how he always asked what she liked and what she wanted and waited with genuine interest in the answer. She knew all the things he enjoyed too and delighted in doing them, relishing in his pleasure.

He was a man of honor and character, who handled his people with genuine care, a man whose smile made her heart stagger. Fie! It was too many things to list at once.

An arrow flashed across the meadow and sank into the grass next to Faye.

She jerked away from it and glared at Kinsey, who stood fifty paces away with her hand on her hip and a smirk on her lips. "I said it was yer turn."

"Ye could have hit me." Faye pushed up to her feet.

Kinsey rolled her eyes. "I assure ye, I wouldn't have."

Faye regarded her sister with suspicion. While Kinsey was good with the bow, her confidence was oftentimes overinflated, resulting in the occasionally missed target. Not often, but it still happened. Faye would prefer she not become the first victim of a wayward arrow.

The clearing was surrounded by forest with enough trees nearby to practice their skills to their heart's content. They were just outside the castle, but it was nice to be away for a bit, a chance to breathe without the weight of her decision squeezing at Faye.

So long as her youngest sister didn't kill her first.

"Kinsey, that wasn't kind of ye." Clara strode toward them, the daggers in the bag at her side clinking. "Although ye are quite skilled."

"Aye, I am." Kinsey pulled her bow off her back and plucked an arrow from where several thrust up from the ground in front of her. She pulled it back with her bow, lining up her site, and released the arrow. It flew towards the tree and sailed passed it. A miss. Several inches from her target.

"That could have been me," Faye exclaimed.

Kinsey turned to her with a grimace. "But it wasn't. And that's really what matters."

"Oh, Kinsey." Clara touched her fingertips to her forehead and closed her eyes.

Kinsey extended the bow toward Faye. "Ye do better."

"Ye know I'm not as good as ye." Faye sighed and accepted the weapon.

"Mayhap I need to feel better about myself now." Kinsey grinned at her.

Months ago, this would have made Faye irate, but now, she couldn't help but laugh at Kinsey's bravado. How much Faye had missed her youngest sister! Even her overconfident impulsiveness and assertive demeanor. Kinsey burned brighter with life than any of them, and it warmed Faye to her very soul.

Faye pulled one of the arrows from the ground and readied her weapon. The bow had never been her weapon of choice. She had always preferred a hidden dagger and her own wits. But Kinsey knew that. They all were familiar with one another's strengths.

And weaknesses.

As anticipated, Faye's arrow went wide, flying past the tree and into a distant stream. Kinsey crowed in delight.

Faye propped her hand on her hip. "My lack of skill doesn't mean that ye still wouldn't have shot me."

Kinsey pointed at her with a wide smile. "But, I didn't." She shifted her focus to Clara. "I think we're both ready to be put to shame."

Clara flushed. "That truly isn't necessary. I've already done some practicing today."

"Ye know Drake tells us we have to practice often to ensure our skills stay strong," Kinsey argued.

"Doesn't he?" Kinsey pressed when Clara did not acquiesce.

She was always trying to encourage their sister to become a mercenary. The idea was laughable. Especially when Clara was such a gentle soul.

Faye felt compelled to come to Clara's aid. "She's already done enough. I think even Drake would be satisfied with the amount of time she's spent throwing her daggers."

Clara shot Faye a grateful smile.

"Have ye made yer decision about coming home with us?" Kinsey lifted her brows.

Faye's mouth fell open. "Don't turn this to me."

"I'll do it," Clara said quickly as she untied the bag of daggers from her belt. "Though I confess, 'tis hard to practice something I don't think I could ever do to another person."

Ever the obedient one, she still drew back the daggers one at a time and released them into the tree. They stuck neatly in a cluster in the dead center of the trunk.

Kinsey whooped with pride and threw her arm around Clara. "Ye're a wonder, do ye know that?"

Clara's blush deepened.

"But have ye made a decision yet?" Kinsey asked.

This time both of them looked at Faye in expectation.

"Ye should come home," Kinsey said definitively.

Faye chewed her lower lip. The decision was not simply made. In the time she took to mull over her options, she'd tried to pull back from Ewan in the hopes that if she did choose Castleton, she wouldn't miss him. At least not as much.

"Kinsey, will ye collect the arrows for another round?" Clara asked. "I think I may try my hand at archery again."

The grin returned to Kinsey's face, and she darted off to eagerly gather the fallen arrows.

"Ye hate archery," Faye said.

Clara offered a helpless laugh. "I do, but I knew this would give us a few moments of privacy." The wind picked up and blew at her dark hair, lifting the loose tendrils. "We'll always love ye no matter where ye live. And we'll always find ways to visit."

Faye's breath quickened. "What do ye mean?"

"I mean, if ye want to stay here with yer husband, then we would support yer decision." Clara lowered her head and looked tentatively at Faye, the way she did when she had something blunt to say.

Trepidation crawled up Faye's spine. "What is it?"

"Ye need to make a decision. Ye canna keep pushing the answer off." Clara's brows pursed with sadness. "'Tis cruel."

"Cruel?" Faye echoed.

"I have them all," Kinsey cried out victoriously in the distance. "Ready yer bow."

"Yer husband greatly cares for ye." Clara glanced to where Kinsey was racing back to them with shafts of arrows jutting out from both hands. "Don't let yer stubbornness and fear of love ruin something good."

Her words were a barb in Faye's chest. And given the apologetic look on Clara's face, she knew it. Which was all the more reason why what she said had such an impact.

Faye nodded in understanding and realized she'd known the answer the whole time.

Kinsey stopped abruptly before she reached them and put a hand up to shield the sun from her eyes, and she looked to the east. "There's a rider approaching."

Faye and Clara both searched and in the direction of Kinsey's stare. Indeed, a lone rider raced toward them on a black horse.

There was only one person she knew who rode a horse with a back that straight, who looked that regal despite a poor upbringing. Before she could stop herself, she was running toward him.

After several days' delay, Drake had finally arrived.

⚜

EWAN WAS IN THE GREAT HALL WHEN SHRIEKS OF EXCITEMENT echoed outside the large doors. Monroe, who had been in the middle of relaying the current farming status of one of the nearby villages, stopped speaking and glanced toward the sound.

"'Tis only the sisters," Ewan explained.

In the last few days, he'd gotten used to the giggles and squeals between the ladies. It warmed his heart as much as it cut him deep. For Faye still had not given him an answer.

What was worse, she was pulling away from him. The quiet moments between them were once more filled with wild passion, where pleasure was sought rather than companionship. She still slept in his chamber with him, but she was gone every morning before he woke.

He was no fool. He knew well why she was taking so long to give him her reply. She was planning to leave.

It eased the pain in his chest to know that in doing so, she would once more find happiness.

After all, she would leave, aye, but she would be back in the summer. And in the days between, he would devote himself to his people as he always had.

The clatter of footsteps echoed off the high stone walls. Three ladies raced into the large room with a tall man between them. He had the same dark hair as the middle sister, Clara, with the same straight nose and generous mouth as the others.

Drake.

Tension wound up the muscles along Ewan's back. He ought to be relieved as he knew he could now present Drake with the Berwick. Except that he suspected Faye was waiting for her brother's arrival to give Ewan her reply.

Unbidden, Ewan's gaze found his wife. Her blue kirtle was the same one she'd worn to his uncle's wedding, and it fit her body so perfectly, it made him want to span his hands over her narrow waist and draw her to him. Sun had kissed her cheeks and lips, leaving them with a lovely glow, and her eyes danced with laughter. She was vibrant and bonny, so much that it made his heart ache.

He approached them and looked at the man. "I assume this is yer brother?"

"Aye." Faye grinned. "This is Drake. The eldest."

Where his sisters were all laughter and bright sunshine, Drake's face was set with seriousness. "Drake Fletcher." He nodded to Ewan politely.

"Ewan Sutherland, Chieftain of the Sutherland clan."

"Well met, sir," Drake replied with a soldier's obedience.

Out of the corner of his eye, Ewan caught Moiré entering the Great Hall. She glanced shyly toward the sisters and hovered near the sidewall, appearing ill at ease among the lot of women.

Their arrival had put Moiré off somewhat, but then his cousin had always been somewhat reticent. Especially when it came to other women. Faye had been considerate to Ewan's cousin, though, and often made time to spend with Moiré.

"I hear ye're Captain of the Guard at Werrick Castle on the English side of the border," Ewan said.

Drake's chest filled with apparent pride. "Aye, I've been fortunate to be in such a secure position."

"I also hear ye're a fine warrior."

"I try, sir," Drake said earnestly.

It was a curious thing to compare this man with his jubilant sisters. But then, from what Ewan had gathered in his conversations with Faye's family, Drake had been their primary provider. Responsibility tempered a man's senses and put his mind to task.

Such men also did not have the liberty to spend large amounts of time away from their duties.

"I presume ye must return to Werrick Castle posthaste," Ewan surmised.

"Aye."

Exactly as Ewan had anticipated. He would need to address the land with Drake immediately.

"I should like to speak with ye once ye've settled," Ewan said. "Faye can show ye to yer room. I'll be in my solar."

Faye's eyes met Ewan's, and she nodded. But her gaze lingered. A jolt of energy raced through him. Was she considering him with interest? Or out of concern?

He roughly shoved aside the thoughts. He'd spent days analyzing every look, every smile, every damn word. It made his brain ache with how much he tried to determine what her decision might be.

Faye waved over Moiré and introduced Drake. It was the

perfect opportunity for Ewan to depart. He could not be near Faye without imagining her soon gone. No sweet smiles in his direction, a cold side of the bed where she once lay tucked in his arms, the absence of her floral scent in the air of his chamber.

He would miss everything, and each little reminder tore at his chest.

It was maddening, this inability to stay away even as it hurt too much to be near her.

He was not in his solar long before a knock came from the door, so efficient and crisp that he knew it would be Drake before the man appeared.

Faye's brother stepped into the room; his footsteps clipped. He didn't gaze around Ewan's solar as most did. But then, the few bits of furniture and simple tapestries were hardly impressive to a man who came from an English castle, which was rumored to be far more ostentatious.

"Ye've cared well for my sister," Drake said. "I dinna know what I'd find when I arrived and was grateful to see her safe. Thank ye."

"I'm afraid it wasna enough," Ewan said candidly. While he would not tell Cait about why Faye had decided to wed him, he knew Drake would need to be informed.

"What do ye mean?" Drake's brows immediately pinched with concern, and his shoulders squared.

Ewan indicated the chair, and the other man lowered himself to the seat.

"Ross said if Faye dinna wed me, he would force one of her sisters," Ewan replied. He'd prepared for this moment, an opportunity to keep Faye's sisters safe. While he tried to reassure her Ross wouldn't find out, he couldn't be entirely certain what the other chieftain might do, and if Faye left, Ewan would be too far away to provide protection. "While I wouldna wed them in a similar condition, there are other clan chieftains who would readily agree."

Drake's lips thinned. "That's how he convinced her to marry ye."

"Aye." Ewan pulled the parchment from the desk drawer. "I dinna want her to do it, but I had no choice."

"Faye has her own mind," Drake replied.

Ewan chuckled. "Aye, she does that. But I wouldna put it past Ross to still try to get to yer sisters, especially Clara."

Drake drew in a deep inhale. "She's a good soul. Mayhap too good. I'll ensure no harm comes to anyone in my family."

Some of the weight eased from Ewan's shoulders at Drake's ardent reply. Faye and her family would be safe.

"There's more." Ewan untied the parchment and unrolled it. The remainder of the information had been completed, with Drake's name where Ross had expected his to be.

Drake's gaze lowered to the desk.

Ewan explained how the agreement to wed Faye had included giving Berwick to the Ross clan. "I dinna trust yer grandda," he said in conclusion. "But from everything I know of yer family, I trust ye and have deeded the land no' to yer grandda, but to ye."

Drake's focus snapped up to Ewan. "Me?"

"It will be safe in yer hands," Ewan replied.

Drake stared at the document, not speaking. Finally, he cleared his throat and nodded. "Thank ye."

"I know ye must prepare for yer return trip to Werrick," Ewan said, offering the man an excuse to depart should he want it.

"Aye. Now that I know Faye is safe." Drake stood and locked forearms with Ewan before leaving the room.

An emptiness filled Ewan upon Drake's departure. Berwick had been a pressing concern; one Ewan had wanted resolved prior to Faye's departure. Now he need only receive her answer, however much that filled him with dread.

❧ 16 ❧

Despite Ewan's trepidation over Faye's reply, he had enjoyed the evening meal. By the time it drew to a close, his cheeks hurt from jesting and laughing with her family.

Even when his brother and da had been alive, they had not possessed a bond like that of the Fletchers. It was easy to lose oneself in their chatter and long to belong to their tight-knit closeness.

If Faye chose to be with them, her decision would be understandable.

She slid her hand into his beneath the table and glanced at him.

"I believe 'tis time to retire," she said.

His loins stirred with anticipation. After bidding good night to all, they rose together and made their way through the halls toward Ewan's bedchamber.

He knew her passion was nothing more than a mask, another barrier she put up between them. But it was hard to resist the heat of her mouth, the flick of her tongue, the way her fingernails raked over his skin and her cries echoed off the walls.

It had been thus since he'd offered to allow her to go back to Castleton, their pleasure being another shield. His brain knew he should deny her even as his cock went hard with need.

He pushed open the door to his bedchamber and secured it behind him. Only this time, she did not arch her body against him once they were alone. Instead, she remained where she stood several paces away, her face tucked downward.

She drew in a deep breath.

"What is it?" Ewan asked. "Is something amiss?"

Her teeth sank into her bottom lip. "I've made my decision."

Ewan's stomach knotted. He'd been waiting nearly a sennight for her reply and now that it was coming, he didn't want to hear it. Once the words had passed her lips, actions would be put into motion. Her items would be packed into trunks, preparations would be readied for her departure, and soon after, she would be gone.

She took a step toward him and reached for his hand. He offered no resistance as her soft fingers curled around his. He might never feel this from her again.

"I've decided..." She closed her eyes and paused, as though dreading what she might say.

Ewan's heart stopped beating for that moment of time.

"I've decided to stay," she said in a rush.

The breath whooshed from Ewan's lungs, and his thoughts spun. She had said it. She had made her choice. She'd decided...

His gaze jerked to hers. "What did ye say?"

"I said I'm staying," she breathed.

He stared at her, disbelieving. "Here?"

"Aye, here." She laughed and put her arms around him.

"With me?" Ewan asked, still unable to believe her words, thinking he'd somehow not heard correctly.

She squeezed him closer to her and gazed longingly up at him. "With ye."

"Why?" he asked. "No' that I want ye to change yer mind, but I thought ye would choose Castleton."

"It doesn't hold the same appeal to me that it once did." She gave him a cautious look. "I want to get to know ye better. And I want ye to get to know me better, as well."

A glow of warmth filled his chest, and a smile blossomed on his lips. "I'd like that too. I've enjoyed having yer family here and learning more about ye through them. I want to make ye as happy as they do."

"Ye're a good man, Ewan Sutherland." She rose up on her toes and pressed a kiss to his lips. "I'd be a fool to let ye go."

Unlike the other kisses earlier that week, this one was chaste and gentle. And though it lacked the sexual intent behind it the others had, it was far more intimate.

Part of him wanted to pull her against him and claim her as fully his, but the more rational part needed to know why, to ensure this was truly what she wanted.

She pulled away slightly after the kiss. "I've been scared, Ewan."

"Of me?"

She nodded. "Of ye. Of us. Of what it meant if I allowed myself to care for ye and give my trust."

He stroked a hand down her soft cheek. "Ye've been hurt before."

Tears welled in her eyes. "Aye. Several times." The tip of her nose went pink.

He thought she would leave it only at that and was pleasantly surprised when she continued, "My da was an English knight."

Ewan nodded, knowing of Drake's desire to follow in his father's footsteps and become a knight. A feat that was difficult for a man with equal parts English and Scottish blood in his veins.

"He died in a battle against the Scottish," she went on. "Losing him was painful. It was made all the more so from people we thought had been our friends. Many of them had lost loved ones in the same battle that took my da. They hated us, Ewan. These people who we thought were our friends, and they turned their backs on us. The butcher wouldn't sell us meat, women blocked the well so we couldn't get to the water, even the priest cast us from the chapel. Through it all, I thought surely, I could trust our neighbors. But when I sought help from my friend for food and comfort..." Her voice went tight with emotion. "She spat on me." She looked at her sleeve as if expecting to find a spatter of spittle there. "She said we deserved to starve."

Ewan remembered Faye as a girl, a sensitive, kind girl whose heart was easily bruised. He didn't know who Faye spoke of, the one who had hurt her so cruelly, but he wanted to punish her.

"We left the village but were met with much of the same hatred all the way up through England and into Scotland, past the border," Faye said. "We stayed in one place for a while, but..."

"But what?" Ewan pressed.

She closed her eyes in clear chastisement of herself. "I told a friend there of how we were avoiding our grandda. The next day, I overheard that her da had gone to the Highlands to seek out the Ross Chieftain. They thought to profit from sharing our location."

She shook her head, her expression so pained, it pulled at Ewan's heart. He stroked a hand down her back, trying to offer whatever comfort he could.

"It was my fault," Faye whispered. "I shouldna have trusted anyone."

"Ye were a lass in need of a friend." He pulled her to him. How he wished he could cradle away her pain.

She nuzzled into his chest, their bodies a perfect fit. "We had to go to the border then, where our accents would be lost among so many of English and Scottish descent, where we could properly hide. But I never trusted anyone again." She looked up at him. "Until ye."

"Ye trust me?" Ewan asked, unable to keep the hope from his question.

Her blue eyes met his and held. She pulled in a long inhale. "Aye," she whispered.

"I'll never hurt ye," he vowed. "I think Kinsey would kill me if I did."

She laughed through her tears at that. "Aye, she would."

Ewan gazed at the woman who had been forced into his life, the one who had been given little option to marry him and yet had decided to stay when she was given the chance to leave. She was attractive enough to turn the head of any man and fierce enough to escape an army of Ross warriors.

He loved her.

The thought struck him like an unexpected blow. And yet even as it did, he knew the realization to be undeniable.

He loved her, but he could not tell her for fear of scaring her off. In time, hopefully, he could confess the depth of his feelings. In time, aye, but not now. Not when it still seemed as if she might be skittish.

He had her trust, but hearts, he knew, were a different matter.

FAYE HAD NEVER CONSIDERED HERSELF A TIMID WOMAN. SHE confronted her challenges and dared them to take her on. But standing before Ewan and baring her soul took a bravery she had never before needed.

The tender, almost hesitant, way he watched her told her he understood her admission had been difficult. He gently brushed his fingertips over her cheek. "Thank ye for trusting me."

She gazed into his eyes, and desire stirred within her. Not like before, where lust had swept through her and drowned everything out. She didn't want to couple with him to forget. She wanted to couple with him to remember—to savor this moment and how hard he'd fought for her trust, how much she willingly gave of herself to offer it and the bond growing between them.

"Ewan," she whispered his name softly.

His thumb stroked over her skin with heart-aching affection. "Aye?"

"I..." The emotions barreling through her were almost too much. Too foreign to put a name to. She put her hand to his chest and her fingers molded over the shape of his muscle there, and his heart tapped a strong rhythm beneath her palm. "I care for ye."

He gazed down at her, and she found herself lost in his hazel eyes, unable to pull away. As if she could stare at him for hours and still crave more. He was a man as beautiful outside as he was inside. And he was her husband.

He had risked so much for her, given her everything she'd asked for, and offered even more. Never had she imagined herself married to anyone, let alone someone who made her feel safe enough to be vulnerable.

And here she was, with her heart peeled raw and her hopes thrown wide.

Ewan cradled her face in his hands. "I care for ye, Faye Sutherland, and I swear to ye, I'll never break yer trust."

He lowered his head, and she rose up on her toes. Their lips met, not with the clash of passion as before, but with a savoring, chaste kiss that became several more. Faye's hands moved over Ewan, needing to feel him, as though reassuring herself of his nearness and desperate to be closer still.

He nudged his chin against hers. The rasp of his cropped beard against her sensitive skin sent a prickle of goosebumps running over her.

"Ye're so bonny, Faye." His breath was warm, where it washed over her lips.

She tilted her face forward to brush her lips over his once more. And again and again and again. Her core pulsed with desire, but more than the need for satiation was the craving for his touch on all of her.

Her fingers moved over his belt, pulling it free. It clunked to the ground and was soon joined by his doublet and leine. Faye paused in undressing him to marvel at his body. Her hands glided over his bare skin, taking note of every detail of him, learning every scar, every swell and valley of hard-won muscle.

Through it all, he watched her, not saying anything, his expression soft with regard that settled into an unfamiliar part of her soul. He put his hands on her shoulders and gently turned her around. She gathered her hair in one hand to allow him access to the ties at the back of her gown.

His mouth swept over the sensitive dip between her shoulder and her neck. Ripples of delight teased over her skin. She pressed back against him as a sigh escaped her lips. He was hard against her bottom, the thick column of his arousal jutting with a need that was echoed in her own core. He continued to kiss her as he unlaced her dress. First pressing his lips to her neck, then her shoulder as it was bared, then the nakedness of her back as the kirtle and sark slid away.

Every kiss was a spark that left her skin humming with delicious heat. Her clothing pooled at her feet in a soundless heap, followed by the soft pop of the ties of his trews being undone and the rustle of leather pushed free from his legs.

He curled an arm around her chest and drew her back against him as he cupped her left breast in one large hand. Though they had been naked many times together, the meeting of skin to skin was even more euphoric. Like the heat of sun spreading over one's face on a cold day.

He kissed her neck again, light passes of his mouth as the hardness at her back swelled. His free hand eased over her waist, her hips, her stomach and down between her thighs. The first connection of his fingers at her center elicited an eager gasp that nearly knocked her knees from beneath her.

He gave a low growl in her ear and curled his finger inside her, stroking her as his lips played over her skin, and his thumb swept over her nipple.

Faye's legs went weak as her body ignited under his ministrations. She arched toward him, yearning to be with him wholly and completely. Slowly, he turned her around and lifted her into his arms.

She gave a little laugh. "Are ye taking me somewhere?"

His eyes locked on hers, and he gave a half-smile that made her heart go soft. "I'm taking ye to bed, wife. But no' like before."

She put her hand to his chest as he carried her and trailed her fingertips over the powerful muscles of his shoulders. His was a body sculpted by the life of a warrior.

"Not like before?" she asked in a husky voice.

"Nay." He settled her on the bed and caressed her in sweeping touches from shoulder to navel. "I want to take my time with ye, to explore every inch of yer body."

She closed her eyes to relish all her senses better. She wanted to lose herself in the spiciness of his masculine scent, in the whisper of his fingers causing waves of tingles over her entire body. She wanted her ears filled with the quiet huff of his breath hitched with excitement. She longed for the saltiness of his skin on her tongue and to watch the shadows play over his powerful body. She craved all of it, all of him. All of *them*.

The bed shifted beneath her, and she realized he was no longer at her side. She opened her eyes to find him crawling down her body. He stopped when his face was near her navel and traced his fingers down her inner thighs.

The delicate muscles there trembled as her legs parted for him, revealing herself to him. He gazed at her center, and heat rose in her cheeks. Then he ran his thumb down her sex in a slow, sensual stroke. A low groan sounded in the back of his throat.

Pleasure rippled through her, not only at his intimate petting but at the delight he took in seeing her. Yet for the first time, she wasn't relishing in the power her body had over him, but in the gratification that she took from knowing he found her so desirable.

His eyes met hers with an intensity that made her bones go soft, then he lowered his head, his mouth hovering over her sex. The tip of his tongue followed the same path his thumb had: gliding over her sex.

Her breath caught.

Before she could protest, before she could even register the bliss of such an intimate kiss in her shocked mind, he licked her again. Her hands clenched into the bedclothes as she suddenly feared she might slide off the earth.

He flicked his tongue over her, probing inside her, circling the little sensitive bud, now swollen with the brazenness of his ministrations. Everything in her went tighter still as an impending release caught her in its grip.

He shifted slightly and eased a finger inside her, stroking her within as his tongue teased over her. It was all too much in the most exquisite way. Faye tumbled away from any element of control and climaxed with an unrestrained cry.

Ewan lapped at her even as she gave way to her crises. Her hips jerked away at the sensitivity of her sex. She laughed lightly. "'Tis too much," she gasped.

He delivered one final lick, then kissed her lower stomach and up her body as he crawled over her once more. She squirmed underneath him, longing for the feel of his arousal pressing into her.

She'd never climaxed without him being inside her, and while it felt good, it wasn't the same without his fullness, without the pleasure of his simultaneous release. He braced himself over her, his gaze still fixed on her, and reached for his arousal.

She whimpered her anticipation. Ready for him. Desperate for the closeness with him. Needing him in a way she'd never known she could need a man.

E wan guided himself toward Faye, watching the pleasure play over her face as he nudged at her entrance.

Her lashes fluttered but remained open. Usually, her head was thrown back, her eyes closed as they took one another hard and fast. Now, though, she kept her eyes locked on his, creating a deeper connection between them.

He eased into her, and the delight that enveloped him was more than just physical. His hands slid over hers, palm to palm, and her fingers interlaced with his. With their hands joined, he took her in slow, steady strokes, their stares locked with one another's, their breathing matched, and their heartbeats in sync as their bodies became one in a new way that touched his soul.

Faye's hands roamed over him as her tight sheath gripped him, sending prickling waves throughout. He savored every thrust inside her, savoring the sweetness of her body beneath him, the way her mouth parted around her moans, the squeeze of her sex.

Her blonde hair tumbled around her shoulders, and she gazed at him as though...as though she was in love.

Something in his chest clenched.

She pulled him toward her, drawing his chest against her. He pushed back, resisting. Lara had hated the press of his body against hers. Such things were impossible to keep from his mind as Faye tried to pull him toward her once more.

He braced his arms more thoroughly. "I dinna want to crush ye."

"I'm not so delicate, husband." She smiled affectionately and tugged at him once more.

He allowed his body to rest over her, skin to skin, her breasts pushed to his chest. Now when his hips flexed forward, his entire body glided against Faye. The closeness brought a new level of intensity. The rub of her soft skin over his, her breath panting in his ear, the sweet floral scent of her all around him.

They moved together, writhing in their shared passion, kissing, touching, loving. Her core tensed around him, and the pitch of her cries changed. His ballocks tensed with the anticipation of his own release. He held her face with his free hand while he drove into her, wanting to see the climax play over her features as he took her.

Her brows flinched, and her lips parted around a cry as her sex spasmed around his cock, coaxing him into a climax as they released together.

Pleasure. Bliss. Euphoria. A taste of heaven. He experienced all of these things and more as they lost themselves together.

As their sated bodies relaxed into a languid state, they remained where they lay, breathing together, hearts pounding chest to chest. Their bodies were slick with sweat, but neither moved away.

Ewan rested his forehead against Faye's. "That was..."

"Incredible," she whispered on an exhale.

His mouth found hers in a tender kiss. Finally, he rolled off her and pulled her into his arms.

She gave a little hum of contentment that nudged against his heart.

Ewan stroked a hand down the impossibly soft skin at her side. "Thank ye for staying in Sutherland."

"I could not bear to leave ye," Faye said.

He tilted his head to look at her where she lay her head upon his chest. "Truly?"

Her smile was shy, and she nodded.

He'd never seen this vulnerable side of her. Nay, that wasn't true. He had seen it before. When she'd been a girl, before her da had died and the world's cruelty had forced her to harden.

"I was dreading seeing ye leave," he admitted.

"Yet ye still offered to let me go." She rested her chin on her hand and looked up at him. "Why?"

He shook his head. "I couldna stand to see ye so miserable when there was a chance ye could be happy."

She reached out and touched his cheek with her small hand. "Ye're better than I deserve," she said.

He shook his head. "Ye deserve all the goodness in the world for what ye've been through."

She shifted upward and kissed him. "Thank ye for giving me the opportunity to leave. I didn't realize what I had with ye until I had a choice."

She settled down against him once more with her head on his chest. He ran his fingers through her silky hair, thankful for the choice she'd made. Having her leave would have torn his chest open.

He only hoped they could remain content, that she would not have doubts. Especially after her family departed.

Faye's breath became deep and even, and Ewan knew she had fallen asleep.

No matter what, at least he was assured that her family would be safe and cared for. With such worrisome thoughts set to rest, he could turn his attention back to his uncle, whom he had been sorely remiss on seeing to the last few days.

Ewan's suspicion of the marriage to the Gordon clan, and

what that might entail, had only grown and he did not wish to be caught unaware. Not when this was finally time for peace.

He brushed Faye's cheek, and she smiled in her sleep.

It was also time for love.

FOR FIVE MORE BLISSFUL DAYS, FAYE WAS HAPPY. TRULY HAPPY. Without an edge of skepticism needling into her thoughts. She had her family with her, save Drake, who had to return to England the day after his arrival, and she had her husband.

But such happiness was not sustainable. Not when her mother and sisters had to return to their life on the border. There was the garden to tend in Castleton and their livestock to care for, all being managed by a servant in their absence. And Faye had to resume her duties as mistress of the keep. Moiré had graciously assumed the responsibility so that Faye could spend more time with her family.

Life had to continue on for everyone.

Only she wasn't prepared for that day to arrive so quickly. The weather was too fine to put off travel any longer, and her family had to pack their belongings for the journey home finally. This time, however, Ewan was sending two Sutherland warriors with them to ensure their safety, and return with Faye's belongings.

It had not taken long for Faye's sisters and mother to prepare as they had taken only a few effects with them when they'd left Castleton in their haste to find her. All too soon, the horses were being readied while they waited in the Great Hall.

Faye's mother drew her in for a hug, embracing her in the familiar lavender comfort of home. "I'll miss ye, my girl. Ye need only say the word, and we'll be back, aye?"

Faye nodded, unable to summon speech around the thickness in her throat.

"Regardless of whether Faye asks for ye or no', ye're always welcome at Dunrobin." Ewan put a hand to Faye's shoulder after her mother released her, offering his strength and support, of which Faye desperately needed.

"We will visit for certs, thank ye." Clara offered one of her sweet, genuine smiles, and it stuck fast in Faye's heart.

Kinsey smirked and opened her mouth, but before she could utter one word, a warrior approached Ewan. "Forgive me, sir, but several riders have approached insisting on speaking with ye."

"Who are they?" Ewan asked.

No sooner had he spoken than a booming voice broke through the silence of the hall. "Sutherland!"

Faye stiffened at the familiar voice of her grandfather. She was not alone. Her mother's gaze shot to the doorway. None of them had time even to consider where to go before Ross strode confidently through the entrance.

He caught sight of them and stopped short. His expression flinched as though seeing them wounded him to his core. "Cait." He said her name softly, displaying more emotion than Faye had thought him capable of.

"We were just leaving." Mum nodded to Clara and Kinsey, and they all strode toward the entrance.

He reached out and wrapped his fingers around her arm, his touch gentle.

Faye's mother glared down at his hand that remained on her. "Release me, ye bastard."

Ross's brows lifted. "Bastard?" He barked a laugh and looked to Sutherland. "Do ye hear how she greets her own da?"

Mum jerked her arm from Ross's grip. "Aye, ye heartless bastard. I hate ye. I told ye to leave Faye be, and ye stole her from us. Ye stole her and dragged her all the way here to force her into marriage."

As she spoke, her face colored a shade of red Faye had never seen on her before.

Ross's mirth vanished, and he sucked in a hard breath as though she'd struck him. "Cait."

"Ye stole my child from me. *My child*," Mum ground out as tears glittered in her eyes. Her words embedded into Faye's chest and ripped open a fresh wound of pain.

Ross's face colored to the same red as his daughter's. "Listen here, aye? I'm yer da—"

"I have no father." Mum's declaration rang out on the stone walls.

"Damn it, Cait." He reached for her again.

This time, she lashed out, striking him in the face. Faye pulled her dagger free and raced to her mother's side. She was not alone. Both her sisters were with her, their weapons ready as well. And in front of them all, blocking the lot of them, was Ewan.

Kinsey's bow was drawn, an arrow nocked. "Do that again, Ross, and I'll put an arrow in yer eye."

"'Tis time for ye to leave," Ewan said to the Ross Chieftain.

Faye reached behind with her hand extended to offer support to her mother. Mum took it, her fingers trembling in a way that created a fresh wave of hurt, clenching at Faye.

"I'm here to see ye," Ross said to Ewan. "About my land."

"Monroe," Ewan called. "Take Ross to my solar. I'll join ye anon."

Monroe stepped forward from where he'd been lingering by the doorway and beckoned. Faye's grandfather hesitated and stared behind Ewan in an attempt to see Faye and her family.

Suddenly, his face fell, and hurt brimmed in his eyes. No longer did he appear to be a power-hungry chieftain, but an old man withered by life's burdens. "Cait, I..." He looked at the ground, and when he glanced up, his lower lip trembled. "I'm sorry." His watery gaze shifted to Faye. "I'm sorry."

Mum's hand tightened on Faye's.

"Ye may claim to no' have a da," Ross continued, his gruff

voice barely audible. "But I have a daughter who I will never forget and who will always hold my heart."

Faye glanced behind her and found tears in her mother's eyes as well.

"Ye've done too much wrong," Mum replied in a choked voice. "To my bairns and me. I dinna know that I can ever forgive ye."

Ross lowered his head and gave a resigned nod, a strong man defeated. "I love ye, Cait."

His endearment was not reciprocated. A hollow silence settled over the Great Hall. Monroe approached the aged chieftain, indicating Ross should follow him to the solar. Much to Faye's relief, Ross did not protest and allowed himself to be led from the room.

Faye and her sisters turned to their mother.

"What was that about?" Kinsey asked.

Faye and Clara shared a look. Kinsey had voiced the question they were both clearly thinking.

Exhaustion creased Mum's face. She appeared as defeated as Ross had. "'Tis a tale for another time."

"I'll say my farewells here," Ewan said apologetically as his gaze slid toward the doorway where Ross and Monroe disappeared.

"Thank ye, Ewan." Mum embraced him, going on tiptoe, so he didn't have to bend down. "Ye're a good man. Truly." She released him and smiled at Faye. "I hope the two of ye will be happy."

Clara came next, embracing Ewan and thanking him for everything he'd done for them as well as Faye. Kinsey did not embrace him but instead offered her forearm to clasp. If nothing else, it was a start.

Kinsey held him to her for longer than was necessary. "If ye hurt her, I'll hunt ye down and kill ye."

"Kinsey," Mum cried.

Faye opened her mouth to protest her sister's violent claim, but Ewan spoke first, his gaze meeting the wildest of the three sisters directly in the eye. "I'd expect nothing less."

He reached out and tenderly stroked Faye's cheek with one calloused hand and departed to join Monroe and Ross. Though the touch was brief, it said so much more than words ever could. A pleasant warmth hummed through Faye. Not physical desire, but something deeper, more meaningful.

"I think ye could fall in love with him," Mum said softly at her side. "If ye let yerself."

Faye lifted her brows. "If I let myself?"

Mum rolled her eyes in a very Kinsey-like manner. "Dinna look at me like that, ye stubborn lass. Ye know well what I mean." She reached for Faye's shoulders and leveled a stare at her as she spoke, the same as when Faye was a bairn. "Dinna push yer emotions away for the sake of fighting. Ye've done that yer whole life. Let go and allow yerself to be happy."

It was on the tip of Faye's tongue to say she already had, that she'd made her choice to stay at Sutherland, after all. But there was a truth to Mum's words that echoed within a cavern inside Faye. One she knew was still raw and open.

"I know ye've seen my hurt at losing yer da," Mum continued when Faye didn't reply. "I know it scares ye."

Faye glanced away rather than confess the truth her mother apparently already knew.

"I would love him again with the same intensity if I had to do it all over again," Mum said vehemently. "Even knowing I would lose him in the end. Such pain was worth the glory of so much love. Dinna fear it, aye? Let yerself be happy."

"I'll try." Faye slid her gaze back to her mother.

Her mother smiled. "That's all ye can do, my girl." She pressed a kiss to Faye's forehead.

The stable lad appeared in the Great Hall and gave a small bow. "The horses are ready, my lady."

Faye braced herself against his words and what they meant. Her family's visit had come to an end all too soon.

She tried not to think when she might see them next and

instead led her family from the Great Hall, out into the sunshine of a perfect spring day. One by one, she embraced each of them, her sisters and her mother, each of whom she loved with the whole of her heart.

She stayed there as they rode off and did not turn to leave until they disappeared in the distance. An emptiness rang through her.

Had she made the right decision?

And if she had, could she release the fight as her mother had suggested, and allow herself to fall in love?

If such a thing even existed.

She had avoided it for so long that now, unlike before, not only did she hope love did exist, but that she could find it with Ewan.

❧ 18 ❧

E wan's temper blazed hotter with each step he took toward his solar. Where Ross was waiting for him.

By the time he pushed through the door, he was practically ready to kill the other chieftain. Peace be damned. Ross glared at him as he entered, evidently of a like mind.

Monroe stood off to the side with measured patience that indicated he'd rather be nearly anywhere else but there in a room with two irate chieftains.

"Ye're lucky I dinna throw ye out right now," Ewan growled.

Ross leapt up from the chair he'd been sitting in, his body tense for a fight. One Ewan would gladly give him.

"They're my family," Ross protested. "My daughter. My grand-daughters. Ye've no right—"

"No right?" Ewan repeated, incredulous. "Ye lost all rights the moment ye shackled yer own granddaughter and dragged her against her will to yer castle."

Ross narrowed his eyes. "Ye still married her."

Ewan grabbed the other man by his leine and shoved him back against the wall. Fire lit in Ross's eyes, but the older man's strength was no match for Ewan's.

"Because ye threatened her family," Ewan spoke in a low, even voice that made Ross's protests go silent. "If ye ever get near any of them, ye'll live to regret it."

"Are ye threatening me now?" Ross demanded.

"Aye." Ewan put his face directly in front of Ross's and shoved him away.

Ross managed to catch himself before sliding to the ground. He staggered to his feet and angrily adjusted his clothing back into place. "Where's my property? Ye said ye'd sign Berwick over to me."

"I said I'd comply with the agreement," Ewan amended. As much as he'd been dreading telling Ross what he'd done with Berwick, he was now anticipating it with renewed gratification.

"I've deeded the land to Drake," Ewan said with great satisfaction.

Ross blinked in shock. "My...grandson?"

"And Faye's rightful guardian."

Ross's jaw clenched, and the familiar vengeful red blossomed over his face once more.

"Ye've done enough to that family," Ewan said. "Do ye have any idea what they've been through?"

Ross's gaze slid away.

"Ye knew, dinna ye?" Ewan demanded, his anger doubling.

"All they had to do was come back to Balnagown, and I'd have cared for them," Ross erupted.

"Aye, so ye could manipulate them and auction off the lasses for marriage." Ewan shook his head. "For once in yer miserable life, do some good for this family. Allow Drake to have Berwick."

Ross pressed his lips together and remained silent so long, Ewan thought he would refuse. Finally, Ross sighed and nodded. "Aye, I'll let the lad keep it."

Ewan nodded. "Now remove yerself and yer men from my castle."

Ross speared him with a look and shoved past Ewan on his

way out the door. Monroe immediately followed him out to ensure he departed without issue. While Monroe was sharp with numbers, he was also incredibly skilled with a blade, enough to handle the likes of Ross should the older man choose to resist leaving.

Ewan braced his hands on his desk while he settled his thoughts. As his temper cooled, Faye pushed to the forefront of his mind. Her sisters and Cait would be gone by now. No doubt, she would be upset.

He pushed out into the hall and nearly ran into Moiré. She screamed in surprise and brown liquid sloshed from the cup in her hands, splashing the floor.

"Forgive me, Moiré." He backed up to give her some space. "I was on my way to see Faye."

She put her hand to her chest as though to calm her racing heart. "I was of the same mind." She offered a sad smile. "I imagine it must be hard for her family to leave after such a pleasant visit."

Ewan indicated the half-full mug. "Was that for her?"

"Aye." Moiré lifted one shoulder, brushing off her considerate act. "I thought it might help." She looked down at the dark liquid staining her red skirt. "Would ye mayhap take it to her?"

"Aye, of course." Ewan accepted the hot cup.

"Thank ye." Moiré smiled gratefully at him, as though he'd done her a great favor. She'd been so helpful while Faye's family had been at Dunrobin.

Ewan nodded. "I'm sorry about yer kirtle."

Moiré waved him off, her demeanor as pleasant as always. "Ye need no' worry after me. Go on to yer bride."

He didn't need to be told twice. He turned on his heel and swiftly strode toward his chamber before the tea in his hand could cool. Once there, he rapped softly on their shared door, entering only when she bade him to.

She lay upon the bed with her back facing him.

"Moiré made ye some tea," Ewan said.

Faye turned to him, her face reddened and tear stained. Dread washed over him. Mayhap she was regretting her decision.

"I can bring it to ye if ye like," he offered.

She shook her head. "Please set it on the table."

He did as she asked. The heavy mug settled on the table with a loud clunk in the quiet room. He hesitated, uncertain what to do next.

"Is there anything else I can get ye?" he asked.

Her mouth curled up in an unexpected smile. "Ye."

Relief replaced dread. Her request was one he could readily agree to.

He eased onto the bed, and she rolled toward him, so her head settled on his chest. She put her arms around him, not in an embrace, but as though she clung to him. He rubbed her back in soothing circles, the way his mum had done when he was a lad.

She hummed in quiet contentment and nestled closer.

Her mouth pressed to his chest, just above his heart, then again at the neckline of his leine. The next kiss was on the skin at the base of his throat. Tingles of pleasure warmed its way to his core as need coiled within him.

She shifted over him, straddling him, her lips brushing his neck, his chin. The heat built to a roaring flame. He caught her face in his hands and stroked her tongue with his.

"Make me forget how I feel right now," Faye whispered breathlessly between kisses.

I love ye.

The words teetered on the edge of his heart and caught at the tip of his tongue. He wanted to say them in her ear as he claimed her body or whisper them to her as they cradled in one another's sweat-slick embrace after.

"I care for ye," he said instead.

She arched her body against him with desperate need, and he was glad he'd kept those passionate words to himself. After she had sacrificed everything, the last thing he wanted was to frighten her with the force of his emotions.

He tugged at the fabric of her skirt and drew it upward as her fingers worked over the ties of his trews, liberating him. He thrust up into her as she rode him, their cries hoarse with passion, his heart tangled in its throes. Despite the throb of lust consuming him, he could not stop the worry from threading through the background of his mind that she would regret her decision to stay.

৩৯৬

FAYE WALKED SLOWLY THROUGH THE CASTLE WITH AN ASSESSING look. It had been three weeks since she'd resumed responsibilities as mistress of the castle after her family's departure. There had been several errors on her part: laundry days switched from the usual days resulting in confusion with the servants, an order for the larder gone wrong, several bolts of fabric used for the wrong things.

All small things. Certainly not to the extent of the blunder the eels had been, though now she and Ewan laughed over the memory.

Eventually, she'd devised a system to double-check tasks before they could be executed to ensure no more issues arose. Only then did everything begin to run smoothly.

She was just leaving the kitchen when Ewan's voice sounded behind her. "There's the bonny Lady Sutherland."

She turned to him with a smile stretching over her lips.

He was as handsome as ever in a pair of black leather trews with his gray doublet opened at the throat to reveal his leine beneath. "And there's the handsome chieftain of us all."

He flashed her a bright white grin and pulled her into his arms. His brows drew down with concern. "Ye look tired, wife. I wish ye'd slept later this morn."

"Flatterer." Faye pretended to push him away. "And I'd already slept plenty late."

In truth, she was embarrassed at how far into the morn it was when she was finally able to pull herself from the bed. Especially when she had always been one to rise with the sun. But regardless of how much she slept, she was unable to wake rested.

Ewan grabbed her back toward him. "Ye know I think ye're the loveliest woman in all of Scotland. I only worry about how hard ye work."

"Says the hardest working man in all of Scotland." She pressed a kiss to his lips. "Off with ye now, I've got a few more tasks to see to."

He cradled her face in his palm and met her eyes with a look that made her heart soften like heated wax.

"I think ye could fall in love with him...if ye let yerself." Her mother's words echoed in her mind.

And mayhap, she had.

In the last three weeks, Ewan had given her all of him. He'd found reasons to need to see her in the middle of the day with a kiss and a smile. He'd left flowers by her plate at meals and had fine fabrics ordered for new kirtles. There had even been a gift of a bejeweled dagger, ornate enough for a lady to wear on her belt with a blade sharp enough for a warrior.

More than all those physical goods, though, were the intimate moments between them. Some nights, he took his time as he worshiped her body; other times he coupled with her hard and fast in a way that left them both breathless. Regardless of how they came together, he always cradled her in his arms afterward, which was where she stayed through the night, in the protective embrace of his arms.

He looked at her often as he did now as if he wished to convey declarations of his heart. Mayhap even of love. It would be so much easier if he said it to her so that she might be free to say it aloud in turn, to test the delicacy of such words against the gradual opening of her heart.

"I care for ye." He searched her eyes. "So verra much."

Her pulse hitched. "And I care for ye, husband." She opened her mouth, wanting to say more even as she feared doing so.

Her stomach clenched, and a wave of nausea washed over her.

"Off with ye or neither of us will ever see to our tasks," Faye said with a forced laugh.

He hesitated, his focus on her sharpening.

"Good morrow, sir." Monroe entered the room and nodded respectfully to Ewan first, then to Faye. "Good morrow, my lady. I trust this morn finds ye both well."

"Aye, thank ye," Faye lied. She certainly did not feel well. Not of late. She pulled Ewan's arm, tugging him toward Monroe. "Off with ye, or we'll be supping on eel."

He grimaced and hastened his steps toward Monroe.

"That's what I thought." She chuckled at her husband's antics. There was a silliness to him that she found endearing. How so powerful and masculine a male could still behave in such a way made her laugh, even when she felt as poorly as she did.

He tossed a final charming grin in her direction and departed with Monroe. No sooner had he left than a fresh roll of nausea caught her. Sweat prickled on her brow. She was going to be ill. Her hands moved blindly, finding the stone wall to brace herself against as she fought to keep the contents of her stomach in place.

"Faye?" Footsteps rushed toward her. "Is something amiss?"

The surprise of Moiré's sudden appearance provided Faye with the thread of control she needed to wrangle in her need to purge. She could hardly allow herself to be ill in front of someone else.

Faye pressed her face to the stone and reveled in the coolness that greeted her. "Forgive me. I need a moment." She sighed.

Moiré put a hand to Faye's brow. "Ye dinna feel warm. Are ye well?"

"'Tis been like this for several mornings." Faye swallowed thickly, desperate to be free of the unpleasant clench to her stomach.

"Have ye been tired as well?" Moiré asked.

Faye opened her eyes and regarded Ewan's cousin with suspicion. "Aye."

"Ye do know where my questions are leading, aye?" Moiré tilted her head. "Have ye had yer courses?"

Faye's mouth fell open. Was it true?

Quickly, she thought back to her courses and realized she hadn't had them since a sennight into her miserable journey to Balnagown Castle. Now with the exhaustion and the illness...how had she not realized?

Moiré blinked, as though with shock. "Ye're with child." Her words were flat, absent the joy and wonder dawning over Faye.

"A child..." Faye pushed away from the wall and brought a hand slowly to her stomach. A babe grew within. Her babe. With Ewan.

Tears welled in her eyes.

Their child.

"I have to tell Ewan." Faye put her palms to her cheeks to cool their blazing heat.

Moiré shook her head. "No' yet."

Faye drew back and frowned at Ewan's cousin, who had been acting strange since she pieced together why Faye had been ill.

"Why not tell him?" Faye asked.

Moiré sighed sadly. "'Tis no' a story I want to tell. But I dinna want Ewan hurt again." Her eyes dulled with sorrow. "Lara thought she was with child once. She told Ewan as soon as she suspected, but it was simply that she missed her courses and was ill. Realizing she wasn't in a delicate way devastated them both, and their marriage fell apart."

Faye sagged back against the stone wall. Such news must have been painful for Ewan. Worse still, that their union had suffered in the wake of such loss. She cupped her hands protectively over her womb, certain a child grew within her.

And yet if she were wrong...

Doubt crowded in the fogginess of her tired mind.

"Mayhap 'tis best to tell him when ye have missed yer courses a second time?" Moiré suggested.

Faye hesitated. Surely Ewan's affections couldn't be so fickle as to falter if she weren't with child. Especially when the draw between them was so strong. And when he had never loved Lara.

But could she put him through such hurt again?

She had never been with child, nor did she know anyone who had been. No one save her mother, and Mum was too far away to seek counsel. Faye had no way to know for certain.

Slowly, she found herself nodding in agreement with Moiré. "I think ye're right."

Moiré clenched her hands to her chest. "The moment ye truly know, ye'll make him the happiest man in all the world."

Faye forced a smile to her lips. Was it possible to keep her suspicions from her husband for another fortnight?

❧ 19 ❧

Ewan watched Faye as she slept, the nip of worry at the back of his mind getting progressively sharper and more insistent. For the last few days, she lay in bed a little longer each morning, sleeping deeply. Despite the amount of rest she had received, smudges of exhaustion still bruised the delicate skin under her eyes.

A gentle knock came at the door.

He answered the door and found Moiré with a mug of steaming liquid in her hand. "Is she still unwell?" she asked.

Ewan nodded. "Aye, I think 'tis time to send for a healer."

"I'd give it a bit more time," Moiré replied with a certainty that offered some comfort. "Give her this. It should help."

Ewan took the cup and cradled the hot beverage in his palm. "Do ye think..." He shifted his weight from one foot to the other. "Do ye think she's with child?"

Moiré pursed her lips. "I'm no' certain," she replied slowly.

"We should call for the healer," he said with finality.

"Mayhap, ask her?" Moiré suggested. "A woman knows if she requires a healer or no'."

Ewan nodded, thanked her and quietly closed the door.

174

"Faye," he said softly. "I've got a tea for ye from Moiré." He sat on the bed and gently squeezed his wife's silky shoulder.

Faye's eyes blinked open, heavy with fatigue.

"Moiré sent this tea for ye." He held it out.

Faye wrinkled her nose. "Toss it out and tell her I drank it, please."

"Do ye no' like it?" He sniffed at a tendril of steam and was hit with a musty odor and an underlying sharpness that made his nose burn.

His face puckered with disgust.

Faye laughed, and she pushed up to a sitting position. "'Tis how I feel about it. I took a sip once and immediately was ill."

Ewan set the mug aside. "Speaking of being ill..." He took her hand and found it warm from sleep—hopefully sleep, and not a fever. That thought chilled him. "I'd like to call a healer."

She shook her head and gave a wan smile. "I'll be fine soon. I just need a few more days, aye?"

"I'd feel better if we call a healer." Ewan frowned. "Faye, I'm worried about ye." He moved his thumb over the back of her hand, stroking it.

How he loved touching her smooth skin, reveling in the softness of it under his own callused fingers. Her lips lifted at the corners. He loved that too, her reaction to his touch.

He leaned toward her and nuzzled his nose next to hers before tilting her head back gently for a brief kiss.

I love ye.

He needed to say those words to her one of these days. But every time he thought to do it, he feared it might be the one thing to frighten her off. Faye might feel things deeply, but she was slow to express them. It was best for her to say it first, to allow her the control of stating her heart before he did.

"I care for ye, Faye." He kissed her again. "So verra much."

She stared up at him, her eyes soft with an affection that grazed the depths of his heart. "I care for ye too, Ewan."

"Promise me ye'll summon the healer if this doesna improve," he said. "I dinna want anything to happen to ye."

She nodded.

"And if ye're no' better in sennight, I'm calling the healer."

She opened her mouth to protest, but he shook his head. "Nay, lass. This has already gone on long enough. I should call for her today." Regret effused him. He shouldn't have listened to Moiré and given Faye an option. The thought of waiting even longer made an unpleasant knot tense in his gut.

"'Tis fine, truly." Faye slipped from his grasp and eased up from the bed. "Do ye see? I'm fine."

He didn't reply. Something was amiss, and he didn't like it.

"Go on about yer tasks, husband." She pulled him to standing from where he sat on the bed. "And leave me to mine."

He drew her toward him and inhaled her floral scent. "I'm worried about ye."

She smiled up at him. "Ye needn't be." She kissed him once more, then nudged him toward the door.

He left with a heavy heart and waited a moment after the door closed behind him. As expected, the painful sounds of her retching came from the other side. He frowned. Surely, she was with child. It had to be why the women were acting so strangely. Why then wouldn't Faye allow a healer to see to her?

The question plagued him all through the day as he met with Monroe and saw to tenants on his land. It rolled around in his mind, a rock worn smooth with worry, even as he finally went to his solar to tend to his correspondence. A folded parchment lay on his desk, its wax closure absent a signet marking.

He cracked the thick seal and swept away the small flecks that littered the surface of his desk. The parchment whispered in his hands as he unfolded it, as though confiding its secrets.

Careful handwriting looped over the page. His gaze slipped first to the end and found Blair's signature at the bottom. A warning prickled at the back of his neck. What did she want?

He skimmed over the contents, and his hand tightened into a fist. He'd been correct. His uncle had been up to something. Blair had information to share but couldn't write it in a missive in case Cruim found out. She asked to meet him in two days' time at a cottage near the Shepherd's Flock tavern in the village.

Faye wouldn't like him meeting with Blair, but the note held no insinuation of seduction, and he had need of the knowledge she wished to share. He only hoped she wouldn't play coy with him again, offering a trade of information for his affections. It was too steep a price to pay.

Monroe entered the solar with a ledger in his hand.

"Did ye leave this missive for me earlier?" Ewan asked.

Monroe looked at the folded note in Ewan's hand and shook his head. "Nay."

Ewan slipped the note into the locked drawer of his desk. "If ye would, find out who did."

Monroe nodded. "Of course."

Mayhap whoever had delivered the letter would have information Ewan could glean. "Until then, I'd like ye to call a healer," Ewan said.

"For Lady Sutherland," Monroe guessed.

Ewan sighed. "Aye. I know she willna be happy about it, but I canna ease my worry."

"I'll see to it on the morrow, sir." Monroe opened the ledger to the most recent page of accounts.

Ewan listened with half an ear and even less of his brain. His thoughts were too fixated on Faye. Once the healer saw to her, he knew he could set his mind to rest. He only hoped Faye would forgive him for going against her wishes.

By midafternoon the following day, Faye was exhausted. Fortunately, the worst of the nausea ebbed, which not only provided a reprieve but also solidified her certainty that she was indeed in a delicate way.

Moiré joined her outside in the kitchen garden and gave her a smile. "How are ye feeling?"

Faye shook her head and led Moira to a nearby bench. "Still not well."

Moiré's lips tugged downward. "Are ye drinking the tea I've been giving ye?"

"Aye," Faye lied. "I'm still plagued with illness. I think…I am nearly certain I'm with child." She sat on the stone bench, ensuring there was enough space at her side for Moiré to join her.

"Nearly certain?" Moiré settled on the stone beside her.

"'Tis foolish to not tell Ewan." Frustration burned at Faye. Its heat sent a ripple of queasiness lapping over her again.

"'Tis safer, to ensure he willna have to go through the heartache of realizing ye're no' actually with child if ye're no'." Moiré's gaze was sympathetic. "He tried to summon a healer for ye, but I told him the healer was in another village and couldn't come." Moiré giggled conspiratorially.

Faye touched her cool hands to the heat of her cheeks, but it did little to quell the threat of sickness. "I think I'd like to see her. She will know better than me."

"Verra well, but I would still be mindful of telling Ewan, especially lately."

Faye got to her feet, but the sensation did not abate. "What do ye mean?"

"Have ye no' noticed he's been acting a bit off?"

Faye's brows furrowed as she thought back to Ewan's behavior. There had been nothing unusual that had stood out in her mind. But then, she'd been so preoccupied with the possibility of being pregnant or not.

"Nay, then." Moiré chewed her bottom lip with apparent concern. "Mayhap 'tis only me putting worry where it shouldna be."

"I'll pay more attention to be certain," Faye vowed.

The worry on Moiré's face smoothed. "Ye're a good wife, Faye."

Her praise warmed in Faye's chest, and she found herself smiling. "Thank ye."

With that, Ewan's cousin took her leave, and Faye went back into the keep and wound her way through the halls to her chamber. Once inside, she was preparing to lie down when she heard movement in the chamber beside hers. Ewan was within, most likely. Her heart quickened with happiness.

She rapped on the door connecting their two rooms, and it opened almost immediately, revealing Ewan. He grinned down at her and pulled her into his arms. "'Tis a lucky man who can see his bonny wife midday."

He pressed a kiss to her forehead. "I must confess something to ye," he said. "I tried to have a healer brought in to see to ye despite ye saying ye dinna want one."

"Did ye?" she asked.

"I hope ye're no' upset about it." He stroked the back of his hand down her cheek. "I've been worried about ye."

Faye closed her eyes against the caress, enjoying the sweetness of the gesture. Moiré had been incorrect about his acting strange. He was as charming and perfect as ever.

"I'm not," Faye replied. "I confess, I think I should like to go to a healer as well."

Her heartbeat quickened. She ought to tell him. Moiré's warnings be damned. Ewan should know her suspicions on the possibility that they might soon be parents. Especially when he was so eager for a babe.

"Moiré says the healer is not in the village at present."

Faye did not share what she knew about the healer being there still and Moiré's lie. "Mayhap, we can go on the morrow. We can go to the village together."

Ewan hesitated. "I canna go then. Any other day, aye, but no' that day."

Faye leaned against the doorframe, feeling the weighted drag of her exhaustion suddenly. "What is happening then?"

He lifted his shoulders in a quick, nervous shrug. "I have to see about something."

Faye eyed him. There was an anxious energy about him. He worked his thumb over his right hand, popping each knuckle in turn.

"What are ye doing?" she asked. "Sounds very important."

He shrugged again. "I canna tell ye about it until afterward."

"Is something amiss?" she asked.

He shook his head vehemently, confirming something most definitely was. "Nay. What of ye?"

Fie. The reminder of her own secrets emerged with an ugliness she did not have the energy to face. She shook her head slowly as the secrets settled between them like boulders.

They kissed once more and parted, widening the gap spreading between them. Anxiety settled in Faye's stomach. It was an uncommon emotion in her dealings with Ewan, and she found she did not like it.

No longer tired, she resumed her duties as mistress of the keep. There was far too much to do to rest anyway.

Moiré found her later after Faye had met with the chatelaine. "Good news," she said brightly.

Faye regarded Ewan's cousin with wariness. It seemed good news was thin of late.

"I was able to secure a time for ye to meet with the healer on the morrow." Moiré beamed at her.

Faye nearly staggered in relief. She had no idea how anxious she'd been to get a healer's opinion on her condition until the tension lifted from her shoulders. She laughed with delight and caught Moiré in an embrace. "Thank ye."

"Of course," Moiré replied. "I'm glad ye'll know soon."

"As am I," Faye replied.

Despite the occasional flicker of doubt, she suspected the healer would tell her exactly what she felt in her gut: she truly was with child. And once she was certain, she would finally be able to tell Ewan.

❧ 20 ❧

Finally, the day came that Faye would go to the healer. She rode with Moiré to the small village on the outskirts of the castle. Though Faye had no confirmation on her condition yet, she continued to cradle her stomach with the flat of her palm.

Through the scrape of seconds and minutes and hours until Faye's visit to the healer, Ewan proceeded to act even more strangely.

"Do ye know what occupies Ewan's time this afternoon?" Faye asked.

Moiré gazed out toward the tops of the thatched houses as they approached the village. "Nay, but I think 'tis important. He seemed verra distracted this morning."

Faye said nothing. She'd thought the same of Ewan. His mouth had been set in a hard line as it did when his mind was weighted with important matters. Energy charged through her veins like lightning, crackling and snapping until she was restless with agitation.

"'Tis this way." Moiré indicated a hut set off from the main village.

A plume of dark smoke rose from the roof's center and billowed up into the clear blue sky. Nervous excitement jittered in the pit of Faye's stomach as they dismounted before the small hut. She would finally know.

A woman not much older than Faye answered the door. Her long brown hair was bound back in a thick rope of a braid, which she swung over her shoulder, and bade them enter.

The air inside was warm and scented with the sweetness of herbs whose names Faye could not recall. Bundles of dried stems and leaves hung from the rafters, and a cheerful fire blazed at the hut's center in a small pit lined with stones.

The woman offered a shy curtsey to Faye. "I'm so pleased to meet ye, Lady Sutherland. I'm Sorcha, the healer. Ye dinna have to come here. I could have gone to ye."

Faye waved her hand. "I've never been one for putting on airs."

Sorcha's face radiated with a healthy glow. "I've heard ye were a bonny woman but had no idea." She flushed. "I can see why ye've stolen our chieftain's heart."

It was Faye's turn to blush. "I don't know that I've stolen his heart..."

"As much as he talks about ye when he's with the villagers, I assure ye, ye have." Sorcha gave her a wide grin.

It was uncommon for Faye to like anyone from the first meeting. But Sorcha had a genuine, open demeanor that reminded her so thoroughly of Clara's goodness that Faye immediately was drawn to the healer.

"If ye dinna mind...?" Sorcha looked to Moiré then glanced toward the door.

Moiré frowned. "I'd like to stay here for Faye."

Faye gave a grateful look to her cousin-by-marriage. "'Tis fine, Moiré. I'll be but a moment."

Moiré's lips turned downward in an uncommon show of churlishness, but she did not protest again as she left the small hut.

"Ye think ye're with child, do ye?" Sorcha asked, her blue eyes twinkling.

Faye nodded, unable to stop her smile. "Aye. I've been ill for the last fortnight and have been tired. My courses haven't come in some time. At least in a month and a half."

"And how does yer bosom feel?" Sorcha asked. "Do ye have tenderness?"

Faye nearly laughed at the accuracy of the question. "So much that I can scarcely stand for my bodice to be too tight across them. Which seems to be happening more often of late."

"Because they seem swollen as well?" Sorcha surmised.

Faye's eyes prickled with tears as she nodded again. "Does that mean…?"

"I canna say for certain until several months have passed and the child quickens in yer womb. But 'tis a strong possibility ye are when ye're showing so many of the signs."

Faye's happy excitement dampened. "Ye don't have a way to find out?"

Sorcha shook her head, her expression apologetic. "There's some who think a pregnant woman's morning waters will rust a needle, but I've seen that happen with women who are with child and those who are no'."

The elation Faye had been swept up in only moments before dissolved into tears. She had wanted so badly to tell Ewan. To have one less secret between them. Then mayhap he might share his with her.

"Lady Sutherland, what is it?" Sorcha asked.

The entire story of how Faye feared to tell Ewan came out. As she talked, Sorcha prepared a tea for her, this one sweet and rich with green herbs that left a lingering nuttiness on her tongue. Far better than the brew Moiré prepared for her daily.

"Ye say Ewan's first wife was with child?" Sorcha took the empty mug from Faye with a frown.

Suspicion prickled at the edges of Faye's awareness. "Aye."

Sorcha tapped a finger on the mug, as though warring with a decision.

"What is it?" Faye asked.

"'Tis only..." Sorcha shrugged her shoulders. "I dinna know she was ever with child. All the times I saw to her were to offer herbs to help find a cure for her barrenness." "I see," Faye replied. But, in truth, she didn't. Mayhap Lara hadn't gone to the healer, but why would she not?

"I'm sorry I couldna be more help," Sorcha said.

Faye rose from the wooden seat by the table she'd settled into during her discussion with the healer. "Ye've been plenty helpful. Thank ye."

She paid Sorcha her fee, which the healer tried to decline, and Faye insisted she take and went outside to where Moiré waited by the door.

"Is all well?" Moiré asked anxiously. "That took far longer than I'd anticipated."

Faye nodded. "I'm with child." There was a certainty to her words, ones that felt right to say aloud. She'd known in her heart she was.

"That's wonderful," Moiré said in a flat voice. Her gaze was set in the distance, her eyes narrowed.

Dread settled over Faye's shoulders. "What is it?"

"I saw Ewan." Moiré indicated a nearby cottage.

"In the cottage?" Faye asked.

Moiré nodded.

Faye's heart gave a joyous leap. "Let's go to him. I can tell him the happy news now."

A smile widened over Moiré's pretty face, and she set to work untethering their horses. They rode together toward the small hut where Ewan's black horse was already secured out front, but as they drew near, another rider approached and dismounted.

The woman wore a dark cloak over a blue kirtle. The wind blew at the hood of her gown, pulling it back just far enough for

Faye to make out the flash of red hair beneath and an ample amount of bosom exposed from the lowcut neckline.

The breath sucked out of Faye's lungs as she realized the identity of the rider meeting her husband.

Mistress Blair.

֍

EWAN HATED THE SECRETIVE NATURE OF HIS MEETING. NAY, IT wasn't the nature of it, but the woman involved. Blair.

What was more, he hated having lied about it to Faye.

His heart clenched to think of his wife, of how tired she'd been and her determination not to go to a healer. He wanted to end this meeting quickly and return to her.

Agitation churned restless anxiety in his gut. He paced the cottage, winding around the empty, dark fire pit, back and forth. There was nothing within the deserted home, all the bits of furniture and belongings long since cleared out. Dots of sunlight shone in from the rafters above, and a musty chill hung in the air, speaking of its long-ago abandonment.

The door rattled on rusty hinges as the handle was gripped, and the warped wood swung inward, revealing Blair. Her gaze fixed on him, smoldering with intent.

Damn it.

She pushed the door closed, secured the latch and drew off her cloak. Her blue kirtle was cut far too low over her breasts, nearly exposing the edge of her nipples as the tortured globes were squeezed over her neckline.

"Ewan," she breathed. "I've been waiting to hear from ye for so long."

He crossed his arms over his chest, uncomfortable with how hot the icy room had suddenly become. And even more uncomfortable with how her gaze raked over him. "Ye told me ye had news of my uncle," he said.

"I have all the news ye want." She bit her lower lip, and her stare dropped to his groin.

Jesu.

He shifted slightly, but there was no way in the openness of the empty home to adequately block her probing eyes. This must be what it felt like for women being ogled by men.

She sauntered toward him, her hips swaying with seduction, her long red curls bouncing.

Ewan stepped back. "This wasna the meeting I intended."

"Then why did ye come?" Blair grabbed his doublet and pulled him toward her. "Do ye know how many nights I laid awake thinking of ye? The man who should have been my husband. How many times I slid my fingers—"

"Enough." Ewan pulled away from her, his face burning with the intensity of his unease. "Ye wrote to me saying ye had important news of my uncle ye couldna discuss anywhere else."

She blinked at him. "And ye wrote to me telling me how ye couldna stop thinking of me. How ye longed to feel my body upon yers."

His jaw dropped. "I dinna write a letter like that."

Hurt flashed in her eyes. "Ye dinna?"

"Nay, and I wouldna," Ewan said gently. "I love my wife." He paused after the declaration. It was the first time he'd said those words aloud. "I love her," he repeated vehemently.

Tears glittered in Blair's eyes. "Ye were supposed to love *me*, Ewan."

Guilt twisted in his chest for the woman who had been a pawn in this game of marriage and love, easily shifted to whatever side increased the likelihood of winning.

"I'm sorry, Blair." His voice was so quiet that it was nearly inaudible in the empty room.

"Dinna think to ever seek my forgiveness." Tears streamed down her cheeks. "I'll never give it. No' after ye agreed to my marriage to yer ancient uncle. I was supposed to be happy." A sob choked up from her throat. She put her head in her hands. "I was supposed to be happy with ye," she whimpered.

Ewan stood by, uncertain of what to do. He had been the source of her misery. It was he who had decided to marry Faye instead of Blair, changing his mind just as the negotiations with the Gordon Chieftain were nearly complete. All of this had been his fault.

He opened his arms to her in an attempt to offer comfort. She sagged against him, nuzzling her face into his chest as she breathed in deeply.

"This was all I've ever wanted." Her arms curled around his back, locking their bodies together. "Ye are all I've ever wanted."

"Blair," he said in an attempt to recall her to her senses.

She ran her hand over his chest and gave a shuddering sigh. "Kiss me, Ewan." Her face tilted up to his.

Before he could disentangle himself from her, the door flew inward with such force that splintered wood skittered across the hard-packed floor. Ten warriors entered the single room cottage with Ewan's uncle behind them.

"I knew it," he cried.

The warriors surrounded them, but Cruim broke through the circle of men and ripped Blair away from Ewan. Cruim staggered slightly as he held Blair by the back of her kirtle.

He glared at her, his gaze going to her nearly exposed breasts. "Ye willna even kiss me, but ye play the role of leman to this whelp?" A rattle in his chest followed his angry words.

"I never wanted to marry ye," Blair said vehemently.

An older man with bulging muscles stepped forward and restrained Blair, holding her arms behind her back. Her chest pushed forward, and her breasts swelled with each jagged breath.

"Release her," Ewan ordered.

The man did not. In fact, he didn't even look at Ewan.

"These are not yer men," Cruim said. "They are in support of me becoming chieftain."

Ewan looked at each man in the room, none of whom met his eyes. "Ye're all traitors," he said with a voice of authority. "And when this is all over, ye'll die for yer betrayal."

Cruim scoffed. "When this is over, they'll be my most trusted warriors. And I'll be the chieftain." The rattle in his chest resumed, and he gave a wet cough.

There was a grayness to his pallor, and he seemed unsteady on his feet.

"Ye have this wrong," Blair said. "Someone told us to meet here."

Cruim looked at her, his expression blank. "I'm sure ye'll say ye both got notes to come here, aye?"

Blair's mouth fell open. "Aye, that's what happened."

"Which is exactly what I thought ye would say." Cruim shook his head with disappointment. "'Tis how she said ye would try to talk yer way out of this."

A chill crept down Ewan's spine. "She?"

"Aye." Cruim's lip curled in disgust. "I wouldna even know about yer affair, or how ye'd both lied to me, had my daughter no' been good enough to come forward. It wounded her to do it, especially when ye'd always been so close."

Ewan went mute with shock. Why would Moiré tell her father about an affair that did not exist?

Why, unless… His blood turned to ice in his veins. Unless she was part of the plot to overthrow him and put his uncle in charge. And if that were the case, then Faye was in grave danger.

F aye raced through the cold stone halls of Dunrobin in a world blurred by tears. She had never been one to run from her troubles. They'd always been faced head-on and with determination.

At least, until the moment that Blair had entered the small, empty cottage with Ewan. The wind had caught her cloak and pushed it aside, revealing a salacious gown whose purpose was clear: seduction.

All the energy had whooshed out of Faye at that moment, dousing the fire that would have risen to the occasion. She ignored Moiré's placating suggestions that there was surely a good explanation and that all would be well. Instead, Faye turned her horse and galloped the short distance back to the castle, not stopping until she was shuttered in her chamber.

It had been her intent to fall upon her bed and weep. For her and her lost marriage, for the child whose father had lied to them all, and for her pathetic heart that had finally cracked itself open to the possibility of hope. Of love.

What a fool she'd been.

She had trusted him. After a lifetime of disloyalty, she should have known better.

A missive sat atop her pillow with her name scrawled over its back. She stopped short and reached for it with shaking hands before carefully unfolding it. A whimper emerged from a throat swollen with sorrow.

Faye,

I tried to make the best of the union we were forced into but can no longer deny my feelings for Blair. You may return to your family posthaste as you are no longer required here.

Forgive me for telling you I loved you when I clearly do not.

- Ewan

The strength bled from Faye's knees, and she sat down hard on the edge of her bed. The jeweled hilt of her dagger dug into her side.

He'd lied to her. Betrayed her.

The pain in Faye's chest was horrific, a searing ache so large, it was difficult even to draw breath. She gasped for air. The hilt pinched at her side with each breath. With an irritated huff, she pulled it out and tossed it across the room where it clattered somewhere under a table. The energy bled away from her, as though that single act of anger was all she would ever have the strength for again.

"Faye?" Moiré appeared at her side. "What is it?"

Faye nudged the letter over the bedsheet, lacking the might to even lift it. Moiré's gaze skimmed over the contents. Through it all, Faye studied her friend's expression, eager to see disbelief in those brown eyes, to hear her refute the message and declare that Ewan would never do that.

Instead, her eyes filled with tears. "Oh, Faye," Moiré said softly.

"It can't be true," Faye protested. "Can it?"

"I have a way to find out." Moiré prodded a key at the ring on Faye's belt. "'Tis to the locked drawer in his solar. I've seen him put many things within. Important letters and..." she hesitated before adding apologetically, "missives he doesn't want anyone else to see."

The idea lodged uncomfortably in Faye's stomach. What might be in there? If there was confirmation of a relationship with Blair and Ewan, did she even want to see? To purposefully drive a new spike of hurt?

"We must know," Moiré said vehemently.

"We already know," Faye replied.

"I'm going." Moiré held out her hand. "Give me the key. I'll tell ye what I find."

A flicker of strength nudged Faye to her feet. She couldn't allow Moiré to see such things without her.

They went to Ewan's solar; the space was familiar with his large wooden desk and the simple space that smelled achingly of him. The spiciness that used to make Faye's pulse quicken, sensual and masculine and wonderful. Now it was the blade that twisted into her heart.

The words from his note cycled through her mind, flitting about restlessly without ever fully settling. She approached the desk, and her trepidation swelled, like a living, breathing, all-consuming thing.

You are no longer required here.

As if she were a servant being readily dismissed.

She put the key into the locked drawer and slowly turned it. A metallic click pinged as the hasp sprang free.

Forgive me for telling you I loved you when I clearly do not.

It was that line that bothered her the most, which cut her the deepest.

She slid open the drawer and found a neat stack of notes bound with a green ribbon that matched the one Blair had worn on her wedding day. Faye inwardly winced even as she reached for the stack.

They were indeed from Blair. Six missives in all.

Faye sank into Ewan's chair, as her legs couldn't support her properly anymore, and read each note. Every word, every profession of love and passion between Ewan and Blair, scraped over the rawness inside her.

It was all too much.

Her stomach clenched, as though the pain in her heart was slowly sinking lower.

Forgive me for telling you I loved you when I clearly do not.

Those words prodded at her brain, through the fog of grief. They echoed back at her now and burrowed in her mind like a burr.

Not with pain, but with doubt.

Ewan had never told her he loved her.

A new need arose within her, to rifle through the other contents in his desk and compare the letter he'd written her to his other correspondence. The note sat heavy in her pocket, but Moiré's stare was heavier. Like a millstone looming over Faye.

How was it that Faye had happened upon that cottage where Ewan met with Blair at exactly that moment? Especially after it had been Moiré who had convinced Faye not to tell Ewan about her pregnancy?

Sorcha's words back at the hut rose in Faye's mind regarding Lara. *"All the times I saw to her were to offer herbs to help find a cure for her barrenness."*

Faye's breath came faster, filling the room with the frantic puffs. She glanced down, discreetly seeking Moiré's fingertips. Splotches of black showed against her fair skin.

Ink.

A chill tingled over Faye's skin.

"I'd like some time alone," Faye whispered. "I...I need to understand all of this."

Moiré nodded. "Take all the time ye need." She leaned over Faye and gave her a brief hug, squeezing her shoulders.

Faye tried not to stiffen. "Thank ye."

She waited until Moiré quit the room before quietly easing open the other drawers and rummaging through. Finally, she came across several letters midway through, a mundane one detailing the purchase of livestock.

Exactly what she'd been looking for.

She jerked the note free from her pocket and unfolded it. Even as she did so, she was hit by the certainty of her suspicion. She flattened the letters beside one another, her gaze darting between the two.

While her note had been written in a hand clearly attempting to imitate Ewan's, it was decidedly not his handwriting. The t's were too looped, the n's too flowy against the bold, sharp scratch of Ewan's handwriting.

Faye settled her hand over both parchments as the realization slammed into her.

Moiré.

It wasn't Ewan who had betrayed her.

All this time, it had been Moiré.

৩১৯

"L<small>ET US GO</small>," E<small>WAN SAID IN A LEVEL VOICE</small>.

Cruim smirked. "Seize him."

The Sutherland warriors, men who should have been loyal to Ewan, stalked forward with purpose.

"I am yer chieftain," Ewan tried again. "This is a direct order to cease this at once or ye'll all pay with yer lives."

Two slowed, but the remainder pressed on. Indeed, it appeared they quickened their pace. Ewan didn't move until they were upon him, allowing them a final opportunity to back down.

The first man, one from the lower part of the Sutherland lands, reached for Ewan's arm. Instead, Ewan captured the man's hand in his fist and met his gaze. "Craig, what would yer da think of such disloyalty? He gave his life to protect our lands."

"Aye, a life buried under yer da's rules," Craig growled and ripped himself from Ewan's grasp. "I'll no' live such a strict life."

The strictness he referred to was no doubt Ewan's refusal to allow him to raise sheep on prime farming land. The absence of crops could be detrimental should another blight come upon them. As Ewan had detailed to the man.

"Rules are made to keep people safe." Ewan had spent too damn long questioning his decisions, and his ability to be chieftain without the training others had received. He knew the decision he'd made had been correct, that it was done to ensure the safety and protection of his people.

"They dinna have rules at the border," another man said. Ewan had known the man since boyhood but couldn't recall his name. But Ewan did remember he'd been punished some time back for stealing from his neighbors.

"And they live in a constant state of war," Ewan protested. "Is that what ye want for Sutherland?"

"My land willna be like that," Cruim said arrogantly.

Ewan stepped back. "I dinna want to fight my own people when we should stand united."

"'Tis already done," declared the man from Ewan's boyhood.

Together they lunged for him. Ewan pulled his sword from its scabbard, but they had arrived with targes and armor. He had not thought to come prepared for battle when meeting with Blair.

"Nay," Blair shrieked. "Leave him be."

Her foot stomped down on her captor's, and she spun around as he released her. In a flash, she had his dagger in her hand. Before she could plunge it at him, one of the men threw himself at her.

That was all Ewan could see, for three men rushed at him then, thrusting their blades with vicious intent. He was able to block them all at once with a mighty sweep of his sword. It was an impressive defense, but not one he could maintain. Indeed, it had been a lucky strike.

Suddenly, blades were striking at him in numbers too great to fend off, forcing him back, back, back until his heels hit the hard wall. Outnumbered, overpowered and bleeding from several gashes, he had no choice but to keep fighting.

A sharp cry cut the air, and the men faltered.

"Nay," Cruim said in a low moan. "Enough."

The maelstrom of jabbing blades and fists ceased, and the men eased away.

Blood dripped from Ewan's left hand to the floor. His body roared with energy, even as his knees did not feel strong enough to support him, ready to fight to the death. He put his hand against the wall behind him to steady himself in preparation for yet another onslaught, his blade raised.

An eerie silence fell over the cottage. Ewan followed everyone's stare and found Blair lying on the ground with Cruim standing over her. A dagger jutted from her throat, and her blue-gray eyes stared sightlessly upward.

"Blair." Cruim fell to his knees with a choked cry that blossomed into a wracking cough.

"I...I dinna mean...to," a man stammered. "She was attacking me, I meant only to keep her off, but she moved—"

"Kill him," Cruim shouted, his face contorting with rage.

His men hesitated to obey his order.

Cruim leapt to his feet and flew at the man with an unholy speed, plunging a dagger into the man's throat, as had been done to Blair. A wet choking sound emerged from the man's mouth in a spatter of blood. He crumpled to the ground in a pool of blood that spread toward the one beneath Blair.

"Take him outside," Cruim said to his men. He looked pointedly at Ewan. "I wouldna struggle if I were ye."

Ewan couldn't pull his gaze from the two bodies, the man who had supported Cruim only to be killed by him. And Blair, who had sought to save herself.

Cruim was mad. And dangerous.

The fear for Faye washed over Ewan anew.

"Where's my wife?" he demanded.

"Ye need no' worry about her." Cruim lifted his head from Blair's body. "Moiré is seeing to her."

Rage and fear tangled against one another at the thought of what Moiré might do to her. "If she's harmed..."

"She's no' any of yer concern." Cruim coughed, a thick rattling coming from his chest. It was followed by a harder hack that made his entire body spasm.

"Take him to the manor," Cruim ordered through a wheezing inhale. "We'll put him in the cellar for now." He indicated the bodies on the ground. "And bring them with us. I'll no' have my wife rotting in a village hut." His jaw clenched as he stared at her one final time before turning and leaving the small cottage.

Ewan wanted to fight, to throw his fist and his blade at each of the men. But it would be a battle he would not win. One that would cost him his life. And his life, however long or short it might be, would be used to keep Faye safe.

Even as he thought her name, his chest squeezed with a visceral ache. Surely Moiré would not harm her, not after the time they'd spent together, after the bond of their friendship. But then, he truly didn't know Moiré at all. For he would have never anticipated that she was capable of devising a way to betray him to his uncle in such a manner.

Cruim's men caught Ewan in a hard grip as two men lifted Blair's body. The sword was wrested from his hand, and his wrists were bound with a rope. The fibers were thick and coarse, working against his bare skin like a bevy of splinters. A sack dropped over his head, leaving him blind and momentarily disoriented, as he was shoved forward.

Light punctured through the loose weave of the sack and told Ewan he was outside. He walked several steps before he was pushed violently. Unable to see, he fell and landed against a hard edge. Before he could right himself, a loud thwack sounded over his head and dulled out all noise. The sweet smell of freshly cut wood filled his senses.

A box.

He'd been put into a box. Most likely, something akin to what Faye had been forced into on her journey to Sutherland.

He gritted his teeth against the pain lashing through him. What did Moiré intend to do with Faye? Metallic fear lingered in the back of his throat and overwhelmed the physical hurt of the injuries his body had sustained. He writhed in the small, coffin-like space. The action pulled at the ropes on his hand, so they bit into his flesh.

He didn't care. He wouldn't stop fighting. Not until he was free and could find some way to get to Faye. To save her.

Ewan waited for the telltale lurch of a cart being drawn onward before he resumed his attempts to liberate himself. He fixed his mind on Faye as he worked, using the sweet cherub's bow of her lips to take his mind from the sting of the ropes. The silkiness of her hair luxuriously slipping through his fingers kept him from thinking of the sticky dampness from the cuts on his hands.

But the ropes were bound too tightly, and the box too small to properly move. Still, he struggled in vain. And as he did, he recalled the way she looked at him, her blue eyes soft with words neither of them had said: *I love you.*

A knot formed at the back of his throat.

He should have told her. He'd been so damned worried about scaring her off, and now he might die without telling her what she meant to him. Determination fired through him.

He had to stay alive. For Faye.

❧ 22 ❧

Faye stared at the parchment in her hands as the stark truth curled around her. Moiré had written all the letters. Even the ones claiming to be from Blair. The letters all shared the same looping t's and flowing n's.

But why?

Fear gripped her heart in its icy fingers.

Moiré didn't want Faye to go looking for Ewan. Events from the last few weeks came together in Faye's mind. How Moiré had been seen leaving Finn's rooms after a tryst. Moiré's suggestion that Faye not tell Ewan she believed she was pregnant, lying about Lara to ensure her compliance. Even how Moiré had suggested Ewan had been acting strange, planting the idea into Faye's mind to make her question everything and believe the deception.

And how easily Faye had been led along.

Tears stung her eyes at the realization. Moiré was obviously helping her father take the chieftainship from Ewan, and they had all been ignorant to it. How foolish Faye had been, and now Ewan was in danger.

Her brain scrabbled for purchase on a plan while she numbly stacked the letters and returned them all to the drawer. The shuffle of footsteps sounded outside the door, and Faye realized Moiré was waiting for her.

Faye reached for her dagger at her side and found the sheath empty. Frustration welled in her throat like a scream. Now she would be facing her enemy without a weapon.

Quickly, she scratched out a letter to Monroe, detailing what she'd uncovered and expressing her fears that Moiré had done something with Ewan.

It was a risk she had to take as an idea slowly came to her. Especially when danger lay in wait on the other side of the door.

Faye got to her feet and said a silent prayer that her plan might work. A band of tension squeezed at her chest.

She pushed through the door and found Moiré was indeed waiting in the hallway, her gaze tight with concern. "I'm so sorry this is happening to ye," Moiré said in a honeyed voice.

Faye studied the woman she had once called a friend. She wanted to curl her fingers around the other woman's neck and squeeze until all the secrets spilled forth.

"Ye needn't worry after me," Faye waved her hand. It was a dismissive gesture she figured Moiré would ignore. "I'm sure ye've better things to do."

Moiré put a staying hand to Faye's forearm. It was all Faye could do to keep from jerking away from the wicked woman. Faye had used attraction and her own sexuality to manipulate people for years, but never once had she done so to inflict harm. Not like Moiré, who wielded her sweetness, with endearing platitudes and ready trust, in the cruelest of weapons.

Moiré smiled. "What would possibly require my attention more than aiding my cousin's wife?" There was an underlying bitterness to her words. Had it always been there, and Faye had not noticed it?

"I need to speak with Monroe," Faye said. "To ready plans for me to depart."

"I'll speak with him for ye," Moiré said affectionately.

It was as Faye had expected. Still, confirming Moiré would try to block any opportunity Faye used to notify someone was like a blow. Which was why she'd come up with another plan.

"I confess," Faye said. "I'd hoped to go to the cottage where Ewan is. I want to confront him."

Moiré hesitated, and Faye could practically hear her thoughts shifting how a change of location might work to her advantage.

At least in this way, Faye could get to Ewan, to find some way to help him. And get to a servant who could tell Monroe about the note.

"Of course," Moiré replied at last. "Though we ought to hurry if we plan to catch him."

She and Moiré rushed to the stables to gather their horses once more. As anticipated, they didn't see a single person on the short trek. But the stable lad was there. Also, as anticipated.

"I've left a missive on my husband's desk," Faye said to the boy. "See to it that Monroe gets it immediately."

The boy nodded.

Moiré's stare darted to Faye.

Faye offered an apologetic smile. "I simply told Monroe about Ewan's infidelity and my desire to leave. I'd written it before ye said ye'd handle it for me."

"I'm sorry 'tis come to this," Moiré said with such affected sorrow that it almost made Faye second guess her assumptions.

But nay. She'd seen the handwriting with her own eyes. It had truly been different. And mayhap Ewan was not in danger, but if he were, at least it would be a way to save him.

They rode out to the village in silence. All the while, Faye's mind raced with scenarios. What would happen if she were attacked? Or if Ewan were already dead?

Or if there truly were an affair, and Ewan and Blair were meeting for a tryst?

The horses were no longer tethered at the cottage when Faye and Moiré arrived. But before Moiré could try to turn her horse back toward the castle, Faye dismounted and rushed into the cottage. Her stomach twisted into anxious knots over what she might find.

She pushed through the door and stopped. The odor of blood rushed to greet her. A massive dark stain had spread over the hard-packed floor. The hut was empty, but it was obvious someone had been there. And someone had been killed.

She staggered inside and caught herself against the rough wall. On the opposite side of the home, highlighted in a slice of sunlight streaming in from the open door, was a bloody handprint smeared against the dingy whitewash.

The door slammed closed, plunging the hut into near darkness, save for the light limning the broken shutters.

Faye spun around, her whole world whirling with shock. "What's happened to him?"

A sob choked out of Moiré.

"Where is he?" Faye asked. "What have ye done?"

"I'm sorry," Moiré's face crumpled. "'Twas my da."

Faye shook her head, not understanding.

"He wants the chieftainship," Moiré said amid her tears.

"What's happened to Ewan?" Faye demanded. Her words reverberated off the stark walls and echoed back to her.

Moiré put her face in her hands, and Faye took a step closer to better hear her. Fast as lightning, Moiré withdrew a blade from her sleeve and shoved it to Faye's stomach while pressing at her lower back with her other hand.

Faye froze, at the mercy of the madwoman. If only Faye had her dagger—if only it hadn't jabbed at her side and she hadn't thrown it away from her. She wasn't entirely helpless, of course. She could attack Moiré, hit her with an elbow, toss her to the ground and put a foot to her throat.

And if Faye weren't with child, she would immediately do those things. Except there was a sharp blade at her belly. One ready to take her babe's life before it could even be born.

"Get outside," Moiré said in a hard voice. "And if ye so much as sigh, I'll plunge my dagger into yer belly."

A shudder of fear consumed Faye. She would do nothing to put her babe at risk. And so it was that she allowed Moiré to lead her from the village and through the woods. Faye walked, tripping over tree roots, her feet made clumsy by her terror—for her husband and for her babe. Moiré remained at her side with the damn dagger put to Faye's belly. But while Faye had no idea where she was being taken, she knew one thing for certain: she would not die without putting up a fight.

EWAN TENSED AS THE WAGON DREW TO A STOP.

The top was thrown from the crate, revealing a clear blue sky. Hands reached into the box and roughly dragged him out. They threw him downward, off the cart and to the unforgiving cobblestones below. A shadow fell over Ewan.

He looked up, squinting against the sun, to find Cruim standing over him. "This is yer fault," his uncle accused. "If ye hadna lain with my Blair, she wouldna be dead." A vein throbbed at the center of Cruim's brow. His cheeks huffed out in a restrained cough. "See to his wounds and send him to the cellar. I want him alive."

Cruim's gaze slid to the other wooden box on the cart. One that had been meant to transport Blair, no doubt. She lay within it now. Or so Ewan presumed, dead within the other crate.

Cruim's men came forward obediently and dragged Ewan down to the small, barred hold in the cellar of the manor. It had been meant to store dry goods, not usurp a chieftain.

One of the men stayed with Ewan and patched up the wounds with bits of linen as best he could. If nothing else, the man's rudimentary application staunched the blood flow. Once done, the man left, abandoning Ewan to the still, dark room.

The iron-barred room was black as pitch and held a mustiness of wet earth floors and cold stone. His fate would yet be determined.

He waited thus, his eyes searching futilely against the press of darkness, his wounds aching. Time dragged on at an indeterminable rate.

They wanted him left alive.

Why?

And what of Faye? What did Moiré intend to do with her?

Footsteps approached and Ewan straightened. His hands searched in front of him, seeking out something, anything. A warm golden glow lit the empty room as someone with a light approached. All at once, the brilliance of it came into view and left Ewan's eyes stinging with the same sensation as looking up into the sun on a particularly bright day.

Ewan grunted and staggered back with his hands thrown over his eyes.

A wheezing cough gave away the person's identity. Cruim.

Ewan lowered his arms from blocking his face and stared just beyond the flicker of a single candle flame to where he knew his uncle's face would be.

"Release me," Ewan demanded, squinting.

"Ye had an affair with my wife," Cruim spoke so passionately, a cough rose up in his chest and choked its way free. "'Tis yer fault she's dead."

"Ye know I dinna," Ewan said angrily. "Moiré has been playing us all for fools. Dinna ye see it?"

"Moiré has always looked out for me," Cruim said. "Which is more than I can say for ye."

"What is it she's done for ye?" Ewan's eyes had adjusted to the light enough to meet his uncle's gaze from between the bars.

Cruim blinked. "She's cared for me after her mum died. She's told me how ye've tried to oppress me, how even yer gift of this manor was to keep me close, to watch me even as ye threaten me."

Ewan stared hard at him, unable to believe his ears. "I threaten ye?"

"I know about the plots." Cruim coughed into his fist. "It was ye who made me sick. To remove me from the line of succession for the chieftainship, so yer bairns will never have a valid rival. I never even wanted the damn chieftainship."

Ewan stared at his uncle in shock. Cruim had never been the threat. In truth, his meddling had never made sense, not when he hadn't shown an aptitude for cleverness. It was why Ewan had discounted him so often, assuming Cruim couldn't be conniving enough to pull off an elaborate stunt.

Ewan never had even suspected Moiré.

"I dinna ever intend ye harm," Ewan said. "It was Moiré."

Cruim scoffed. "She's helped me, Ewan. She even helped my marriage with...with Blair." He winced. "Moiré said the arrangement would help her wed Finn." Cruim's voice went tender with an apparent affection for his daughter. "She said doing that would secure my alliance with the Gordons and protect me from ye." His lower lip trembled.

"Cruim," Ewan said in an even tone. "She's been using ye, manipulating ye as she'd done to everyone else." He shook his head in stunned disbelief at how readily she'd fooled them all. "Even me."

His uncle shuddered, and a cough erupted from his mouth so violently, it appeared to have surprised even him. He fell against the barred door, dragging in choked breaths as the cough overtook him.

He'd lost a considerable amount of weight recently, his arms like sticks, his shoulders slender where the doublet hung loose around them.

"Let me out, Cruim," Ewan said. "I believe Faye to be in danger."

Cruim's hands curled around the rusty bars as though holding himself upright with them. "She's no' a good woman," he panted. "Just like Lara."

A chill descended down Ewan's spine. "What about Lara?"

Memories rushed him all at once. How Moiré had been the one to see Lara teeter over the cliff before coming to him, distraught and scratched from her attempt to save her.

Lara hadn't killed herself. Moiré had murdered her.

And if Ewan didn't get free of his cell, he knew in his gut that Faye would also be killed.

Metal rang against metal in the distance. Ewan jerked at the discernible sound of battle. Men's shouts rang out with alarm in the distance.

"Let me out," Ewan demanded. "Moiré is going to try to kill Faye. The same as she did with Lara."

"Moiré knows best," Cruim said weakly. Another cough took him, leaving his shoulders trembling.

Spatters of blood glistened in the dirt. Whatever plagued Ewan's uncle, it would surely kill him.

Ewan slipped his hand through the bars and jerked the keys from Cruim's belt, along with his dagger. The older man did nothing to stop him.

Ewan tapped the key on the opposite side of the iron door, seeking the lock. It clattered inside clumsily, and he wrenched it to the left. A metallic click sounded, and the door creaked open. He stepped out into the hall. Still, Cruim did not move.

It entered his mind to put his uncle inside the cellar, but with the way the man was curled in on himself, blood dripping in strings of saliva from his mouth, Ewan knew it would do little good. His uncle would be no threat. Not when he was dying.

Instead, he crouched by his uncle and gently squeezed his shoulder. "May God forgive ye for what has been done, Uncle."

Ewan straightened and backed away before charging up the stairs to where the sounds of battle increased—the clashing of weapons and armor and cries of war. A line of warriors appeared in front of him, backlit by light, so they were set in the shadows. At least a dozen men ran to him. Too damn many to take on with a single dagger.

Ewan gritted his teeth and held his ground. If saving Faye lay beyond them, he'd kill every damn one to get to her.

"Sir?" A familiar voice said.

The men stopped.

"Monroe?" Ewan squinted as he raced forward, so the light washed over the faces of his trusted advisor and strongest warriors.

Monroe's dark eyes went wide. "What's happened—"

"Moiré," Ewan ground out.

"We know." Monroe's lips thinned beneath his black beard. "Lady Sutherland wrote me a note telling me what happened. We found blood in the cottage she sent us to, and we assumed it had to do with Cruim. Lady Sutherland's horse was still bound near the hut, as well as Mistress Moiré's."

"Where is Faye?" Ewan demanded.

Monroe's brows shot up. "She's no' here?"

Ewan shook his head. "No' that I'm aware. She wasna brought to the cellar." He turned his attention to his warriors. "Most of ye search here and take every traitor prisoner. Send two men to Dunrobin to look for Faye. Monroe, ye come with me."

The warriors split up in immediate compliance with their orders.

"Where are we going?" Monroe asked as Ewan led him through the Great Hall of the manor to the large doors exiting outdoors.

"To the cliff," Ewan said as a savage pain twisted through him. "Where Lara died."

Where Faye most likely was. He only hoped they would not be too late.

"There's something I think ye should know." There was an

almost gentle note to Monroe's voice that made Ewan pause and regard him with concern.

"What is it?" Ewan's heart locked mid-beat as he waited for his friend to respond.

"In the letter Lady Sutherland wrote, she confessed something I think ye should know." Monroe glanced down at his hands, then lifted his gaze to Ewan. "She's with child."

❧ 23 ❧

The air was tinged with the brininess of the sea, and the hushed roar of crashing waves sounded in the distance. Faye continued to put one foot in front of the other, allowing Moiré to guide her to the unknown location.

The dense forest cleared away, revealing a cliff that spilled out to a vast sea.

Fear clutched at Faye's heart, and she faltered. "Where are we? Where is Ewan?"

"I've spent my life being weak." Moiré pressed the point of the blade to Faye's stomach.

The tip pricked Faye's skin beneath her kirtle and made her continue the slow march forward.

"I'm the daughter of a second son." Moiré gave a mirthless laugh. "Destined to be a servant to my kin for the rest of my life. Do ye know that babe in yer belly will have a better advantage in every way than I've ever had?"

Faye hated that she couldn't put her hands over her belly to protect her unborn child. It left her so much more vulnerable than she'd ever realized possible. "So, ye'll kill me? And Ewan? Why? For power?"

Moiré pulled in a deep breath, her chest puffing with pride. "To be chieftain."

Faye gaped at Moiré. "Will ye kill yer own da as well?"

A pained look crossed Moiré's face. "He was already dying." It was said so defensively, Faye knew Moiré had a hand in helping his illness along.

"It was why I planned to do this," Moiré continued. "I didn't have to hurt ye as well until ye told me ye were with child." Tears welled her large brown eyes. "I tried to save ye, but the tea I made ye dinna work."

The tea.

Horror chilled Faye to her bones. "Ye were trying to kill my child?"

"Dinna look at me like that," Moiré snapped. "As though I'm a monster. I couldna allow an heir to come between me and the chieftainship. And I dinna want to kill ye."

They were near the cliffs now. The wind gusted with more force, billowing against their faces, and carrying with it the salty mist of the ocean.

"And now ye think ye have to kill me?" Faye's voice was quiet, but her thoughts screamed through her brain with a multitude of scenarios to free herself.

Moiré nodded and sniffled. "I'm sorry."

"Why lie to me about Ewan?" Faye demanded. "The letters..." She shook her head. "I know about them."

Moiré thinned her lips. "So ye wouldna question why he dinna return to Dunrobin, so I could find a way to give ye a tea that would work with the new herbs I took from Sorcha's garden." She gave a frustrated sigh. "I tell ye, Faye, I was trying to save ye. But after we came across the blood, after ye demanded to be answered...I couldna keep it a secret any longer." Her arm at Faye's back tensed. "Especially no' with that babe in yer womb."

"What about Ewan?" Faye choked.

"He's alive," Moiré offered graciously. "For now. Cruim insisted he stay a prisoner rather than kill him outright. My da has a tender heart. One that willna beat long enough to see all this through, I wager."

Faye staggered under the force of her relief. Ewan was alive. Her thoughts flicked back to the cottage. Why had there been so much blood?

Could Moiré know for certain that he'd not been killed when she'd been with Faye the entire time?

She slowed her pace as they neared the edge. The deep blue sea stretched endlessly beyond, and the breaking waves over the rocks below filled their ears. Faye's heart slammed in her chest, its rapid-fire beat so loud, it drowned out nearly everything else. It was a pain more vicious than anything she'd ever felt.

Her mother's words rushed back to her, the reminder that the glory of love was worth the pain of loss. Such a thought hadn't fully registered with Faye. Not until that very moment.

But she wouldn't think of Ewan being dead. She couldn't.

"What about Lara?" Faye asked.

Moiré narrowed her eyes. "Ye're too clever. Mayhap, 'tis a good thing ye've interrupted my plans." She lifted her shoulder. "Lara's womb finally took root."

It was too much. Faye's feet stopped moving forward. She wouldn't die like Lara had.

"Walk." Moiré prodded Faye in the belly with the dagger, her hand at Faye's back pressing even harder.

This was exactly the reason Faye's eldest brother had insisted his sisters train so hard. To ensure they were never in such a position. She couldn't think through the moves too much, not when each thought resulted in a new way everything could go so horribly wrong. She had to trust that she was strong enough, skilled enough. Or the cost would be her life as well as that of her unborn child.

Faye jerked sharply to the side as she swung her elbow into Moiré's face. The blade sank reflexively into Faye's side, more pressure than pain. Moiré put her hand to her face where she'd been struck.

An opportunity to run.

One Faye would not waste.

She sprinted back toward the forest. Warmth washed over her side where she'd been sliced, but she forced her thoughts from it. She was nearly halfway to the tree line when a solid weight knocked into her back and sent her landing hard on the ground. Pain shot through her side and dazzled her vision from where the wound at her side absorbed the impact.

Faye kicked her feet out, hitting one foot square into Moiré's chest. Moiré staggered backward. But not far enough. Before Faye could scramble to her feet, Moiré was on her again.

Her fists came down on Faye, merciless and unending. Faye blocked them as they came, each one stinging at her forearms, unable to get a hit of her own. She thrust her hips up and pushed with all her might. The action sent Moiré crashing to the ground beside her.

This time, Faye managed to get to her feet. Something caught against her toe, tripping her, so she sprawled forward. The thing at her foot pulled. Moiré, dragging her backward, toward the cliff.

But Faye wasn't done fighting yet.

⚜

THE CLIFFS WERE VISIBLE IN THE FAR DISTANCE. EWAN LEANED closer to his horse, urging the beast onward. To Faye. And their bairn in her womb.

The agony in his chest was so intense, it made drawing air difficult. He couldn't lose her. Not when he hadn't told her he loved her. Not when they were just starting their life together.

As they grew nearer, Ewan fell prey to despair. No figures were visible as they approached the spot where Lara had died.

And then he saw it, a woman in a yellow kirtle with brown

hair pulling another person backward by her leg, a woman with blond hair.

Ewan's heart caught.

Faye.

And Moiré.

Ewan cried out to his horse in an effort to make him go faster, but the beast was already going as swiftly as was possible.

Faye kicked at Moiré, who continued pulling her to the cliff's edge. Ewan watched, helpless as Faye struck out at Moiré. She fell, and the two rolled on the ground together, arms lashing out, legs kicking.

Ewan's pulse ticked with frenzy. They were still too far.

All at once, Faye sent Moiré flying off her, as she scrambled to her feet and ran. It looked like she might escape when Moiré lifted something and threw it at Faye's head.

Faye dropped, unmoving.

Ewan cried out, but he was still too damn far away, his voice drowned out by the wind.

Moiré pulled Faye by her feet, so her skirts bunched up as she was dragged. Still, Faye did not move. Not even when Moiré was poised with her at the edge of the cliff.

Ewan was closer now. It would be mere moments until he could help.

But before he had the opportunity, Moiré shoved at Faye, so her body rolled to the very edge of the cliff.

Nay.

Ewan wanted to call out to them again, but he couldn't. Not with his heart lodged in his throat. He pulled his dagger free and rode with such haste, the world bounced around him.

It would be difficult to strike Moiré from his current position, but not impossible. Ewan held his breath to steady his hand and released the dagger.

It sailed through the air toward Moiré, its path true. Just as it was about to connect, she bent, and it flew over her head. His insides crumpled at his failure. And of what it might mean.

Oblivious to what had happened, Moiré shoved at Faye. A startled scream carried on the wind toward Ewan.

He found his voice and bellowed against the wind for Moiré to stop. She doubtless couldn't hear him over the roar of the waves crashing against the rocks below the cliff, for she didn't even turn. Nay, she kicked her foot hard at Faye with an impact that sent her rolling over the edge of the cliff.

"Moiré." Her name tore up through his soul, raw with rage and horror.

His cousin spun around just as a hand shot out and grabbed her by the ankle. In one moment, she was standing there, gaping in surprise at Ewan and the next, she was gone. A shriek caught on the wind and died away.

But it was not his cousin he feared for. He dismounted and ran toward the cliff, his heart caught in a fist of desperation and dread. After all, how could Faye survive a fall such as that?

She was gone. In that one instant, the woman who had brought so much passion and joy and love to his life was gone. And in her womb, she'd carried their babe, a mere blossom of a bairn and a symbol of the love they had never spoken, but he knew they both felt.

Tears stung his eyes.

He'd been a coward. And a fool. There had been so many moments he could have told her he loved her.

Faye.

His Faye. With her golden blonde hair that he'd stroked as she slept in his arms. There were too many stories of her life he'd never hear, too many kisses he'd never share with her again. There was a child neither of them would ever meet.

A knot ached in the back of his throat. He made his way to the cliff's edge on legs that threatened to buckle. Each footstep brought a new memory of the woman he loved, the life they had shared.

What he would never have again.

That life was gone.

All he had left was regret.

❧ 24 ❧

Faye's fall stopped abruptly as her hands found purchase. Pain seared at her side, where Moiré had managed to cut her.

Faye blinked, her mind still reeling with shock. One moment, her hands were out, grasping first at Moiré, then at air and the next, they closed on firm stone. A flutter of yellow kirtle rippled past her, accompanied by a scream of terror as Moiré plunged to the rocks below.

Faye averted her gaze. Not only did she not want to witness Moiré's demise, but she also couldn't bear to see what her fate might await her, should her hands give out.

The cliff face was directly in front of Faye, its surface comprised of rock and soil and stubborn bits of grass. She was close enough to stretch her feet out and meet a narrow ledge. The small movement burned like fire at her side, but the ground held firm underfoot. She relaxed her grip on the stone somewhat, but not releasing it entirely.

A prickle stung her palms where the rock had scraped her skin —the slight hurt was insignificant in light of her life having been spared.

Her arms trembled with exhaustion, even just from the small amount of time she'd been hanging on. She didn't dare relax her grip anymore, though. Not when the ocean roared beneath her, like a monster's gaping mouth, ready to swallow her.

A shiver of fear threatened her composure. She scanned the cliff face. Any hope she might have had to climb out was dashed away by disappointment. Aye, she'd managed to stop herself from falling, but what could she do to return herself to solid ground?

She was at least eight feet below the cliff. Too far to stretch a hand or try to jump. Nor were there any more visible bits of rock like the one she clung to.

She could scarcely feel her arms, and her fingers had begun to ache. She couldn't hang there forever with a toehold on a small ledge.

But what of Ewan?

An ache balled at her throat as she thought of her husband. Had Monroe found her letter? Had he gone out to find Ewan? Was he safe?

Tears of frustration burned in her eyes. She had to climb up, to save Ewan, to be with him.

The memory of the bloody handprint flashed in her mind, brilliant red against the whitewashed wall. And all that blood on the floor.

He might be injured. Mayhap already dead.

Nay. She could not think about such horrible things.

There had to be a way out. She stretched her foot farther to the right, and her weight shifted, threatening to pull her from the rock she held. Her fingers clenched the stone tighter, and she eased her toes back to the small ledge. The emptiness at her back seemed to pull at her, eager to drag her to her death as it had Moiré.

It was impossible to move without letting go of the rock.

"Faye," Ewan's voice came from overhead.

She looked up, shocked to find her husband's head peering

over at her.

"Ewan." Her hands nearly slipped from the rock with relief.

"Monroe, I need a rope," he called while leaving his gaze fixed on her. "Stay there, my love. Dinna move."

My love.

Tears ran down her cheeks at the sentiment. She'd been a fool to hold back on her emotions for so long. And for what? To have nearly died without having told him.

"I love ye, Ewan Sutherland," she cried against the wind. "I love ye."

He blinked rapidly. "And I love ye, Faye Sutherland," he choked out.

A rope appeared over the edge of the cliff with a loop tied at its end. It lowered down to her, dangling within arm's reach where it danced about in the wind. Sweat tingled at her palms, but she slowly released the rock with her left hand. A gust billowed up and threatened to pull the rope from her, but her hand closed around the roughhewn fibers, and she drew it toward her.

The act had been minor yet had left her panting for breath as fear sent an unnatural energy racing through her. She needed to thread her foot into the loop.

Cautiously, she lowered her gaze to where her toes rested on the stone ledge. Beyond it was the danger of a fall that would go on for too long. How many breaths would she take before being smashed upon the rocks?

She tightened her grip on the stone.

"Dinna look down," Ewan said.

A cry choked from her, wrung out by her terror.

"Faye, look up at me," he said in a soothing voice.

Her gaze lifted to where he stared intently at her with his beautiful hazel eyes.

"Use the feel of it," he instructed. "Ye've got the rope, bring it to yer toe. Ye can do this. Ye're the bravest lass I know."

She moved her left shoe, and the rope bumped clumsily

against it. Her toe searched blindly before the loop brushed either side of her foot, and she knew it was in place.

Ewan nodded. "Aye, like that. Is it secure?"

She tentatively pressed her weight on the loop. The rope tightened around either side of her shoe. "Aye."

"Now let go of the stone," he said.

Her palms went damp, one curled around the rope, one clutching at the hard stone.

"Do this for our bairn," he said. "Do it for me. I canna lose ye." His voice broke. "I canna lose ye, Faye. No' when I love ye so much."

So powerful was his love, it overwhelmed her fear and forced her hand from the rock that had saved her. She swung out, spinning wildly. Her other hand gripped the rope, and she squeezed her eyes shut to avoid seeing everything whirl around her. To refrain from the macabre curiosity of looking down.

One foot dangled disconcertingly, while the entire weight of her body was braced against her arch in the rope. A simple loop of rope—the only thing keeping her from plunging to her death.

The rope shifted up. Once. Twice. Over and over, it hefted higher until solid, warm hands closed around her forearms. She opened her eyes, and Ewan was there. Like a wish that had materialized into reality.

His hold braced over her, guiding her to him until the earth was solid under her torso, and then under her feet. "Faye." He blinked as tears filled his eyes.

He pulled her to him in an embrace that nearly smothered her, and she gladly dissolved into it, into him. The sobs shuddered through her then as she gave way to all the emotions churning inside her. The thoughts that she might have lost him, the horror of how closely she had dangled toward death. The fear that she would never see him again.

"I love ye," she whispered into his chest between sobs. "I've loved ye for a while but was too foolish to say it."

He moved back slightly and lifted her face up to his with the pressure of his fingertips under her chin. "And I love ye. With all my heart. And our bairn..." He put his hand to her lower stomach and a muscle clenched in his jaw. "Faye."

Concern flashed in his eyes, and he looked down between them where his hand was red with blood. All at once, the pain of Faye's injury rushed back. "'Tis a cut on my side. I turned in time to keep Moiré from reaching my stomach."

Ewan wasn't listening. He'd swept her into his arms and was already running to his horse.

The ride to the village was so much faster than the slow march Faye had endured with Moiré when she'd been forced toward her own death. Within minutes, they were at Sorcha's hut.

The healer rushed out to answer Ewan's calls and immediately took Faye inside.

⚜

EWAN DIDN'T HAVE TO WAIT LONG BEFORE THE DOOR TO Sorcha's hut opened, and Faye emerged. He went to her, eager to hold her, to confirm she was a healthy as Sorcha had guaranteed him. Yet, he was hesitant to do so lest he caused her further harm.

His own wounds pulled uncomfortably and ached, all minor injuries he could see to later.

"It was merely a nick on my side," Faye said as if it were of little concern.

"The babe?" He tried to keep the anxiety from his voice.

Faye took his hand and placed it to her flat stomach. "The babe will be fine."

He couldn't ease the tightness of worry from his chest. Not when he'd come so close to having lost her. Having lost *them*.

"What happened to Blair?" Faye asked. "Is she with yer uncle? Was she harmed?"

Ewan's mind flinched at the memory. "One of Cruim's men

killed her. She tried to take his weapon. I...I dinna see what happened."

"All that blood," she whispered.

"Ye saw it?"

Faye nodded, her eyes wide. "I had to keep pushing it from my thoughts. I was too frightened it was ye—that ye'd been killed. What happened?"

He told her how the men had taken him, and of being injured in the process and how Cruim had insisted he be seen to before going into the cellar. "I dinna think he knew what to do with me, aside from locking me in the cellar." For the first time, grief penetrated through the haze of the day's ordeals. "He was never eager for my chieftainship. It was Moiré. She told him I was plotting against him."

"Ewan." Faye touched his face with her slender fingers. "I'm so sorry about Moiré. I didn't mean to grab her when I fell—"

"If ye dinna kill her, she would have stopped at nothing to kill ye." Emotion welled inside him, the anger at how she'd tricked them and even the sorrow for the loss of the person he'd thought her to be. "She fooled us all." He pressed a kiss to Faye's forehead. "I think I understand now why ye were so slow to trust."

"My inability to trust almost led to never telling ye I loved ye." Her hand settled on his chest, directly over his heart. "I'm glad I had a second chance."

He pulled her to him, and her head rested against his chest. "I love ye, Faye."

"And I ye." She curled her arms around him, securing them together. "I'm only sorry I foolishly took so long to say it."

"Ye werena the only one who dinna say it when ye felt it." He kissed her smooth forehead. "Are ye ready to go home, lass?"

She nuzzled against him, enveloping him in her sweet floral scent. "Aye, there's nowhere I'd rather be." She looked up at him from where her head rested on his chest. "And no one I'd rather be with."

EPILOGUE

August 1341
Sutherland, Scotland

Faye paused by the ewer and rested her hand over the growing bump of her stomach. Ewan approached from behind her, still warm with sleep, and curled his strong arms around her in an embrace.

She settled back against him as his palm cradled her stomach. "How is our bairn this morn?"

"Active." Little flutters flickered inside her stomach as if to confirm her statement. The babe had quickened a fortnight ago and had become more insistent on making his presence known. Or hers, as it may be.

"I'm going to the surrounding areas today, including Torish." Ewan turned her around. "Would ye like to join me?"

She beamed at her husband. She always enjoyed seeing Torish, as he well knew. Not only for the realization that the land had been hers and would pass down to their child. She also enjoyed seeing how the villagers' lives had improved under Ewan's leadership. The people were well fed, their homes repaired and their land and livestock better tended.

"I'd love to." She kissed him. "After I see to the meals for today."

"Of course." He grinned. "Can we expect eel?"

She swatted a hand at him playfully. "Ye don't ever need to expect eel again."

But her jesting covered an underlying flash of pain at the reminder. For it hadn't been a mistake with the venison running out, as the cook had said. The servant admitted after Moiré's death that she had insisted he do it and keep quiet about it. She'd encouraged him to do other nefarious little acts as well, but he'd refused or ensured it was thrown out before it could be eaten. And sadly, he was not the only servant manipulated by Moiré.

All those mistakes Faye thought had been her doing had been Moiré's hand in an effort to make Faye think she'd been doing a poor job.

It was only a sampling of Moiré's perfidy. It had been confirmed she was the one behind her uncle's traitorous acts. The man had been ill for a long time, and she used his seclusion as an opportunity to poison his mind. God rest his soul. Cruim had died the night Ewan escaped from being locked in his uncle's cellar, upon hearing of his daughter's death.

Moiré had used him not only to turn men against Ewan but to encourage an alliance with the Gordons, who had agreed to support Cruim in taking the chieftainship, which would have left it open for Moiré upon his impending death. Her depravity knew no depths. Several herbs were found in her room that Sorcha confessed were used to aid in getting rid of pregnancies...and for conceiving. It appeared that while Moiré tried to kill Faye's child, she was also trying to get with child from her time with Finn. No doubt to force him into a marriage.

Ewan smoothed a lock of hair away from Faye's brow. "Have I told ye how much it pleases me to see ye so healthy?"

"Every morning." She kissed him and turned to the ewer to pour fresh water into the bowl. The sickness and exhaustion from the early stages of her pregnancy had dissipated, leaving her practically glowing with energy.

She lifted a fresh square of linen and nudged aside the letter next to it to ensure it didn't get wet.

Ewan's eyes caught the movement, and he lifted his brows. "Have ye answered yer grandda yet?"

Faye shook her head and lifted the linen to her face. The cool water swept over her warm cheeks, waking her up fully.

Her grandfather had wanted to come visit as soon as he found she was expecting a child with Ewan. He'd claimed it was to restore their good faith, especially after she had nearly been killed. But while Faye had learned to open her heart to the idea of trust, she was no fool.

After all these years, she finally understood her mother's decision to keep them from their grandfather. Starving and fighting for life was better than being puppets to a man like him.

A spike of protection for her unborn child jabbed her back straight.

"I don't want him here," she replied. "Or near the babe."

Ewan pulled on his trews and gave a supportive nod. "I think it's for the best to keep him from our daughter...or son."

"Any wagers?" Faye asked with an intentional coquettish slide of her eyes to her husband.

His gaze swept down her body. "What will I win if I guess true?"

She loved that he looked at her like that still, hot with attraction and love. "Anything ye like, husband."

He lifted his brows. "I think 'tis a bonny wee lass like her mum."

"And I suspect he's a brawny warrior, like his da." She ran her fingers down Ewan's powerful chest.

A quiet knock came at the door connecting their rooms.

Faye bid her maid enter, and Gavina came in with a letter held high in the air. "Yer family has written to ye."

Faye crowed with excitement and readily took the letter from Gavina with a word of thanks. She cracked open the seal and read through the contents.

But as she read, the smile slipped from her face.

"What is it," Ewan asked.

Faye shook her head and read through it again. Ewan's strong arm came around her shoulder. "Faye?"

"'Tis Kinsey," Faye replied. "She's left home."

"Left home?" Ewan frowned. "Where did she go?"

Faye lowered the missive, frightened by the frantic scrawl of her mother's normally neat script. Her fear and panic were evident in the way she'd written, as she begged Faye to help out in any way possible.

"Kinsey has always been of the mindset that the English deserved to be punished for everything they've done to us and Scotland." Faye put a hand to her chest, but her heart still pounded beneath the letter in her fist. "She's left to join the fight against England, to reclaim Scottish land."

"Drake," Ewan said softly.

Faye nodded as tears brimmed in her eyes. "Drake is employed by Lord Werrick, an English earl, and an English March Warden. If Kinsey is fighting against the English, she's fighting against my brother. They're enemies."

Ewan hugged her to him. "Kinsey wouldna compromise Drake."

Faye tucked her head against him. "I hope ye're right."

"I can send some of my men to yer mum to help," Ewan said. "But 'tis too long a journey for ye."

Faye pressed her lips together to ward off the protest that

immediately rose up. He was right, of course. Going to Castleton and coming back would take a month and a half, at least, mayhap more with the colder weather that would sweep in soon. And that was assuming Kinsey could be found quickly.

Faye knew her sister too well to think she might be easy to locate. After all, Kinsey never did anything without fully committing herself. If she'd joined the war, she would be in deep.

Instead, Faye nodded. "Aye, please do send some men. My mum will need help. As will Clara."

"I'll do it straight away," Ewan promised. "She'll be safe. Both she and Drake."

Faye embraced her husband, grateful for his support and his readiness to aid her family. But even as he offered reassurance, she was plagued by doubt. For in the end, what would win out? Kinsey's love for their brother, or her hatred for the English?

Faye only wished that her sister might settle down with a good man as she had and allow herself to be truly happy. It was times like this, Faye was grateful she had opened up to her husband so that he might know the truth in her heart.

"I promised to protect ye," Ewan said. "And that extends to yer family as well."

She closed her eyes as a tear eased down her cheek, for she knew his words to be true. For Ewan Sutherland, the man that she'd married, father to their unborn child, was indeed a man worthy of her trust. And now she had a life where love was not a vulnerability, but a strength, and worth every risk she'd taken.

Thank you for reading FAYE'S SACRIFICE! I read all of my reviews and would love to know that you enjoyed it, so please do leave a review.

Faye's siblings all have their own stories too:

- Kinsey in *Kinsey's Defiance*
- Clara in Clara's Vow (info coming soon!)
- Drake in Drake's Honor (info coming soon!)
- If you want more stories that take place on the border between England and Scotland, check out my Borderland Ladies series and meet Drake, starting with *Marin's Promise*

Check out Kinsey's story next in KINSEY'S DEFIANCE where Kinsey leaves home to help with the Scottish rebellion against England, an archer for a laird's son too handsome and charming for his own good.

***Keep reading for a first chapter preview of KINSEY'S DEFIANCE**

KINSEY'S DEFIANCE

KINSEY FLETCHER IS A WOMAN WHO STANDS UP FOR OTHERS who can't fight, so it's no wonder she jumps at the chance to be an archer in the war to reclaim Scottish lands alongside the handsome laird's son.

William MacLeod is a man all women love, one out to prove his worth while also catching the eye of the feisty and fiery Kinsey who pretends to want nothing to do with him.

With tremendous odds against them, can a love blossom and make them stronger together, or will their conflicting goals tear them apart?

SIGN UP FOR MY EXCLUSIVE NEWSLETTER TO STAY UP TO DATE on the latest Borderland Rebels news. Sign up today and get a FREE download THE HIGHLANDER'S CHALLENGE.

www.MadelineMartin/newsletter

KINSEY'S DEFIANCE
Chapter 1 Preview

July 1341
Castleton, Scotland

Kinsey Fletcher never cared much for market days. They were loud, crowded and filled with Englishmen trying to stir up trouble.

Like the two bleary-eyed sods pointing at them as Kinsey and her older sister, Clara, walked by.

"Ignore them," Clara said gently. "They mean us no harm."

"They would if given a chance." Kinsey narrowed her eyes at the men, who grinned salaciously in return. The arrogant fops.

"Ye can't go around picking a fight with every man who looks at ye." Clara led them away from the carpenter's stall they'd been perusing, and through the crowded streets. "Ye'd never get any rest."

Kinsey scoffed. "I'm not the only one they're looking at." Though sisters, their vastly different appearances went beyond the blue shade of their eyes to their hair, with Clara's being dark and silky straight while Kinsey's curls were bright red. Regardless, they both seemed to draw a significant amount of notice.

Not that it was anything Kinsey couldn't handle. Indeed, it was the exact reason she insisted on wearing her bow and a quiver of arrows to the market.

"Come, we're nearly done." Clara took the basket from Kinsey and examined the contents. They needed only a few nails and a bit of wool, and then they could finally return to their stone manor on the outskirts of the village.

Some English lived in the village as well, given that they lived so close to the English-Scottish border, where the two nationalities had a tendency to blend. How could they not when the lands were stolen by either country, then taken back, only to be stolen again?

But reivers often spilled over from England in greater numbers on market days. Some seeking items from the traveling merchants; others in retaliation for some raid against them, which had been a retaliation for another prior raid. On and on it went.

One day, someone would need to put a stop to it. And Kinsey wouldn't mind taking a stab at trying.

Regardless, they all somehow wound up at the tavern with too much ale sloshing about in their heads and a keen determination to woo whatever lass they came upon.

Kinsey and her sister stopped at the blacksmith's booth, where Clara bent to inspect a small bin of nails.

"They're all straight, miss." The blacksmith folded his arms over his broad chest. His gaze wandered appreciatively over Clara's slender pale hand, then up her arm to her face.

"Ye always do fine workmanship, I know," Clara offered by way of reassurance. She lifted her focus to him, then her cheeks colored with a blush as she apparently noted his attention.

Kinsey shifted from one foot to the other in agitation. This was why they were always getting into trouble during market days. Clara was the type who wouldn't ignore anyone speaking to her. Not the vendors, who she politely declined when she passed, nor the men who approached her to compliment her. Clara would blush prettily, a genuine response she could never stifle, while offering a "Nay, thank ye" that was far too sweet to be taken as an actual no.

This only made the men press harder, then Kinsey would have to step in to demonstrate the might of true discouragement. Usually with her bow and arrow.

It wasn't Clara's fault, of course. She was a beauty, though she never believed it no matter how many men tripped over their hanging tongues as she passed. It was more than her wide, pale blue eyes and the full mouth they'd all inherited from their mum.

There was an innocence to Clara, a demeanor of genuine kindness. Mayhap that was why her good sister drew the worst men.

Kinsey wasn't as oblivious when it came to men's notice. She knew they watched her as much as they did her sister. But she didn't blush at their flattery. She sliced them with the blade of her tongue and set them back a few paces.

The two Englishmen were still there, pointing at them now. One caught her notice and gave a cheeky wave with the tips of his plump fingers. Kinsey practically growled her irritation.

"Do ye think these will be enough?" Clara asked.

Kinsey grudgingly examined the twenty or so pointed nails in Clara's cupped hand.

Kinsey nodded, though she had no idea how many were needed. Their eldest sister, Faye, had always been the one to attend the village on market days. Not only did she enjoy the task of shopping, but she also managed to procure the best deals. Except now, Faye was married, living in the Highlands with a bairn on the way. And there was nothing for it but to attend the market in her stead.

Clara paid for the nails and thanked the blacksmith, who gave a slow, besotted smile as he took the coins.

They had only a length of wool to purchase, and then they could leave. Kinsey's shoulders didn't relax though, not with those men nearby. She glanced about and realized she'd lost them. Mayhap that meant they'd given up and—

"You're absolutely lovely." One of the two Englishmen stepped from the surrounding crowd and approached Clara.

A flush of color blossomed over her cheeks, damn her.

"Thank you," Clara replied with a shy duck of her head.

Kinsey didn't bother to hide her huff of aggravation. Clara would eventually get them both killed.

"I bet you're far sweeter than any honey I could buy here."
The man stepped closer, swaying a bit. His friend stood behind
him, saying nothing as he offered them a smile that looked like it
was going to slide off his homely face.

Clara shook her head, her smile wavering with uncertainty.
"Nay, I—"

Kinsey stood before her. "She's not interested."

The man didn't bother to hide his lust as his gaze slithered
down Kinsey's body. "And I bet you've got the right amount of
spice to offset that sweet, eh, Red?"

She resisted the urge to cross her arms over her chest to shield
herself from his foul stare. Not only would she not give him the
satisfaction of knowing he unsettled her, but she also wanted to
ensure she could draw her bow quickly.

"I'm also not interested." She notched her chin a little higher.
"We'd like ye to leave."

"What if I want to stay?" He licked his lips.

She slung her bow off her back, drew an arrow and sent one
into the dirt just before his feet where he stood several paces
away. He stepped back, and a second arrow landed where his foot
had been.

"The next one goes a little higher." She nocked another
arrow, aimed it at his groin and smiled. "Is that enough spice
for ye?"

"Kinsey." Clara's voice held a note of warning.

Kinsey could already hear the admonishment. Though, with
Clara, it was more a careful reminder than a chastising.
"Remember what the constable said—the next time you bring out
your bows, you'll be fined."

But Kinsey wouldn't be fined. The constable made the threat
often enough for her to know it held no weight. Then again, she'd
only ever shot the ground. Would he continue to be as forgiving if
she actually shot someone?

Eventually, she just might find out.

Today would not be that day, for the Englishman and his friend scowled and staggered away.

The cloth merchant was at the end of a line of booths, beside a cart touting jars of honey.

"Do ye need any assistance?" A voice asked from behind Kinsey.

From an Englishman to a Scotsman. If only the taverns would close on market days. Surely, the lack of alcohol would set some minds toward their proper function.

God, how she hated market days.

"Fine timing." She glanced over her shoulder.

The man was lean and tall, his brown hair neatly styled to the side, his high cheekbones evident with the hint of a smile on his lips. He was the most handsome man Kinsey had ever laid eyes on. And he knew it.

What was worse, he was undoubtedly a nobleman. His clothes were too fine to be a reiver. Too fine to be even a merchant from the border.

Before she could open her mouth to offer a smart retort to send him off, Clara spoke up. "Nay, but thank ye for offering to help."

Kinsey gave her sister a long-suffering look, which Clara met with a patient tilt of her head. How was it she never got riled?

"Then mayhap ye can help me," the man said.

But Kinsey was already turning away, pulling Clara to the cloth merchant who would undoubtedly take far too much of their time.

"Can we get the wool next week?" Kinsey asked under her breath.

"I'm almost finished with the new dress I'm making for Mum." Clara navigated the crowd of people as they walked. "I need only this last piece of wool for it to be complete."

Her older sister slowed just before they reached the cart laden with bolts of colorful fabrics. "I know ye don't like market days, and aye, the people can be...coarse, but Kinsey, I worry about ye. The constable said—"

"Excuse me, miss." The handsome stranger appeared at Kinsey's side once more. He smiled at her in a way she was sure other women found charming.

To her, it made him look like a false apothecary, selling off a bottle of common loch water as a cure-all potion.

Still, whatever he had to say would at least be more interesting than yet another discussion about the constable and his flimsy threats. She nodded to Clara to go on without her. After all, the vendor was only a few paces away. She would be able to keep watch on her sister.

Clara hesitated, but Kinsey waved her on, and she finally made her way to the cart. The man was still smiling when Kinsey returned her gaze to him.

"I'm William MacLeod," he said as if he thought the familiarity of his name would warm her to him.

It didn't.

"Ye caught my eye," he continued. "I had to come to talk to ye."

And here it went.

"Ye're an exceptional archer."

His compliment took her aback.

"I beg yer pardon?" A quick glance confirmed Clara was at the cloth merchant and being left alone.

"I saw how confidently you fired those shots." He nodded the way men do when they're impressed. "Ye're damn good."

Heat touched her face. "Thank ye," she replied.

Was she really blushing and thanking him? She was getting as bad as Clara. But then, no man had complimented her skills with a bow before.

"I have need of a good archer," he replied. "How would ye like to join my men and me in the fight against England?" He looked over his shoulder to indicate a group of men outside the inn before returning his attention to her. "To rise with the return of King David and reclaim the land that the English have stolen?"

Her blood charged in her veins at his words.

She'd heard of King David's return to Scotland after his exile in France. He'd been there so long that she couldn't remember a time when he had been on Scottish soil. She'd also heard of his determination to take back what belonged to them.

And she could be part of that army.

How long had she wished to exact vengeance on the English for their betrayal of herself and her family after their English father was slain in combat? How often had she lain awake in the manor, craving something more out of their quiet life?

This would be the ideal opportunity. The decision ought to be easy.

She glanced to where Clara sifted through several bolts of fabric with a careful hand.

Could Kinsey leave her family? Especially with their brother, Drake, already working for an earl on the wrong side of the border, and Faye being so far away?

And yet how could she not fight for Scotland after so many injustices?

WILLIAM MACLEOD HAD SPIED THE FIERY LASS FROM ACROSS the market. What man would not?

Hair like fire, sapphire blue eyes that sparkled with a challenge, high firm breasts...aye, he'd have noticed her anywhere. But then she'd brought out that bow, quick as a snake's strike, and expertly pinned the arrows into the ground right before the man's feet.

That was the kind of archer William needed in his command.

A bonny lass to warm his bed would be an added benefit.

And yet she appeared hesitant.

"If ye join my men and me in our efforts to regain Scottish land from England, I'll, of course, pay ye." He winked at her.

She frowned slightly, almost appearing as though she found his charm off-putting. Strange.

Her fine lips pursed with shrewdness. "If ye pay me to do the job of a man, I'll take the wage of one."

There was something in the way she spoke that made her sound English. The Scottish burr was there, yes, but her words were less lyrical, crisper. He'd bet his life that she had mixed blood running through her veins, which meant neither country had likely been kind to her. He could use that to his advantage.

He considered what she'd said. While most men might balk at such a brazen demand, William found the logic of her request sound. "Consider it done. The pay of a man for the work of a man."

"And I want armor." She glanced behind him, where his men stood in their chainmail.

"Of course."

Her eyes narrowed with a look of cautious intensity. "How do I know I can trust ye?"

He studied her, taking in the blue linen kirtle hugging her well-curved frame. The garment was fine enough, but not grand. Certainly, it was absent fraying hems or worn spots. Which meant she was not poor, but nor was she rich.

Her bow and arrow were of better quality, mayhap the best he'd seen on the borderlands.

She wasn't unfounded in her lack of trust, especially on the border between England and Scotland, where treachery was prevalent, and reivers left everyone on edge.

She flicked her attention to where her lovely dark-haired companion pulled a bolt of fabric from a stack and handed it to the merchant with a generous smile.

William was running out of time.

"My father is Laird of the MacLeod clan on Skye." He indicated his family crest on the hilt of his blade, the bull's head expertly carved into the gold.

"And ye're his heir?" The weight of her assessment settled over him.

William squared his shoulders. "Why would I no' be?"

In his father's eyes, there was one primary reason—disappointment. It had started early on when William was a boy. The knowledge that nothing he ever did was good enough to satisfy his father. After a time, William gave up trying.

He'd stopped caring. Or so he told himself. But with his father now threatening to name someone else as his heir for the lairdship, he had no choice.

This was his one opportunity to prove his worth by assisting King David in reclaiming Scottish land. And William would stop at nothing to ensure he succeeded.

"I must go." The lass said abruptly.

"Can I no' get an answer from ye?" he pressed. "What's yer name?"

She smirked. "If I decide to join ye, I'll give it then."

"We leave at dawn tomorrow." A sense of urgency always helped spur prompt decisions. "Meet us by the inn."

Except she didn't take the bait. She lifted a shoulder with a maddening air of indifference. "I may be there. I may not."

She began to turn away, and he knew she would be lost if he didn't press his cause.

"Have ye or yer loved ones no' ever suffered at the hands of the English?" he asked.

She slowly looked back at him, and he knew his gut had been right.

"Ye've no idea," she ground out.

"Then why let them win?" He stepped toward her. Her eyes sparked in a way that told him he'd struck a note, one he could readily play.

There was a sweet, powdery scent about her. Markedly feminine. He could envision himself gliding his lips over the hollow of her naked collarbone, breathing her in.

"The English have had their way with Scotland for too long," he said. "Starvation. Raids. Homes burned. Lives stolen." He shook his head. "No more." His hand balled into a fist. "King David will reclaim Scotland, and I'll be there. Will ye?"

Her breath quickened, evident by the swell of those lovely breasts against the neckline of her simple gown. "Dawn?"

He nodded, and she said nothing more, leaving to rejoin the dark-haired woman. Though she hadn't committed to accompanying them, she would be there.

Or at least he hoped.

Hiding a smile, he put his back to her despite the temptation to watch her depart and approached the inn.

All his men had entered, except the largest warrior who merely lifted his brows at William's arrival. "Will she join us?" Reid asked.

William shrugged and tried to pass it off as though she were of little concern. "She says she'll think about it."

"That's as close to a nay as ye've ever had from a lass." Reid pulled his auburn hair back into a thong, away from his sharp-featured face. "What do ye think?"

"She'll show."

Reid smirked. "An early dawn departure, then?"

It was a tactic William had employed before. A highly effective one.

William simply winked. "Did ye secure the rooms for us?"

"Do ye even have to ask?"

William threw his arm around his second-in-command. There was a reason he'd asked his boyhood friend to be his right-hand man in going up against the English. Reid was resourceful, with a knack of accomplishing any task.

They entered the inn together for a bit of hot food and a few ales before settling in for an early night. As William ate and drank with his men, he couldn't stop his mind from wandering back to the bonny redhead who spoke with a blended accent. She was fine to look at, aye, but many lasses were.

If her archery skills were as good as she'd exhibited, she would be invaluable as a warrior. They were in an age where a strong bow could give them an advantage, plucking off enough of the enemy to change the tide of battle.

She could be the pivotable role that helped him impress his father.

William hated the twinge in his chest at the thought of his da. He shouldn't crave the man's approval the way he did, not when it had never once been given before. But mayhap this time...

He knew the night would be a fitful one as dawn slowly approached, to see if the lass would join them or not. And he hoped to God she would.

AUTHOR'S NOTE

The idea of a bedding ceremony has always fascinated me with a mix of curiosity and horror. I can't imagine a new bride's nerves, often times meeting her husband for the first time, being made to endure such a terrible event.

Which is why I had to write about it.

Technically the first recorded bedding ceremony occurred in the 1400's, which is a century later than this story takes place. However, it's not uncommon in history prior to the 1600's to not have written record of events taking place due to the high cost of vellum (See the Author's Note in Ella's Desire for more information on this). Notes about life in general are hard to find because it didn't seem worth the expense or time to write down such things that were then considered mundane. Ergo, even if something wasn't recorded until a later date, it didn't mean it didn't exist then. This is an overriding theme in history regarding accuracy.

The bedding ceremony was done for two reasons. The first of which was as we all guessed: to confirm consummation and prevent any future attempts at annulment. But there it was also done as part of community. I know it sounds weird to think about your family and friends gathering around you in such an intimate setting, but for some, it was their really weird way of offering comfort and support. I know, I know... No, thanks! LOL

Generally, the couple changed behind screens into their night clothes, then tucked into bed in front of many watchful eyes. Now, men would typically be wearing night shirts as well. And, yes, they did look like nightgowns. Sometimes they even wore night caps too. In this story, Ewan is naked from the waist up and that is 100% creative liberty, because let's face it – even Ewan in a night cap and nightgown would be decidedly unsexy.

Once tucked into bed, the couple was blessed by the priest, the curtains around the bed were drawn shut and the couple was left alone. This is a generalization of the chain of events. Sometimes there were additional rituals incorporated, like the bridesmaids throwing stockings on the bed to see who might marry next, or food being eaten after they were put to bed and before everyone left. Sometimes the couple was even expected to come back to the wedding party when it was done.

It definitely is a piece of history better left in the past. I can't even imagine how uncomfortable it must be to go through something so socially awkward. I hope you enjoyed this little tidbit in history and how I used it to in Faye's Sacrifice.

ACKNOWLEDGMENTS

THANK YOU TO my amazing beta readers who helped make this story so much more with their wonderful suggestions: Kacy Stanfield, Janet Barrett and Tracy Emro. You ladies are so amazing and make my books just shine!

Thank you to Erica Monroe with Quillfire Author Services for the consistently amazing edits.

Thank you to Janet Kazmirski for the final read-through you always do for me and for catching all the little last minute tweaks.

Thank you to John and my wonderful minions for all the support they give me.

And a huge thank you so much to my readers for always being so fantastically supportive and eager for my next book.

ABOUT THE AUTHOR

Madeline Martin is a USA TODAY Bestselling author of Scottish set historical romance novels filled with twists and turns, adventure, steamy romance, empowered heroines and the men who are strong enough to love them.

She lives a glitter-filled life in Jacksonville, Florida with her two daughters (known collectively as the minions) and a man so wonderful he's been dubbed Mr. Awesome. She loves Disney, Nutella, cat videos and goats dressed up in pajamas. She also loves to travel and attributes her love of history to having spent most of her childhood as an Army brat in Germany.

Find out more about Madeline at her website:

http://www.madelinemartin.com

 facebook.com/MadelineMartinAuthor
twitter.com/MadelineMMartin
 instagram.com/madelinemmartin
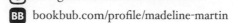 bookbub.com/profile/madeline-martin

ALSO BY MADELINE MARTIN

BORDERLAND LADIES

Ena's Surrender (Prequel)

Marin's Promise

Anice's Bargain

Ella's Desire

Catriona's Secret

Leila's Legacy

BORDERLAND REBELS

Faye's Sacrifice

Kinsey's Defiance

Clara's Vow

Drake's Determination

REGENCY NOVELLAS AND NOVELS

Earl of Benton

Earl of Oakhurst

Mesmerizing the Marquis

HARLEQUIN HISTORICALS

How to Tempt a Duke

How to Start a Scandal

HIGHLAND PASSIONS

A Ghostly Tale of Forbidden Love

The Madam's Highlander

The Highlander's Untamed Lady

Her Highland Destiny

Highland Passions Box Set Volume 1

HEART OF THE HIGHLANDS

Deception of a Highlander

Possession of a Highlander

Enchantment of a Highlander

THE MERCENARY MAIDENS

Highland Spy

Highland Ruse

Highland Wrath

Manufactured by Amazon.ca
Bolton, ON

13914948R00146